D0675960

**REA**

D0677446

Dear Readers,

Roses, candy, and champagne are wonderful—but they're not the same without the Valentine of your dreams. This year, celebrate the quest for true love with four spectacular new romances from Bouquet!

Nothing's better than an unexpected—and unexpectedly perfect—romance. In talented Vanessa Grant's **Think About Love,** a businesswoman with an orphaned baby niece plans to cut a deal with the boss for some time off, until she discovers her boss has a deal of his own to offer—matrimony! In Sandra Madden's uproariously funny—and teasingly sexy—**Since You've Been Gone,** a young widow who's started over finds there's only one problem with her plans for the future when her "dead" husband walks in the front door!

Sometimes when one dream comes true, others take the hint. That's certainly true for the spunky heroine of Kathern Shaw's **Make-Believe Matrimony.** Winning the lottery has resulted in dozens of very determined suitors—and the live-in protection of one very attractive, very single cop. And in Lynda Simmons's **Just the Way You Aren't,** an important commission at a famous hotel is sure to land a young artist the attention she needs to rev up her career—but attracting the attention of the hunky hotel project manager is much more appealing!

Enjoy!

Kate Duffy
Editorial Director

ROMANCE

# BOOK YOUR PLACE ON OUR WEBSITE AND MAKE THE READING CONNECTION!

We've created a customized website just for our very special readers, where you can get the inside scoop on everything that's going on with Zebra, Pinnacle and Kensington books.

When you come online, you'll have the exciting opportunity to:

- View covers of upcoming books
- Read sample chapters
- Learn about our future publishing schedule (listed by publication month *and author*)
- Find out when your favorite authors will be visiting a city near you
- Search for and order backlist books from our online catalog
- Check out author bios and background information
- Send e-mail to your favorite authors
- Meet the Kensington staff online
- Join us in weekly chats with authors, readers and other guests
- Get writing guidelines
- AND MUCH MORE!

**Visit our website at
http://www.zebrabooks.com**

# JUST THE WAY YOU AREN'T

*Lynda Simmons*

**ZEBRA BOOKS**
Kensington Publishing Corp.
http://www.zebrabooks.com

ZEBRA BOOKS are published by

Kensington Publishing Corp.
850 Third Avenue
New York, NY 10022

All Kensington Titles, Imprints, and Distributed Lines are available at special quantity discounts for bulk purchases for sales promotions, premiums, fund-raising, and educational or institutional use.

Special book excerpts or customized printings can also be created to fit specific needs. For details, write or phone the office of the Kensington special sales manager: Kensington Publishing Corp., 850 Third Avenue, New York, NY 10022, attn: Special Sales Department, Phone: 1-800-221-2647.

Zebra, the Z logo, and Bouquet Reg. U.S. Pat. & TM Off.

First Printing: February 2001
10 9 8 7 6 5 4 3 2 1

Printed in the United States of America

*For Sylvia McNicoll,*
*and friendship that goes above and beyond*

## ACKNOWLEDGMENTS

Special thanks to:

Cathy Miyata and Hedy Czuchnicka, who know how to deliver a thump on the head when needed; Sheila King and Victoria Pearce, for taking me inside the world of an artist; and Andrea Watson, for introducing me to the world's best butter tarts at Watson's Tea Room in Hamilton.

# One

She had a wonderful mouth. Full and soft. Lips always moist, slightly parted, like an invitation to sample, to taste, to take what he wanted one more time. And who was he to refuse?

He propped himself up on an elbow and kissed that mouth, slowly, deeply, breathing in her sigh as he drew the sheet down, exposing milk-white shoulders and small round breasts, the nipples taut and waiting. He smiled and touched his lips to her breasts, her belly, inhaling his own scent on her skin as he moved lower, pushing the sheet ahead of him and stroking her thighs, parting her legs, teasing her with his fingers, his lips. Taking his time and building his own need as much as hers.

She swallowed hard when he took her close to the edge again and drew away once more. "Bastard," she whispered, making him laugh.

"I'll take that as a compliment," he said, watching her kick back the rest of the sheet and rise up on her knees.

He closed his eyes, content to let her take over while a light breeze drifted through the terrace doors beside the bed, billowing the sheers and bringing the distant sounds of the street into the penthouse bedroom—the plaintive cry of a garbage truck in reverse, the howl of a car alarm, the call of an early-morning road crew setting up the first traffic barriers of the day.

Sunrise in Manhattan. Never peaceful, but never dull either.

Kind of like sex with Trisha.

He opened his eyes when she threw a leg over him, straddling his hips while she reached her hands behind her neck, lifting her long dark hair from her shoulders and stretching her arms up over her head, putting on a show that promised a hell of a finale—and maybe a curtain call or two.

Trisha Dale was old money with new ambition—a real break for the Mozart chamber orchestra that had hired her as their publicist. He had met her a year ago at the opening of his latest project, the Chicago Concord Hotel. She'd been on the first leg of a tour, he'd been at the end of his stay, but they'd talked, laughed, and ended up spending the night in his room, something they'd been doing on and off ever since. Whenever they were in the same city they'd get together, share a few laughs, a bed—an ideal arrangement for two people with heartache in the past and no illusions about the future. No promises, no expectations, no need to worry about where they'd be spending Christmas or anything else for that matter. Just a good time. She kissed his lips, dipped her tongue in his mouth. A very good time.

She moved her hips in slow, sensuous circles and raised a brow when he groaned. "You still want to take this slow?"

He wasn't gentle, simply grabbed her hips and lifted her up, positioning her exactly where he wanted her. "Up to you," he said, wondering just how long he'd be able to play at this himself.

She leaned forward, sliding her breasts across his chest. "Come on, then," she whispered, and the game was officially on.

He held her fast, rose to meet her—

"Mr. Wolfe?"

They froze. Both heads turned at the second knock.

"Mr. Wolfe? It's Duane Nugent. Your new assistant? Head ⁀ice sent me. I'm here to help, sir."

Michael let her go and sucked in a long breath, willing his blood to cool and his mind to think while Trish rolled over on her back and laughed.

Duane Nugent. The name rang no bells, but that wasn't surprising. Michael's last assistant had quit a week ago, claiming they couldn't pay him enough to work for an overbearing, slave-driving, son of a bitch—the usual whine. Michael had told head office he'd find his own replacement this time, but there was a new CEO in charge and with new management came new policies, new procedures, and now Duane.

"Mr. Wolfe? Are you there, sir?"

"Of course I'm here. And you're early, Nugent."

"The files indicated you're an early riser yourself, sir. So I took a red-eye. Didn't want to miss a thing. Especially today. I also have an envelope from head office, sir."

"And so it begins again," Trish whispered. She kissed him lightly, then threw her feet over the side and grabbed her dress from the floor. "I've got a meeting in a few hours anyway." She plucked her bra from the bedpost and flashed him a smile. "Don't forget to ask me about London later."

Michael grabbed his jeans from the nightstand. No hurt feelings, no recriminations. Just complete understanding.

How perfect was this woman?

Of course, it wasn't the first time they'd been interrupted. As project manager for Concord Hotels, Michael Wolfe was responsible for the renovation and restoration of each new property added to the list of luxury, boutique hotels. He was the company's man-in-the-hole, living on-site for the duration of the project, coordinating the trades and making sure the job came in as planned on time and as close to budget as possible.

An odd arrangement perhaps, but well suited to the wealthy and eccentric woman who owned the company, and a man whose only fixed address was a post office box in Maine.

And Duane's third knock was just part of the day.

"Mr. Wolfe? Shall I come back later, sir?"

"Just wait there," Michael called, fastening his belt as he scanned the room for his shirt.

"In the living room," Trish whispered. "With my underwear."

He grinned, remembering. "Why don't you come back after the meeting? Come to the opening with me tonight." He bent over the nightstand and read from the invitation lying next to his wallet. "A masquerade tribute to the many extravaganzas held at the Brighton Hotel during her heyday."

The owner of Concord Hotels had always made sure her openings were affairs to remember. Strictly black-tie and blue blood, with a sprinkling of celebrities to guarantee a good turnout and set the standard for future functions. Although her estate had sold the firm to Grant Hall Resorts a few months ago, the tradition had continued. Head office staff and guests would start arriving this morning, and at eight o'clock tonight, the bands would play, the champagne would flow, and the old Brighton Hotel would officially become the new Brighton Concord.

And Michael couldn't think of anyone who would make the evening more tolerable than Trish.

He grabbed a fresh shirt from the closet. "So what do you say? We'll sip champagne, avoid the accountants, then come back here and pick up where we left off."

"Love to, but I can't."

"Why not?"

"Ask me about London," she said and closed the bathroom door.

"What about—"

"Mr. Wolfe?" Duane called. "There was a mix-up with my room. Where shall I put my bags?"

"Not in here," Michael muttered, and rounded the corner into the living room.

He'd occupied the suite for close to a year now, but other than the crushed shirt on the sofa, not much in the penthouse belonged to him. None of the Queen Anne furnishings or gilt-edged prints. Certainly not the crystal eggs or glass ornaments. Just the laptop on the desk and a few books in the Queen Anne secretary desk.

Travel light was his philosophy. No baggage, no holdups, no unscheduled stops. Only Trisha, now and then. He walked to the desk by the window, knowing exactly where he'd find those black silk panties.

"And Mr. Wolfe? May I say right now, sir, that I've been briefed on your work both in the past and here at the Brighton, and I count myself lucky to be part of your team, sir."

"That's the kind of dedication I like to hear. So how about you start by getting us some coffee?"

"You want me to bring coffee, sir?"

Michael couldn't help smiling as he switched on the computer. The new guy wouldn't last a week.

"Two, please. Black for me and double cream for Ms. Dale."

"I take milk," Trish said, running a brush through her hair as she came through from the bedroom.

"I knew that." Michael raised his voice again. "Make that one black and one double milk. And two bagels with cream cheese."

"Pumpernickel with light ricotta," Trish called, and shot Michael a pointed look. "I quit white flour in February."

"I knew that too," he said. Then he hollered, "And Nugent. Could you hurry?"

"Why do you do that?" she asked.

He shrugged and glanced at his monitor, checking for e-mail and smiling when he saw a message from his brother's sons, complete with attachments. More pictures, he hoped, since he hadn't seen the kids in close to two years.

He turned back to Trish. "I suppose I'm tired of assigned assistants. I'd like to find my own again—"

"I meant why do you even pretend to remember anything about me?"

"What are you talking about? I remember lots of things." He held up the panties. "Need these?"

She snatched them out of his hand. "If your memory is so good, what city did I ask you to remind me about?"

"Paris. No, wait. Brussels."

"London," she whispered, and his shoulders slumped.

"All right, I admit I forget the little things. But I do remember what a good time we had at the last opening." He sat down at the desk, tapped the keyboard. "Are you sure you can't come tonight? I could send Duane out for a costume. Guarantee that he quits by tomorrow."

"I'm sure." She sat down on the edge of the desk. "Tell me something, Michael. Are we a couple?"

"Not like other couples, I suppose—"

"But where do you see us in a year from now?"

"They've just taken over a property in Sundridge, near San Francisco, so—"

"I mean where do you see *us* in a year's time?"

He looked up at her, the skin on the back of his neck prickling. "I don't have time for this right now."

"That's always the problem, isn't it? Time."

"That's the way it's always been. We see each other on the fly, when we can, and move on. I love the way we are."

"But do you love me?"

"That's not fair and you know it."

"You're right. It's just that lately I find myself thinking about marriage again. And kids." She hesitated, struggling. "I guess this isn't enough anymore, Michael. I want more."

He rolled the chair back from the desk, got to his feet. "I've had more, Trish. And all I want now is less."

Her smile was sad, her voice soft. "And you've certainly got it."

He glanced around at the plants he didn't tend, the paintings he hadn't selected, knowing exactly what she meant, and seeing no need to change a thing. "I never lied to you."

She looked down at her hands. "Randy pointed that out when he asked me to move in with him. You remember Randy Baker, don't you?"

"Sure. Short guy, plays the flute. Wouldn't stop hitting on you the last time we were in . . ." Michael stopped short.

*Ask me about London.* Of course.

He drew up in front of her. "So Randy wants you to move in?"

"Are you jealous? Don't answer that. Just tell me this. Shall I take him up on his offer?"

He pulled her into his arms. "If it will make you happy."

She sighed and rested her head against his shoulder. "That's what Randy figured you'd say."

"Mr. Wolfe? I've got the coffee, sir. Can I come in now?"

She started to pull back but Michael held her tighter. "Stay," he said.

"What's the point?" she said, already moving away, opening the door, leaving him alone with his laptop and his books.

"Sorry we kept you waiting so long." Trish stepped back from the door with a coffee in her hand. "Thanks for this."

"No trouble at all, ma'am," Duane said, and smiled straight at Michael as he nudged his suitcase through the door ahead of him. "It is such a pleasure to meet you, sir."

He was tall and lanky, no more than twenty-two or twenty-three, his hair spiky but more by accident, it seemed, than design. And who in God's name had dressed him?

Duane handed Michael the coffee, set the bag of bagels on the desk, then went to unzip his suitcase. "I have my résumé here, sir. And the envelope from head office." He hurried back with two manila envelopes. "They said it was urgent."

"It always is," Michael said. He was reaching for the letter opener when he spotted Duane shaking Trish's hand at the door.

"The pleasure was mine, ma'am," Duane said.

She smiled and raised a hand to wave. "Good-bye, Michael."

"Trish, wait."

He caught up with her at the elevator across the hall. She smiled, her eyes soft, filled with tenderness and an understanding he probably didn't deserve. "Good luck, Michael. And don't be too hard on Duane."

He watched her step into the elevator. Watched her press the button. The perfect woman, walking out of his life.

And for one fleeting moment, he was tempted to call out, stop the door, say the words she wanted to hear. But he'd never been a good liar, and there was no denying the sudden rush of relief when the elevator finally closed.

He turned to find Duane watching him from the doorway of the penthouse.

"Women," the young man said, obviously flustered. "Can't live with them, can't live without them. But there are plenty of fish in the sea. Just get back on the horse and ride—"

"You don't get out much, do you, Nugent," Michael said.

"Not lately, sir, no."

Michael threw an arm around his shoulder and led him back into the apartment. "Then you must be looking forward to tonight."

"I admit I'm excited, sir. And a little starstruck too."

"Well, you won't be disappointed." Michael walked to the windows to watch a limo pull up to the curb, and the doorman jump to attention. "From what I hear they've pulled out all the stops for this ball." He turned away when Trish stepped out to the curb. "But first you'll need to pick us up some costumes. Get a tux from Silvers for me, and whatever you want for yourself. Nothing with a head."

"Understood. But does a tux qualify as a costume?"

Michael crossed to the bedroom. "Ever hear of James Bond?"

Duane's face lit up. "Or perhaps you're Fred Astaire. That would work too."

"Believe me, Nugent, I am never Fred Astaire." And if he had his way, he'd be anywhere but at that party tonight.

He grabbed the invitation from the dresser and glanced over at the bed. The sheets were rumpled and the pillows flat. If he let himself, he could still smell Trish in the room. But as she'd said herself, what was the point? They were finished. The time had come to move on, and Sundridge, California, was as good a place as any.

So he'd go to the ball, toast the company's success, and slip out the door. And Duane could dance the night away for him.

The phone on his desk rang. He turned into the living room to see Duane answering the call before the second ring. The kid put the phone on hold the moment he saw Michael.

"The designer's in the lobby, sir." He held out the receiver. "There's a problem with the mantel on the fireplace. Shall I deploy the maintenance team?"

"Not yet," Michael said, taking the phone. "Just out of curiosity, were you in the military, Nugent?"

"The reserves, sir. I have some wonderful memories."

"I can imagine," Michael said. "Just do me a favor, and call me Michael." He handed Duane the invitation to the ball. "This is yours. Whatever you do, don't lose it. Security will be tight as hell tonight. And trust me, without one of those, no one gets in."


"So you're telling me it's no problem to get in." Sunny Anderson dropped her toolbox by the door and headed back to the scaffold in the center of the ballroom. "You've been watching James Bond movies again, haven't you?"

Valerie Conan-Smythe, blond by choice and pushy by nature, followed close behind. "James Bond would never come in through the kitchen. But it's a classic move with a solid success rate, and with me on the inside, what can possibly go wrong?" She folded her arms and stood on the drop cloths Sunny was trying to gather up. "Will you just listen for a minute?"

Sunny left the cloths and looked up into the well-meaning if somewhat narrowed eyes of her best friend and favorite concierge.

They'd met a year ago at the Cobble Hill Gallery in Brooklyn where Sunny was teaching "Sketching the

Nude." Turned out they both lived in the neighborhood, shared a love of the human form, and had a tendency to grin when it was male model night.

The steps from coffee, to lunch, to takeout and a video at Sunny's flat had been short, and when the interior designer for the Brighton finally decided she wanted a mural in the ballroom, Val had been there, waving Sunny's name like a flag. And she hadn't let up yet.

She pointed up at the ceiling. "That is the best work you've done yet, but without a little help, no one will even know it's there."

Sunny laughed, left the drop cloths, and climbed up the side of the scaffold instead. "How can they miss it?" she asked when she reached the top, her eyes moving across the mural she'd finished less than an hour ago.

*Something smart, elegant, and vaguely European,* the designer had said when she hired Sunny. *Make it blend with the drapes and carpet too. After all, we're talking ambience here, not art. And we'll need it in two weeks.*

And Sunny had delivered, coming in just under the wire after three all-nighters, plenty of hot coffee, and loud, jarring music from the sous chef's ghetto blaster. Her fingers ached and her arms and shoulders were numb. But now, where there had only been blank space, there was . . . ambience.

Twenty feet above the ballroom floor, five couples danced on air in a swirl of silk, satin, and diamonds, the eras blending into one another as they waltzed, fox-trotted, and tangoed around the dome at the center of the ballroom.

A 1940s Hollywood starlet in shimmering silver peered over the shoulder of her pretty-boy partner, watching the Victorian wastrel on the other side of the dome frown while the lady in his arms stole a glance at the Regency rake with the Jane Austen flirt beside them. And all the while, the Civil War beauty held on tightly to the ruggedly handsome Rebel captain—a man with a taste for something more brazen. But the flapper in the plunging, fringed dress only had eyes for the dark and dangerous gangster she had come in with, a man with slicked-back hair and a smile he gave only to her—a fantasy man if ever there was one.

But it wasn't the fantasy that lightened the ache in Sunny's shoulders, or brought a smile to her lips. It was pride, because that mural had it all. Passion, intrigue, and of course, a few secrets. Because what was a mural without secrets?

"It's called tunnel vision," Val said, snapping Sunny back as she clambered up the other side of the scaffold. "They'll see the bar, the buffet, and each other. Add to that the fire-eaters, jugglers, and God knows what else they've got planned for entertainment, and you'll be lucky if anyone even remembers there *is* a ceiling." She hoisted herself up onto the platform with Sunny. "What you need is a little *buzz.*"

Sunny gave her thermos a shake. "I'd have to get more coffee."

"Not that kind of buzz. I mean talk. Promotion. Spin." She took a step closer. "In less than fourteen hours, this room will be filled with press and potential clients. It's your chance to make some contacts, get your name out there. Start doing the kind of work you love, full time. And make some real money for a change."

Work she loved, and real money. Now, there was temptation. She could pay off her truck. Set up a college fund for her daughter. Move the two of them out of her parents' house into a place of their own. And never again wait tables at her mother's café.

Val unsnapped the first guardrail and set it down on the platform. "It's a simple matter of schmooze or lose, understand?"

Sunny's fantasy faded to black as reality settled in again. "Have you seen the size of the security guards they've hired? And they'll certainly be watching the kitchen." Sunny laid the second railing down, and unlocked the platform. "Besides, I'm a terrible schmoozer. I can never figure out how to shake hands while holding on to those little sausages and a wineglass at the same time."

"That's why you schmooze first and eat later."

"But I never know what to say."

"I'll coach you."

Sunny sighed and went to work on the side braces. "Val, be reasonable. This evening is about wealth and power. Beautiful people in beautiful clothes. You're tall and sleek, you'd fit right in. But look at me. I'm short and round—"

"Curvy," Val corrected, and started in on the other side. "And I hear curves are coming back."

"Not by eight tonight. Besides, my nails are nonexistent, I've got circles under my eyes, and my last haircut was in my own bathroom with the nail scissors. They would eat me alive."

Val helped her lift the platform and carry it to the door. "All you need is a day at the salon. Manicure, pedicure, frizzy-hair cure—"

"But it's wing night. The guys will be expecting me to play Trivia Triumph at QB's. And Jess will be so disappointed—"

"Sunny, stop. You know your brothers will take her."

All right, so Val had her there. Sunny's brothers, Sean and Hugh, would never leave their six-year-old niece stuck without wings and quarters for the video games on a Friday night. And Val could definitely teach her a thing or two about schmoozing.

As they went back for the rest of the scaffold, Sunny glanced up at the Hollywood starlet, taking in the eyes, the placement of the hands, the slight curve of the lips. Just the right combination of flirting and flattery. Funny how she could capture the essence of the shmooze with a brush, but could never master it herself.

"The answer is still no. I won't go where I'm not welcome. And Michael Wolfe has made it abundantly clear that contractors are not on the guest list."

Val rolled her eyes. "It's a masquerade. He won't have a clue who you are."

"He wouldn't anyway. That man would not recognize me if he fell over me."

Sunny had never met him, although she'd seen him often enough: in the lobby, on the stairway, once in the deli across the street. Of course, he never saw her, never acknowledged her at all. Just kept that nose of his facing forward, heading in a straight line toward his destination. Determined, focused. Oblivious.

As far as he was concerned, she was just another body on a scaffold, like the window washers, or the electricians, all of them there for only one reason—to deliver a service as quickly and efficiently as possible, and expected to leave the same way before the gala event.

It was the same reasoning behind the "no signature" clause in her contract. Did the electrician sign each switch plate? Did the plumber scrawl his name under the sink? Certainly not. And management did not expect to see any telltale signs of the painter left behind either. And if Val thought for one minute that Sunny wanted to rub shoulders with Wolfe or any of his kind, she was sadly mistaken.

They broke down the last of the scaffold and carried the supports to the door. "I'm not going. The work will speak for itself."

"Funny, but I don't hear a thing."

"Then you're just not listening."

"So I guess Michael Wolfe wins."

Sunny glanced back at the mural, smiling at the *S.A. Anderson* she'd worked into the beadwork of the flapper's dress. Discreet, but there. Definitely there.

"Don't mess with the painter," she whispered, but jumped all the same when the door swung back, and the man himself entered.

She took an unconscious step backward as Michael Wolfe swept past. He was tall and dark, not conventionally handsome by any means, but attractive in a driven, obsessive sort of way. While he wasn't her type, she had to admit there was something arresting about him. A magnetism that had always drawn her, even when she wanted to look away, ignore him. Like now, for instance.

His entourage followed him across the room: Yanka, the interior designer, Sam, from Sam's Woodworking, and a young man wearing the strangest suit Sunny had seen in years, all of them obviously flustered and trying hard to catch up to Wolfe.

He didn't pause, or look back. Just kept going, passing under the mural without giving it so much as a glance, and setting a pattern for everyone else.

"I don't think they heard it either," Val whispered.

Sunny merely shrugged. "Wait till they come back."

Michael stopped in front of the fireplace, gave the mantel a quick once-over. "She's right," he said, and turned to the contractor. "The fit is wrong."

The designer's shoulders slumped with obvious relief while the contractor's mouth opened and closed under the weight of the mighty Wolfe's decision.

"It's too late to do anything about it right now," he continued, "but I'll expect a replacement before your bill is settled."

Sunny wasn't surprised when the contractor asked no questions, suggested no compromise. Because Michael Wolfe never compromised, or at least that was the story.

Along with the rumors that he never ate or slept. Just worked nonstop, round the clock, and expected everyone else to do the same. Sunny could almost believe it was true. She knew firsthand how he'd treated his assistant. Running him ragged, making unreasonable demands. The poor guy had sat on her drop cloth enough times, pouring out his heart about the man upstairs. And hadn't she seen him herself only two nights ago? Roaming the darkened hall outside the ballroom, his shirt open as though he couldn't sleep and had just thrown it on carelessly, as an afterthought?

He had broad shoulders and a nice chest—hairy too, not shining and bald like so many models who came into the gallery. He wasn't sculpted either, but appeared naturally trim and strong. Like a man who worked physically for a living, although she knew that wasn't true. He was the general, after all, the one who sent others off to do the dirty work. So maybe he ran. Although she couldn't picture that either. And to be honest, she didn't much care.

She much preferred the gangster on the ceiling.

Tall, dark. Not classically handsome . . . She turned away, startled. Coincidence. Nothing more. If she looked hard enough, she'd probably see George the sous chef, or one of the bellboys up there too. That even a trace of Michael Wolfe was in her gangster only proved how tired she'd been.

She glanced over at Val as the group came back toward them. "This time," she said, but not even the designer paused to look up. They all kept going, marching straight past Sunny.

"Yanka," Sunny called, and felt her face warm when everyone stopped and turned. She flashed a sheepish grin, pointed to the ceiling. "I just wanted to know what you thought."

"The mural, right," Michael said and narrowed his eyes at her. "What's your name again?"

The man was as utterly predictable as she'd expected. "Sunny Anderson," she said, and started to extend her hand.

But he was already on his way back to look at the mural with the rest of the group trailing along like puppy dogs.

"You were supposed to have finished this by six," he called over his shoulder.

Sunny drew up short when she realized she had fallen into step behind him. "I did, but—"

"Then why are you still here?"

Rude *and* predictable. Always an endearing combination. She held her ground. "I needed some pictures for my portfolio."

"Uh-huh."

The group stopped under the dome. Four heads tipped back, but no one spoke before Michael.

"Nice," he said, and looked over at the designer. "You must be pleased."

"I knew she'd come through," Yanka said, shooting Sunny a smile while Sam gave her two thumbs-ups behind Wolfe's back.

Sunny glanced at Val, then took a few steps toward them. "Then perhaps you won't mind if I leave some cards. Have catering put a couple on each table—"

The designer spoke up. "I don't think—"

"It's fine," Michael said, heading for the exit. "Nobody's going to notice it otherwise. And make sure you're out of here in fifteen minutes."

The door closed behind them, and Val had the sense to say nothing.

Sunny drummed her fingers on her leg. The room was awfully quiet. She looked up at the mural. It was time to turn up the volume.

"I'll need a manicure," she said, snatching up her tool-box. "And a really great costume."

# Two

The Lord of the Isles Tea Room had been part of the Anderson family for close to thirty years. With ten tables, a kitchen that gave new meaning to the word *cozy*, and a menu that could shut down arteries faster than you could say "clotted cream," the Isles had outlived a steady stream of trendy cafés and bistros to become a fixture on the street.

Moyra and Jack Anderson had modeled it after Moyra's favorite tearoom in Renfrew, with the cash desk to the left of the entrance, and baker's racks to the right. The kitchen sat in the middle with a window over the counter so the cook could see who was coming in, and a door so those continuing past could call hello before rounding the corner to the lace-covered tables in the back.

Evenutally, a second door had been added to the kitchen, so Moyra could carry teapots straight out to the tables. And when the children came along, Jack put in a staircase so the family could come straight down to the tearoom from their apartments upstairs, instead of using the door on the street. But since then, changes had been few at the Isles.

There were no hissing cappuccino makers and nothing even vaguely foreign on the menu. Just a taste of Scotland with Mary, Queen of Scots above the fireplace, Sunny's mural of the Loch Ness monster by the window, and the kind of home baking that had made more than a few men beg Moyra to run away with them.

But she was there in the kitchen as usual when Sunny came in from the salon, rolling pastry for her famous tarts while things were quiet in the tearoom.

"I'm home," Sunny called, dropping her backpack on the cash desk. "Is Jess here?"

"She's still out with Hugh," her mother called through the window. "And I'm about to kill your father."

To Sunny, Moyra Anderson had always been a bantam hen—small, scrappy, and tough. Her accent was strong, her shortbread tender, and anyone who stepped on her toes did so at their own risk.

"Your mother exaggerates," Jack Anderson called from the back of the tearoom. "I've just been explaining how we need a satellite dish. And a big-screen TV, so we can bring in both the soccer matches and the lads. Of course we'd need a liquor license—"

"No liquor," Moyra said. "And no soccer. This is a tearoom, not a pub."

"But there's a place in Flatbush that's both," Jack said, motioning Sunny to silence with a finger to his lips as he pulled a tape measure from his pocket. "We have to keep up with the times."

Sunny shook her head and unzipped her backpack. If Moyra was the hen, then Jack Anderson was the cock of the walk. Tall, proud, and not always smart when it came to saving his own neck.

"The Isles pub and tearoom," he went on. "Or the tearoom and pub, if you prefer."

Moyra growled, Jack threw up his hands, and Sunny ignored them both. With almost forty years of marriage behind them, it wasn't the first time Moyra and Jack had fought.

Sunny took out the shoes Val had given her from the bag—white stiletto sandals, guaranteed to work with whatever costume Sunny wore. As long as she didn't break an ankle first.

She kicked off her boots, rolled off her socks, and stuffed her feet into the shoes. She stared at the French-manicured toenails poking through the end, then rose slowly, holding the chair for balance and wondering if a pair of fetching sneakers wouldn't do the job equally well.

"We'll ask Sunny's opinion," Jack said as he walked toward her. "Can you picture a pub here, lass?"

"No, she can't," Moyra answered for her, then came to the kitchen door and narrowed her eyes at Jack. "What's this *we* business anyway? This is *my* tearoom. And Sunny, what on earth did they do to your hair?"

"They straightened it," she said and did a careful pirouette. "What do you think?"

"I think it probably cost too much," Moyra said, before turning back to her pastry.

It was her mother's standard response to anything new—haircuts, clothes, friends—and Sunny took it in stride.

"You look lovely," her father said.

Sunny smiled and gave him a quick hug. "Tread lightly," she whispered.

"Aye," he said, and pulled the measuring tape out quietly.

Moyra looked up from the pastry she was rolling as Sunny tottered into the kitchen. "I swear one of us is not going to survive his retirement."

"It's still new." Sunny pressed a kiss to her mother's cheek. "Give him time."

"He's had a month." Moyra frowned as she sprinkled flour and gave the dough a turn. "I'm going crazy having him underfoot all day. What I wouldn't give to be a golf widow."

Sunny laughed. "Count yourself lucky. Your husband still wants to be near you."

"That's another thing." Moyra glanced out into the tearoom then lowered her voice. "The old fool tried to climb into my bed last night. Can you imagine that?"

Sunny tried very hard not to, but as Jack wandered past the kitchen door with his tape measure dangling at his side, she saw how lost he looked, and knew he wasn't adjusting any better than Moyra.

"He just needs something to do," she said. "And maybe a pub's not such a bad idea, only not in the tearoom."

"I'll not be buying more property—"

"You wouldn't need to if Jess and I moved out." Sunny kept her tone light, casual, as though they were discussing the weather and not her future. A future that surely included more than life above the tearoom. "You and Dad could move up to the third floor, open a pub on the second—"

Moyra banged down the rolling pin. "This is your home, for heaven's sake. I won't have you and Jess running off because of your father's crazy notions. If he wants something to do, he can find it elsewhere, and leave us alone."

Sunny nodded and retreated, for now. "Are you two still going to watch Dave and Hazel reaffirm their vows tomorrow?"

"Yes, but I think it's bloody nonsense." Moyra glanced over at Sunny. "Want to have a go at the pastry before it gets busy again?"

Sunny's older brothers, Sean and Hugh, had both joined their father at Anderson's Electric, officially taking over the reins a month ago. While Moyra wasn't ready to bow out yet, it was no secret that she planned for her only daughter to follow in her footsteps as well. But Sunny just couldn't seem to master the secret of her mother's famous pastry. And if tonight went according to plan, she never would.

She wiggled her new shiny fingernails. "Sorry, but the nails won't take it."

Moyra scowled and turned back to the counter. "You'll poke an eye out with one of those if you're not careful. And for what? A party full of fancy people where you'll probably get arrested for trespassing."

"I won't get arrested, and it's good for my career," Sunny said, taking comfort in the lines she'd been feeding herself all day. "I'll make contacts I couldn't make anywhere else. Get the recognition my work deserves."

*And thumb my nose at Michael Wolfe.*

Childish, perhaps. But weren't all the best things in life? She pursed her lips. *What's your name?* Even now, just thinking about it could set her on edge, make her want to write it down and paste it to his forehead. *Sunny, you jerk. Sunny.* Although she couldn't for the life of her say why it should matter so much when the real issues were learning to schmooze and walking in a straight line. And above all, avoiding security.

She drew in a deep breath. Piece of cake, she told herself, and teetered a moment, trying to remember when she'd last worn shoes this high.

Not since Jess was born at least, and she was six now, which would make it seven years . . .

She stopped and looked down at her feet. High school prom. Pink dress, pink shoes, and a boy who wasn't ready to be a father.

"Mrs. Dempster, Mrs. Fitzhenry," Jack said with a snap of his tape measure. "How are you today?"

Sunny pushed the image of Jess's father and a disastrous gala evening from her mind. Tonight would be different. Tonight would be fine. She drew in another deep breath. Oh, please, let it be fine.

"Did you hear about Mary Crane's girl?" Mrs. Fitzhenry called to Moyra as she passed the kitchen. "She's taken up with a married man."

"Says he's going to leave his wife and marry her," Mrs. Dempster added.

Moyra's face softened as she followed them around the corner to the tables. "And the poor girl fell for it?"

"Like a stone," the two women said in unison.

The Glasgow ladies turned their attention to Sunny. The sisters were short, sharp-eyed, and still on the bright side of seventy. They came every day, ordered the same things, and always had the best neighborhood gossip.

"Your hair looks nice today, Sunny," Mrs. Dempster said.

"Not as frizzy as usual," Mrs. Fitzhenry agreed. "And you're so tall all of a sudden."

"It's the shoes," Sunny said, doing her best to walk without wobbling while the ladies settled into the chairs.

"I used to have a pair very like them myself," Mrs. Dempster said. "Wore them to all the dances. The boys loved them." She motioned Sunny closer and lowered her voice. "I used to call them my 'come and get me shoes.' And they never let me down once."

"Of course, she was a tart," Mrs. Fitzhenry whispered.

"Our Sunny's not a tart," Moyra said on her way back to the kitchen. "And she's not after a man, either."

Jack laughed. "Every woman is after a man."

"You be quiet," Moyra called. "And don't think I can't see that tape measure."

Mrs. Dempster turned to Sunny and motioned her to sit next to her. "Where will you be wearing the shoes, dear?"

"A masquerade," Sunny said.

Mrs. Dempster's face crinkled with delight. "Oh, those are always such fun. What are you going as?"

"No idea," Sunny said. "Val's getting me a costume. Although I'm not going for the dancing. Or the men."

"Told you so," Moyra said as she set a teapot on the table.

Mrs. Fitzhenry ignored Moyra and spooned sugar into her cup. "Then why bother?"

"It's a business evening," Sunny said. "I'll make contacts I can't make anywhere else. Get the recognition my work deserves—"

"Come into the kitchen and I'll recognize the work you do with the pastry," Moyra said. "You can't earn a living with a few murals, you know."

True, Sunny thought, and glanced down at her shoes. But a steady run of them would do it.

"Wait till you see what I have," Val called as she hustled through the door with a binder under one arm and a box in her hand. She held up the box and grinned at Sunny. "You won't believe what I found."

As long as it wasn't higher heels, Sunny would be happy.

Val gave Jack a quick hug, pressed a kiss to Moyra's cheek

and nodded at the ladies as she set everything down on their table. "A mask," she said, and stood back while three heads peered into the box.

It was a butterfly half-mask, a delicately contoured confection of luminous greens and blues with a dusting of sparkles on the wings and the softly arching antennae. "This," Val said, "is the absolute latest in costume drama."

"Oh my," the Glasgow ladies said together as Sunny lifted the mask from the box. It was lighter than she'd expected, and made from butter-soft leather.

"Where did you get it?" she asked.

"Never ask a magician for her secrets." Val pulled a chair up to the table and opened her binder. "Okay, we have a lot of work to do. I'll definitely be helping behind the bar tonight, so phase one is under way."

"Phase one?" Mrs. Dempster asked.

"Just a business term," Sunny told her.

"I also heard from the theater," Val continued. "Hugh and Jess picked up the costume, so that's phase two. But the costume *must* be back by five tomorrow. They're doing inventory on Monday morning, and if the costume mistress gets caught loaning things out, she's in big trouble."

"Understood," Sunny said. Val had called in a favor from a theater group in New Jersey, giving them Sunny's measurements and head size over the phone. The costume mistress had promised to find something suitable and Hugh had played the hero, as usual, agreeing to pick up both Jess and the costume.

While Sunny was glad the theater company had come through, she couldn't help thinking about their last few productions: *Oliver, Gypsy,* and *L'il Abner,* and she shuddered to think what could wind up on her head.

"What is the costume?" Mrs. Dempster asked.

"Won't know till it gets here." Val clicked a pen and moved on to phase three. "Now for the agenda. People you *have* to meet."

Both ladies leaned forward. "What's all this?" Mrs. Fitzhenry asked.

"The art of schmoozing," Val said. "An agenda, ice-breakers, the all-important smile." She glanced up at Sunny. "You know how much I love your smile, but can you tone down the wattage tonight? Try something a little more subtle, yet still sincere."

Sunny held the mask to her eyes and tried a sincere but subtle smile.

Val sighed. "Keep practicing. And keep walking. And remember, the key to successful schmoozing is to stay focused and never linger too long. Get in and get out."

"Get in and get out," Sunny repeated, then lowered the mask and started walking again.

Mrs. Fitzhenry pursed her lips. "When I was young we called these things social graces. How to get out of a car, how to sit, how to be witty without being offensive."

"It's all about being poised and graceful," Mrs. Dempster added. "Like a princess."

Val nodded. "A princess, exactly. One who knows about pitching and networking." She pointed at Sunny. "Walk."

Sunny wiped her palms on her overalls as she walked, wondering how a princess coped with sweaty palms.

"Antiperspirant," her father whispered as she went past. "President Nixon used to put it on his face before a speech, so he wouldn't sweat so much in front of the cameras." He gave Sunny an understanding smile. "You see if it doesn't work like a charm. Unscented of course."

"Of course," Sunny said, knowing in her heart that she wasn't a princess. Just a single mom who enjoyed her family, a beer with the boys, and genuine conversations. And how in God's name was she going to smile less?

"What are you doing now?" Val said, her voice unexpectedly soft as she came toward her.

Sunny looked down at the beautiful butterfly mask in her hand and knew she couldn't carry it off any better than she could the heels. "Thinking that I'm wasting your time. That I'm not cut out for this."

Val's fingers were light and cool on her arm. "But you are cut out to paint. And if you pass up this chance tonight, how will you feel when you're waiting tables tomorrow?" She leaned closer. "Don't tell Moyra I said so, but it's definitely time to say good-bye to the tearoom."

Sunny hesitated, torn between what she wanted and what she was. And never had she been so grateful for the sound of footsteps in the doorway.

"We're here," Hugh called, as he and Jess raced past the kitchen to the tables. Hugh dragged a garment bag from his shoulder, and held it aloft. "I have—The Dress."

"And I have The Hair," Jess said, pushing past him with a black box in her hands and a huge grin on her face.

"Together we are . . ." They bowed with a flourish. "Your costume."

Sunny could only laugh. They were Andersons, both. Right down to the red hair and the need to win. Only Jess's amaretto eyes set her apart, and gave a clue to her father's dark, Mediterranean beauty.

"Take it upstairs," Sunny said, following the two of them and Val to the staircase at the back of the tearoom.

"Good luck," her dad whispered.

"Watch your ankles," her mother said.

"What's the costume?" Mrs. Dempster squealed.

"It's divine," Jess called back on a sigh.


At 4:00 P.M. Michael finally sat down at his desk. He'd spent most of the day with service crews and hotel maintenance staff, making sure everything from the air-conditioning to the security systems were up and running, and that there would be no surprises tonight. As a result, he had ten phone calls to return and a queue full of e-mail, along with Duane's résumé and the envelope from head office still waiting to be read. So he went in order of priority and opened the e-mail from his nephews first.

The title was *Guess What?* and the body was short. *Hi Uncle Mike, We have a surprise for you! Nicholas and Ben.*

At five and eight respectively, the boys already knew the

value of brevity, and Michael predicted great futures for both of them.

He clicked on the first attachment and watched the faces of his brother's family appear: Andy, his wife, Jill, and the two kids, blond and smiling, and getting bigger every time he saw them.

For a moment there was envy, a soul-deep longing for the children he would never have. A girl with sleek black hair like her mother, and a boy with ears he would grow into, just as his father had. Michael had seen them both in Kate's eyes for years. But there had always been a reason to hold off, to wait, neither of them dreaming that they didn't have all the time in the world. But Michael was getting better at shaking it off and smiling. Getting on with it, as they say. After all, it had been three years.

He clicked on the second attachment. There were three shots here. In the first, they were all standing in front of a vacant lot, holding a sign that spelled out: WE NEED A HOUSE.

In the second they were checking their watches: WE NEED IT SOON.

And in the last, they were looking forlornly at the camera: CAN YOU HELP US?

Michael typed an equally brief reply. *No. Call Bill Johnson.*

He hit SEND but knew it wouldn't be the last he'd hear from his brother's crew. They were nothing if not persistent, always inviting him to Toronto for one holdiay or another. But Michael hadn't taken so much as a weekend off since joining Concord, and with the California project looming, it didn't look as though things were going to change any time soon.

So if Andy and Jill had bought themselves a lot and wanted a house, there was no better choice than Bill, because Michael had got on with it. And he wasn't in the business anymore.

The front door opened and Michael glanced up from his desk. "Did you get the tux?"

"Affirmative," Duane said, carrying a garment bag and

a box to the sofa. "I asked myself when I was at the store, what would Mr. Wolfe want in a tux?"

"Black and white," Michael said, reaching for the envelope from head office.

"Yes, sir. But beyond the question of black and white, there were still choices to be made. Bow tie or cravat. Cummerbund or vest. Long jacket or short. Striped pants or plain."

Michael slowly raised his head, taking in Duane's own strange suit, almost afraid to see what his final choice had been. "I lean toward simplicity."

Duane smiled. "I knew that, so I let tradition be my guide." He pulled the bag off with a flourish and held up a black tux with a white shirt, a black bow tie, and a cummerbund.

"Good choice." Michael shook his head and pulled a file from the envelope. "What did you get for yourself?"

"I'll be happy to show you," Duane said, stretching his neck for a closer look. "Is that for Sundridge?" He snapped back to attention when Michael glanced up. "I noticed the name at the top."

"Very observant." Michael rose and carried the file to the drafting table. "So what's your costume?"

Duane hesitated a moment, then returned to the sofa and lifted the lid from the box. He pulled out a wide-brimmed hat and a striped serape. Setting the hat on his head, he fastened the string under his chin, tossed the serape over his shoulder, and composed his face into a frown. "Who am I?"

Michael shrugged. "A mariachi singer?"

Duane looked hurt. "I'm Rudolph Valentino in the *Four Horsemen of the Apocalypse*. A wonderful if widely forgotten film."

"I see the resemblance now," Michael said, and flicked on the light above the table. "You should go and get ready."

"If you don't mind, I'd like to see what head office has sent. I've seen your preliminary work on the Carillon Hotel, sir, and I'm looking forward to rolling up my sleeves and pitching in. In fact, I've already assembled a list of mechanical and electrical contractors in the area, along with references for your consideration." He gestured to the unopened envelope on the desk. "I included it with my résumé, if you'd like to take a look."

"Maybe later," Michael said, giving him a smile that had frozen bigger men to the spot and worked just as efficiently with Duane. "I'd like to see how it measures up to the list I compiled months ago. I'm sure your network of industry contacts is every bit as impressive as your enthusiasm."

Duane looked down at his feet. "I used the yellow pages."

"No better starting place." Michael turned back to the file. "Just out of curiosity, Nugent, did the files you read mention that I usually work alone?"

"There were a few notes to that effect."

"Then you'll understand when I say I'll call if I need your help." Michael flipped open the file. "Lock the door on your way out. I'm officially at home now."

Michael purposely ignored Duane's rustlings as he folded his costume back in the box, only looking over his shoulder when the door clicked shut behind him. Michael sighed and glanced over at the envelope containing the résumé. If the kid was as smart as he appeared to be, he'd ask for a transfer tonight. Because Lord knew Michael wouldn't work with himself if he was Duane.

He went back to the file. On top was a photograph of the Carillon, followed by three sketches and a rough, computer-generated plan of the first and second floors. They weren't working drawings by any means, just an artist's impression of what the lobby, the ballroom, and a typical guest room might look like. Attached to the photograph was a yellow post-it note: *From the Desk of Judith Hill.*

Judith Hill was tall, hungry-looking, and the new CEO of Grant Hall Resorts, the firm that had taken over Concord. Her profile at the official announcement of the merger had listed her as a graduate of Harvard, a veteran in the resort industry, and a team player with vision and imagination.

As an up-and-comer in the world of family resorts, Grant Hall had built five hotels in three years, and under Judith's direction, the expansion was to be even faster. While the Concord side would continue as a separate entity, changes were clearly in the air.

*Michael, we're so excited! The Sundridge property is to become the flagship resort in the Grant Hall chain.*

Like many other Concord properties, the Carillon in Sundridge had once been a private estate. Nestled high on a hill and surrounded by sculpted gardens and dancing fountains, the house had been a pink palace filled with marble and crystal. A fantasy built over seventy years ago by a man desperate to keep his wife at home after she'd seen Gay Paree. Unfortunately, the plan hadn't worked and the estate had passed from one owner to another, each time undergoing some sort of renovation or updating, until it finally landed in Michael's lap, destined to become the next Concord hotel.

Michael had submitted his design assessment and a proposal for the new hotel to Concord before the buyout, suggesting the kind of restoration and renovation that had become their trademark. But the sketches Judith had sent reflected none of his recommendations.

*. . . as you know, a Grant Hall resort is all about fun, and what could be more fun than a week at the new Carillon?*

Michael almost laughed. *Fun* didn't begin to describe what they'd done. *Manic* was the word that came to mind.

The nine luxury suites Michael had proposed had become 320 identical rooms in an expansion that wiped out the gardens and replaced the fountains with two swimming pools. A water-slide tower was attached to the main house by a skywalk that led guests to an arcade in the lobby, a screening room, and three themed restaurants. But it wasn't until he turned to the sketch of the ballroom that Michael finally shook his head.

The original ballroom had been designed after the palace at Versailles with vaulted ceilings, gilt edging, and mirrored walls. In Judith's version, that room became a mini-putt with windmills, clowns, and a water hazard featuring snapping turtles.

Michael couldn't help wondering who was part of Judith's "we," and whether any of them knew that a king and the woman he had the misfortune to love had once danced in the reflection of those very mirrors. And if they knew, did any of them care?

*. . . let me know how much you love it. Judith*

He rocked back in the chair, thinking of those dancers at the Carillon and seeing in his mind the dancers on the ceiling downstairs. He smiled as an image of the painter herself came to mind.

Cute and freckled, she looked all of sixteen in baggy overalls and a baseball cap, although he knew she had to be older. Those overalls had made it hard to see much, but he'd had a definite impression of curves. The kind that were soft and full, and couldn't be found on any sixteen-year-old he'd ever seen.

He straightened, called himself a dirty old man, and moved on to the sketch of the guest room, but found his mind wandering, wondering where she'd come from and how they'd found her, and hoping she had indeed left some cards with catering. Because it would be a shame if she didn't get some business out of it.

His eyes were drawn back to the ceiling of the Carillon's future ballroom, a barren expanse broken only by chandeliers that he knew would not be crystal. Which left plenty of room for a mural, a reflection of what the old ballroom had been, perhaps. And who knew? With a push, he might find a way to convince Judith that a mural was worth fitting into the budget. Along with a few mirrors. And a touch of gold here and there.

Michael picked up Judith's note, not sure where that idea had come from or why. What she did with the Carillon made no difference to him one way or the other. He was just along for the ride, which was exactly the way he wanted it.

He'd already had his turn in the driver's seat, with his own architectural firm and fifteen employees—Capitol Designs, because they'd lived in Washington and Kate loved a good pun.

Kate. He said her name out loud this time, but softly. "Kate," as though there was enough magic in the single word to conjure her up, have her walk through that door, sleek black hair framing a face that was delicate and fine boned, and accenting eyes so brown they were almost black.

Katherine Shaw, his wife, his best friend, his only love. Gone, just like the company, the dog, and all their foolish plans. Nothing left now but Michael, a few books, and a house in Maine that he couldn't let go.

He rose, suddenly restless, needing to move, to breathe, to be in California with a new project to think about. Something to keep his mind busy and his heart numb. And if that meant gutting the Carillon and turning the whole thing inside out, so be it.

He dragged Judith's note toward him, scrawled *How do I love it? Let me count the ways* across the bottom, shoved it into a small envelope, and rang for a bellboy.

He hesitated, still not sure why it mattered, then pulled out the note and added a line, *Have you seen the mural in the ballroom?* and shoved the whole thing back in the envelope, telling himself the painter had worked hard and deserved a break. It was as simple as that.


Afternoon sun filtered through the blinds in Sunny's bedroom, casting narrow strips of light against the wall above the bed she and Jess often shared. Their flat on the third floor wasn't large, but the light was good, the rent right, and Jess loved having her nana and grandpa one floor down. And as she climbed up onto the bed with the box, Sunny knew she would have a hard time convincing her they needed a place of their own.

"Utterly divine," Jess whispered into the box.

"Short for fabulous," Hugh said, laying the garment bag on the bed as he peeked into Val's makeup bag. "Do you have pancake in there? We're going to need to get rid of those freckles."

Sunny frowned and set the butterfly mask on the dresser. "I like my freckles."

"You'll need alabaster skin," Jess said matter-of-factly. "To go with hair of gold."

"Hair of gold," Sunny echoed, and opened the box Jess had been carrying. Sure enough, the Styrofoam head inside had hair of gold—a blond wig the color of clover honey shimmering with palest gold—upswept in the back with soft curls at the front. It didn't look like Daisy Mae or Nancy, and it definitely wasn't Fagin. "What show is this from?" she asked.

"*Arsenic and Old Lace,*" Hugh told her.

Sunny screwed up her nose. "The old ladies who killed people?"

"There were other characters," Hugh said, pulling back the zipper on the garment bag. "But I tell you, Sunny, this gown is enough to knock anyone out cold."

Any lingering fears Sunny had of *Oliver* rags or *L'il Abner* shorts faded on a rustle of jade-green satin, short puffy sleeves, and a bodice cut so low, it made her blush just to look at it.

Jess bounced up and down on the bed. "What did I tell you? What did I tell you?"

Val approached slowly, like a supplicant. "You were right, sweetie. Your mom is going to look divine." Val scooped up the dress and wig, and hustled Sunny into the bathroom, smiling at Hugh and Jess as she closed the door. "Excuse us, but we have to make a proper entrance."

Sunny slipped off her jeans and T-shirt while Val climbed up onto the toilet seat with the dress. Sunny raised her arms and closed her eyes as the gown slid down and wrapped around her. The satin was cool and soft, raising goose bumps on her skin and sending a wonderful shiver along her spine.

Val fastened the zipper at the back, pulling the dress in tightly, making Sunny gasp, but the effect was startling. She put her hands to her chest, shocked by the expanse of skin and the soft rise and fall of her breasts. And when Val pulled the puffy sleeves down past her shoulders, Sunny felt herself blush all over again.

She slipped her feet into the sandals and glanced into the mirror above the sink, seeing those bare shoulders, the heightened color in her cheeks, and the sharp, clear green of her own eyes. She'd spent so many years in overalls and blue jeans she'd forgotten the simple joy of dressing like a girl. And she couldn't deny the rush of excitement deep inside, where only dread had been. She felt beautiful, looked beautiful, and she wanted to see herself with hair of gold.

Sunny didn't think twice about covering her wonderfully sleek hair with a white net cap and tucking all traces of red underneath. Then Val slipped on the wig, and Sunny had nothing to say.

The woman looking back at her from the mirror was a stranger. A wonderful, exciting, sensuous stranger, and for some reason, Michael Wolfe came to mind. He wouldn't know her if he fell over her now, but it would be fun to watch him trip.

Which left only one thing missing.

"The butterfly mask," she said, and Val threw open the door.

Sunny swept into the bedroom, her every step rendered graceful by the movement of the dress. Jess stopped bouncing and Hugh got to his feet. It was Sunny's first standing ovation, and she loved it.

Hugh pulled from his pocket a velvet box. Inside was the

most exquisite fake emerald necklace Sunny had ever seen, along with a pair of matching earrings.

"Who are you?" Jess whispered, putting out a hesitant hand to touch the gown.

"Your mom is one of the cool blondes," Hugh told her. "Grace Kelly, Jean Harlow—"

"Grace Kelly," Sunny said, giving Jess's hand a squeeze and winning a smile from her.

"Grace is good, very classy," Val said. "Now we're going to need props for this next part." She motioned Jess to follow her. "Let's go ask Nana for a wineglass and a small plate. And you," she said to Sunny, "keep walking. The important thing tonight will be to stay focused."

Hugh looked over at Sunny. "You ask me, the important thing is to have some fun."

Sunny sighed and reached for the mask. "This night is not about me, it's for my career."

"Sunny, do you have any idea how long it's been since anything was just about you? About having fun, enjoying life? Doing something completely outrageous."

"It's been a while," she said, and glanced over at the window, seeing herself at sixteen, climbing down the fire escape in the middle of the night. Madly in love and defiant as hell, heading out to meet the dark-haired boy her parents had forbidden her to see. The first boy who had ever said he loved her.

"But I'm a mother now," she said. "I have responsibilities."

"And you live up to them every day," Hugh said gently. "Which is why you can afford to let loose a little tonight. Dance with a stranger. Have a moment of madness, just for yourself."

"A moment of madness?" she said and gave a short laugh. "How can I do that when I'm supposed to be figuring out who's worth talking to, who's not? Smiling right, walking right. Getting in and getting out." She fit the mask over her eyes. "Believe me, I'd rather be going to wing night."

Hugh glanced back at the door, lowered his voice. "As much as I like Val, you don't have to do any of those things." Hugh took hold of her shoulders, made her face the mirror. "You're so beautiful, all you have to do is stand in the middle of the room, and look up."

# Three

By 8:00 P.M. the crowd outside the Brighton was as large as the one inside. With each new limousine, Fortune 500 groupies and autograph hounds huddled closer to the velvet cord that lined the red carpet, hoping for a glimpse of a star, any star. Perhaps a smile or a wave, maybe a scrawled signature in their books, before the favored few in feathered masks and glittering costumes were swept through the front doors and into the party of the week.

The ballroom was alive with color, music, and laughter. Four themed bars and buffet tables offered everything from wine and cheese, to umbrella drinks and Polynesian ribs, while white-coated waiters circulated with trays of champagne. Fire-eaters, jugglers, and mimes competed with the band for attention, while roving photographers captured everything on film.

Michael picked up his glass—vodka martini, shaken, not stirred—and pushed away from the bar, knowing he'd have to do the rounds soon if he wanted to be out of there within the hour.

He glanced up at the ceiling as he skirted the dance floor, seeing the mural from yet another new angle and not at all surprised that no one else seemed to know it was there.

"I've been looking for you," a voice called. He turned to see Judith bearing down on him, looking every inch the confident CEO in a costume that was male on one side and female on the other. Disconcerting perhaps, but fitting.

"You were supposed to wear a costume," she said by way of a greeting. "And don't tell me you're James Bond. I wasn't born yesterday."

It was on the tip of his tongue to say that he was Fred Astaire when she took his arm and waved a photographer over. "Smile," she said, and a flash went off in his eyes. "We're starting a corporate newsletter and I want everyone in the first issue."

The band slid into a slow and schmaltzy version of a Beatles tune. Judith took what was left of his martini, handed the glass to the photographer, and said, "Let's dance."

Michael followed her onto the floor, wondering which one of them was going to lead, and was quietly pleased when her feminine side prevailed, for the moment at least.

Sunny gave the kitchen door a push and peeked into the ballroom. She held Val's hand for support, a Kleenex for security—not entirely trusting her father's Richard Nixon story—hoping the band would move into something fast and loud so no one would hear the beating of her heart when she took that first step through the door.

"If you don't go soon," Val whispered, "they're going to start getting suspicious in here."

Sunny checked behind her. The entire kitchen staff was watching her while they worked, still unaware of who she was. No one had questioned Val when she arrived at the service entrance with a glamorous young woman in tow. After all, it wasn't the first time a star or a mistress had come in the back way. And if the concierge was with her, then the only thing needed from the staff was absolute discretion.

"Seems I've got cold feet," Sunny said to them, moving smoothly into an Irish accent to compliment her disguise.

They all nodded and smiled back. As she turned to the

door, she heard snippets of conversation above the clatter of dishes and pots.

"I swear she's that actress who always dies in planes."

"Wasn't she on Rosie last week?"

"No, that was the other one."

"Man, I don't care who she is. That chick is hot."

She smiled out the door. Sunny Anderson, hot. Who would have ever dreamed?

The fact that they weren't really talking about the real Sunny did nothing to dampen her spirit. She hadn't felt this wonderful, this high in a long time, and she wasn't about to let technicalities spoil the fun. Tonight she was the mystery woman. A vixen in green, a siren in emeralds, with cleavage to die for and no past to live down, nor future to live up to. And Michael Wolfe would be lucky if she remembered *his* name.

She squinted through the crack in the door, searching the crowd, wondering if he was out there, but not sure why it mattered.

Val pointed past her head. "There's that guy we saw this morning, remember? Turns out, he's Michael's new assistant. So if he talks to you, be careful." She screwed up her nose. "Any idea what he's supposed to be?"

Sunny shrugged as the wide-brimmed hat and serape moved out of view. "A mariachi singer?"

Val shook her head. "That man needs someone to take him in hand." She frowned at Sunny. "And if you don't go through that door on your own steam in ten seconds, I will take you in hand."

"I'm going, I'm going." Sunny hesitated. "Is there any possibility Wolfe won't be out there?"

"Absolutely none."

"That's what I thought."

So the vixen took a breath, and the siren squeezed Val's hand. But it was Sunny who tossed the Kleenex on faith and gave the door a push.

And there it was, smack-dab in the center of the room:

the mural—her mural—with a crowd underneath, music in the air, and nowhere at all for her to stand.

With Judith still in his arms, Michael blinked and looked again as the kitchen door swung closed. There was no vision standing there, no beauty in green, no enchantress in a butterfly mask. Only a waitress with Princess Leia balls on her ears and an empty tray in her hands, disappearing into the kitchen.

"Got your note," Judith was saying, "and I have to say I'm glad you're onside for the Sundridge project. We've got big plans for Concord, and for you, Michael. I was concerned you wouldn't come over so easily."

"It's your company," he said, pushing the kitchen beauty from his mind as he dipped Judith, finding it quite satisfying when her male side gripped his shoulder in terror.

Her eyes narrowed with suspicion as he settled her back on her feet. "You're not as unreasonable as I'd been led to believe."

"I don't know how these rumors get started."

"Your assistants, for the most part, although I haven't heard any complaints from Duane yet."

He spun her out. "It's still early. Give him time."

She came back, watching him closely. "So I'll expect you at the meeting on Monday morning."

Meeting? He vaguely recalled a memo. Key issues. Group energy. Everything he usually avoided. But this was a new day, a new company. And it made no difference to him one way or the other.

"I'll be there," he said.

She stopped dead and both sides of her looked him straight in the eye. "Don't let me down on this one, Michael. I'm treating these next few days as an executive retreat. A chance to build a solid team, and I expect everyone to be part of it. Especially that meeting." She raised a hand, the dance clearly over. "I want to get a group shot," she said and struck out across the dance floor, obviously expecting him to follow.

He was a step behind when Judith drew up in front of a group of men and women standing near the kitchen door. He glanced over as the door opened again. A flash of white hats and gleaming pots, but no woman in green. He gave his head a shake and made up his mind to get something to eat once the photo shoot was over.

"You all remember Michael Wolfe," Judith said, but went around the circle anyway.

General Patton was the VP of finance, Attila the Hun was the landscape architect, and Scarlett O'Hara was the communications officer, every one of them handpicked by Judith, not a hand-me-down like Michael.

Introductions made, she motioned another photographer over and had them line up. This time, Michael turned before the flash went off.

"Haven't seen much of you," the General said.

"I've been pretty busy here—"

"But you'll be at the meeting on Monday?" Scarlett asked.

Michael smiled at Judith. "Wouldn't miss it."

"Looking forward to talking to you about the Carillon," Attila put in. "Maybe we can get together on Sunday."

"No problem," Michael said, glancing over as the kitchen door swung back one more time. But it was only a busboy, collecting dishes. He turned back to the group, now heavily involved in a discussion of something called a dream mission, when he spotted her at last, the beauty in green. Only this time she wasn't in the kitchen, she was standing not thirty feet away, all alone, dead center on the crowded dance floor, looking up at the ceiling.

So the beauty in green was a mad woman. It figured.

But mad or not, she was the most striking woman he'd seen in a long time. Her hair was blond, her skin like cream, and the glittering butterfly mask lent her eyes depth and drama and drew attention to a mouth that was soft and rose colored.

All around her, couples moved in time to a Bert Bacharach number so mellow it was almost ripe, yet she seemed above it all, floating undisturbed but not unseen. How could a woman so beautiful ever go unseen? And now that he thought about it, she didn't really look mad either, more curious than anything. But what the hell was she doing?

He watched, intrigued, as Wyatt Earp and a dance hall girl who looked like someone he should know from televison stopped beside her and looked up too. That's when she smiled for the first time, a slow and subtle curve of the lips, like a cat who had just spotted the canary. She said something that made them laugh, and it wasn't long before another couple stopped and looked up. Then another, and another, and if he wasn't mistaken, the reporter from the *Times* had just started circling. The little mural painter would have been pleased.

"So Michael, what do you think?" Judith asked.

He was still smiling when he turned back to the group. "I think I suddenly believe in the dream mission. If you'll excuse me, I have something to attend to."

He didn't wait for Judith's blessing, simply headed into the crowd, figuring he could spend a while at the party yet.

The reporter shoved a tape recorder at the beauty in green, and as Michael drew closer he could hear her voice: soft and refined, with a soft Irish lilt he found ridiculously sexy.

"All I know about the artist is what I see." She glanced up one more time. "I'm sure there must be someone around who can answer your questions."

A hand appeared in front of the reporter. "I'm Valerie Conan-Smythe, hotel concierge. Perhaps I can help you."

"I certainly hope so," Judith said, already making her way to the front of the crowd. "Val, nice to see you again. I'm beginning to understand why your reputation precedes you." She offered a card to the reporter. "Judith Hill, CEO of Concord Hotels, and I can tell you we are mighty proud of this wonderful work."

"I imagine you are," the reporter said. "One more thing, miss. What's your name?"

But the vision was already gone, threading her way through the crowd to the bar.

"I'm sure we can answer all of your questions," Judith said, turning the reporter around and leading both him and Val off the dance floor.

The band suddenly let loose with a swing number and the singer took center stage again. Couples jumped and jived, the fire-eater boogied with the bugle boy, and the mural's fifteen minutes of fame were over. But the beautiful blond was still there, standing in a relatively quiet corner by the seafood table with a waiter at her side, downing one glass of champagne while she reached for another.

Michael headed over, picking up two more glasses along the way, in case she was still thirsty.

He drew up behind her, watching the play of light on her hair as she drained the second glass. "Who are you?" he asked, and she choked on the last swallow as she turned.

"I beg your pardon?"

"Your costume," he said, and took a quick step back, giving her room. "I can't put a finger on who you're supposed to be."

She stared at him, her eyes wide behind the butterfly wings, as though she might bolt at any second; then that same mysterious smile slowly curved her lips.

"I would have thought it was obvious," she said, her voice softer, her accent musical again as she came toward him. "I'm Grace Kelly, after the prince. And you?" she asked, her eyes drifting lower, her appraisal so frank and so completely unexpected that his mouth went dry and he found it hard to think.

"James Bond," he managed. "Before Roger Moore."

She took the glass he'd forgotten he was holding and raised it to her lips. "Pity. I rather like the new one better."

He had a nice laugh for a man with no sense of humor. Not a rollicking belly laugh, or one of those annoying snickers, but one that was soft and sexy, and made for the dark.

The kind that winds around you, draws you in, and makes you wish you'd listened to that little voice that started hollering *Run, run, and never look back* when you had the chance. Because all you had to do was look at him to know this guy was nothing but trouble. And haven't you had enough of that already?

*Without a doubt,* she thought, and turned her head, but only to hide a smile of triumph, knowing that for once she had Mr. Wolfe's undivided attention.

She sipped her champagne, tapped her feet to the music, and pretended not to watch him watching her. After all, her work here was done and Val appeared to be handling the rest just fine over at the wine bar. If she hurried, she would still make it home in time to put Jess to bed. Hang the vixen dress in the closet and be Mom again, just like every other night of her life.

She jumped when his breath tickled her ear. "Who are you really?"

She turned, meeting his eyes and feeling the pull, the draw that was so much a part of this man, only stronger this time, more compelling, because all of that energy was focused on her.

"Sonja," she said, unable to come up with a last name or even to move as his gaze dipped lower, skimming over her mouth, her throat, the cleavage she was so proud of, taking his time as she had herself and not looking up until her skin began to warm and her breathing grew shallow.

*Run, run,* the voice whispered. But instead she gave a soft, distinctly un-momlike laugh, picked up a plate, and started round the seafood table, knowing Sonja was starting something Sunny wasn't going to be able to finish, but unable to stop her just yet.

"And who are you in real life?" she asked, spearing shrimp and crab, and feeling her heart beat a little faster when he picked up a plate of his own and followed.

"Michael Wolfe, project manager for Concord."

"Sounds impressive."

"Not really. But I couldn't help noticing your interest in the mural. Are you an artist yourself?"

"I dabble," she said, surprised that he hadn't launched into a long dissertation about his fabulous career, many successes, and oh-so-rosy future as most men would have done. But then, Michael Wolfe wasn't anything at all like most men.

He leaned closer, his arm brushing hers as he reached for a sushi roll. "What do you do when you're not dabbling?"

"I work in a gallery," she told him because it was true, and it was all she could think of when every cell in her body was on alert and her mind was buzzing with contradictory warnings. *Leave now. Stay and see what happens. Is it really safe to eat raw fish?*

She gave her head a quick shake, said no to the sushi and added, "In Boston. I'm in charge of discovering new talent," because that sounded interesting, more like Sonja. "The search always excites me because I never know where I'm going to find the next emerging artist," she added, sketching the portrait as she went along, and adding the details layer by layer. "Naturally I travel extensively. Moscow one day, Rio the next."

"Where do you call home?"

"Wherever I happen to be," she said, because the idea appealed to her. "But I'm very glad I made the stop in Manhattan, or I would never have seen that mural."

"So our painter is on your list of emerging artists."

"Definitely." She kept her eyes on her plate and tried to sound casual. "Do you know much about her?"

"Only that she's a cute kid with a weird weather name. Stormy, Cloudy—"

She bristled. "Thunder perhaps?"

"It's Sunny," a voice said.

They turned and the Bonnie and Clyde couple behind them grinned. "Sunny Anderson," the woman continued, pointing to the wine bar and Val. "That girl over there left the artist's name and number on a card by the swizzle sticks.

Told us to go and check out her work at a Brooklyn gallery too. I'm thinking of calling her Monday, see what she suggests for the half bath in our chalet."

A half bath at the cottage. Sunny sighed. It was a start.

"I'm sure you'll be pleased," Michael said.

"We can hardly wait," the woman said and the two of them moved on to the salmon, also passing on the sushi, Sunny noticed.

"So are you pleased?" she asked, turning back to Michael.

"So far," he said, his voice like a caress as he drew up in front of her.

"I meant with the mural," she said dryly and walked around him. "What do you think of it?"

"It's very pretty."

"Pretty," she repeated and drummed her fingers on the bottom of her plate.

She could let it go. Should in fact, but for some reason it was important that he see what was really up there.

She put the plate down and motioned him to follow her out to the dance floor where she stopped under the dome.

"Tell me what you see," she said.

Michael didn't need to look at the mural again to know the answer. "Five couples dancing," he said, standing behind her, breathing in the delicate scent of her perfume.

"Anything else?" she asked.

He glanced up. "The bad guy with the flapper seems happy."

She swiveled her head to look at him. "Do you think she leaves with him?"

He pursed his lips, seeing the soft rise and fall of her breasts, feeling the warmth of her skin against his chest, and thinking maybe she was crazy after all. "Sonja, it's a mural."

"And a mural is like a person," she said softly. "With personality and conflicting emotions. A past, a present, even a future. When you look at it, you know that something is about to happen, but you don't know what it is.

And like people, many of them have secrets. Including this one."

Michael tipped his head back. "And you see this secret?"

She smiled and pointed to the starlet. "Right up there. In the sequins on her dress."

Michael looked, tilting his head to the right and then to the left. Adjusting the angle, squinting, unsquinting. "I see fish. But then, I can never find anything in clouds either, so—"

She laughed. "Don't try so hard. Just relax, and you'll see it, above the heel of her shoe. Cinderella escaping at midnight."

"Sorry, but I don't—" And then suddenly she appeared, right where Sonja had said. A tiny Cinderella running for all she was worth.

He turned back to her. "How did you find her in all those sequins?"

An odd smile touched her lips. "You'd be amazed what you can find if you look closely."

Michael pulled her into his arms, swayed to the music. "You know, I never did understand why she ran off."

"Cinderella?" Sonja looped her arms around his neck, laid her head on his shoulder. "Because her time was up. The magic was over. What else could she do?"

"Ignore the clock and enjoy herself."

"But what if the prince didn't like what he saw underneath?"

"He went after her, didn't he?"

"True. But it was a fairy tale."

The song ended. Sonja turned to go but he stopped her with a hand on her arm. "How long will you be in town?"

"I'm leaving in the morning." She smiled as she strolled away. "Which gives us about as much time as Cinderella and the prince."

Her feet moved of their own accord and she stared straight ahead, horrified and thrilled at the same time. Wondering where that had come from, and what she was playing at. And not at all surprised when he fell into step beside her.

This was why she wasn't ready to leave, she realized. She was simply enjoying herself too much. Enjoying the fact that as Sonja she could do anything or say anything. Be shocking and sexy, and make Michael Wolfe sit up and take notice.

She glanced over at him as she walked, feeling beautiful, powerful, but most of all desirable. Because if that wasn't hunger she saw in those narrowed dark eyes, then she'd been out of circulation for far too long.

Which was a distinct possibility given that her last sexual encounter had been almost a year before in the back of Vince Cerqua's convertible when the top wasn't the only thing that wouldn't go up. And she'd spent the drive home assuring him that it happened to men all the time; at least that was what she heard in the tearoom.

She turned away quickly, feeling her face warm, and knowing instinctively that Michael's top would never let him down. Not that she wanted to find out. Not really. Not now, at any rate.

"Where will you be going in the morning?" he asked.

"New Jersey."

He drew his head back and she laughed. "There's a theater group I'm rather fond of. After that, it's anyone's guess. I'm just a wanderer. Never in one place long enough to plant a garden as they say."

"Is that what you'd like to do? Plant a garden?"

"Yes," she said, slipping in a touch of Sunny, but staying true to Sonja. "Of course, with so many emerging artists, I'm not thinking about that right now."

He stopped and took her hand. "What are you thinking about?"

Trouble. And sex. Mostly sex. For all the good it did her.

Truth to tell, Sunny wasn't the kind to have a one-night stand. She was conservative in her thinking and cautious when it came to matters of the heart. The biggest risks she took were with the best-before dates on salad dressings.

She was the kind who delivered hampers at Christmas, painted faces at the community center on Halloween, and made sure her organ-donor card was signed. There was no question about it. She was Sunny the good: Balanced. Friendly. And utterly predictable.

But Sonja? Now there was a real vixen. A woman who traveled the world, took risks every day, and was never, ever predictable. And it seemed a shame to make her leave the ball so early when she was only in town for one night. And Sunny had the rest of her life to spend being good.

Michael ran his thumb across hers and the pull was stronger than ever, bringing her back a step. After all, it wasn't as though he was a total stranger, some masked man she picked up at the sushi bar. This was Michael Wolfe, the Beast of Brighton, Terror of the Tradesmen. And she already knew he looked good without a shirt.

And who could tell. Maybe Hugh was right. Maybe a moment of madness *was* good for the soul.

The music changed again, the singer launching into a slow, sultry torch song that begged an answer to the question women had been asking for centuries: what *is* it with men and commitment?

While Sunny had wrestled with that issue herself for years, convinced that the boy she'd loved too much would come back for her one day, pale and contrite, wanting nothing more than to love her the way he should have all along, it wasn't commitment she had on her mind when she twined her fingers with Michael's and gave him Sonja's best come-hither smile. "I'm thinking we should go to your place," she said.

And was sure she was floating as they headed for the door.

# Four

The lobby was a flurry of activity with guests in costume coming and going, bellboys hustling back and forth, and the night watch on the concierge desk talking on two phones at once.

Michael and Sunny were just one more couple passing through and no one gave them a second look when he placed his palm on the small of her back to guide her past the front desk.

Sunny, however, was keenly aware of his touch. Every change in pressure, every move of his fingers felt absurdly intimate under the harsh lights of the lobby. And as they rounded the corner to the bank of elevators, the reality of what she was about to do made her mouth go dry.

She nodded to a group of Jedi warriors exiting the elevator and kept her head down as she and Michael filed into the car with Malibu Barbie, Ken, and Worf. Barbie and Ken were obviously together, judging by the way Ken was holding her hand and looking down her bikini top. Worf, on the other hand, seemed to be there alone, until the elevator stopped and he took Barbie's other hand. And it was only through a conscious effort that Sunny kept her mouth from dropping open when the three of them stepped off together.

She heard a low, throaty laugh as the door closed, and suddenly what she was about to do didn't seem so enormous after all. Just one man and one woman on their way up to the penthouse to do the nasty. No big deal. Tame almost. She jumped when Michael ran his hand up her back, the first brush of his fingers across her bare skin like a shock—hot and electric. Anything but tame.

The elevator slowed and stopped. "This is it," he said, his gaze skimming over her in a way that was casual yet so blatantly sexual it made her knees wobble and her heart pound with equal measures of fear and excitement.

"About time," she said, hoping she sounded seductive and not merely breathless. The door slid open and she told herself to move, to walk. To put one foot in front of the other and get off the damn elevator because now was not the time for cold feet. But Sunny's feet were not only cold, they were frozen. Stuck fast to the carpet with no intention of moving.

She glanced down at her traitorous toes. So much for being unpredictable.

He looked at her curiously. "Something wrong?"

"Just checking my shoes," she said, snapping her head up, determined to be reckless, wild, master of her own feet. "You never know when you'll lose one," she added, and stepped into the hall. "Which way?"

Her step was light and quick, and Michael knew that whatever weight had been holding her down since they left the ballroom had lifted, although he had no idea why or how. And it didn't bother him in the least that he would never have the answer.

He didn't need to know a lot about her. Didn't need to know what side of the bed she slept on, or whether she owned a houseful of cats, or that her best friends still called her Muffin, or Booky, or nothing at all because she had no best friends. He didn't even need to know her last name because none of it mattered. The only thing he really needed to find out was what it took to make sure she had a good time, because that's all they were doing.

"Directly across the hall," he said, taking the key card from his jacket and inserting it into the lock on the door marked IMPERIAL SUITE.

"Now I'm definitely impressed," she said.

"Don't be"—he held the door so she could go in ahead of him—"because it's not mine."

The apartment was dark and still, and her eyes were instantly drawn to the row of tall, narrow windows and the lights of the city below. "What a fabulous view," she said, stating the obvious to fill up the silence and give her something to think about besides the fact that they were all alone now. Just the two of them with the whole night ahead and not a thing to stand in Sonja's way.

"That's why they call it the Imperial Suite," he said, already shedding his tie and jacket as he moved past her, switching on a few lamps and the CD player, revealing a taste for big band music, walls the color of soft morning sunlight, hunter-green love seats, and black lacquer chairs covered in leopard print fabric.

The effect was vibrant and cheeky—surprising considering that the tone in the rest of the hotel was subtle and elegant—and she wandered between the chairs and tables, pausing to touch a ruby-red pillow here, a gilt-edged box there, intrigued by his office.

"Will you miss this place?" she asked and glanced back, half expecting him to be at his desk or checking messages, the workaholic back in his lair. And her pulse jumped when she saw him at the bar, watching her openly as he uncorked a bottle of wine.

"Not at all," he said, taking two glasses from the shelf behind him. "I hope you like red. It's all I have."

"Red is fine," she said, and swallowed hard, might even have whimpered as he came toward her with the wine. She took the glass he offered, clinked it with his, and said, "Cheers," and moved off again, her steps slow and measured but heading for the Queen Anne secretary's desk in the farthest corner all the same.

She stood with her back to him, sipping wine she couldn't taste and absently scanning the shelves; aware of his eyes on her even now, and the faint humming in her blood that this man could start without even touching her.

Sunny moved her shoulders in an unconsciously feminine gesture but resisted the urge to look back, to see where he was. She reached out and picked up a small jeweled box. "What is it that you don't like about the penthouse?" she asked, setting the box down and picking up a brass candleholder instead, suddenly curious about his tastes in homes, in trinkets. In women.

"Nothing particular. I just prefer things a little more understated."

She glanced over. He was leaning against the bar. The glass in his hand was empty. "Nothing here is yours then?" she asked.

"Only the computer and some books." He refilled the glass and brought the bottle with him as he crossed the room. "I travel light and call wherever I am home. Just like you."

"Right," she said, remembering. Sonja the wanderer. No kids, no pets, nothing at all to weigh her down.

Of course, Sunny had only been fantasizing. In truth, she couldn't imagine a life without weight, without roots, without Jess. If she'd thought about it longer, she would probably have given Sonja a place of her own somewhere. Small, not too expensive to heat, but close to the people who loved her, with ties that bind and sometimes chafe, because it was just too sad to think of anyone having nothing and no one.

She glanced up as he came to stand beside her. "Surely you have a home base. A place to store your things and go back to when the job is over?"

He shrugged and topped up her glass. "The jobs usually run back-to-back and I don't have a lot of things."

"But what you *do* have must be somewhere."

"Why?"

"Because it only makes sense."

He set the bottle on the desk and said nothing, simply looked at her for so long she could feel the heat rising into her face. "I'm sorry. I shouldn't—"

"It's in Maine," he said at last. "On the coast."

She turned back to the desk, thinking he'd suit the coast with its moody skies and rugged cliffs. She even had a picture forming in her mind of a lone figure, a regular Heathcliffe standing on a rocky ledge, dark and brooding . . . She stopped mid-picture and leaned forward, her eyes narrowing as she read the titles of the books on the top shelf. And she had to make a few alterations to her picture because while she could imagine Heathcliffe reading one of the horror novels up there, it was more difficult to picture him with *The Far Side* or *Monty Python*. And even harder to imagine him curling up with *Greenhouse Gardening*.

She glanced back as he drew up behind her. "You have an eclectic taste in books."

"The horror is mine but the cartoons are my brother's idea." He ran a fingertip down between her shoulder blades, making her arch and smile. "He thinks I need to lighten up."

"Do you?"

He unclipped one of her earrings and set it on the desk with his glass. "Not always."

Sunny stared at the earring as he ran his hands down her arms, his fingertips brushing the sides of her breasts while he pressed soft kisses across her shoulder. "So," she managed, "do you always read horror?"

His breath was warm in her ear. "Do you always talk so much?"

"Only when I'm nervous."

He touched his lips to the sensitive hollow of her shoulder. "Do I make you nervous?"

"And curious." She took a step away, nodded at the books. "I have to know. Are you really a closet gardener?"

Michael looked up at the shelf. "My wife used to garden," he said, and wished he hadn't when the inevitable questions and answers began.

"You're married?"

"She's dead."

"I'm sorry."

"Me too."

"Anything else you'd like to know?" he asked, and headed back to the bar.

"No, that about does it," Sunny whispered, watching him fill his glass a third time and once again altering the picture in her mind. Making it two people on that rocky shore. One a woman. A wife. Maybe even a mother. And realizing how very little she knew about him.

Rumors mostly, from the contractors and his own former assistant. Tales of a tyrant told over coffee or a beer, but nothing of substance, nothing to reveal the man himself. Yet she'd believed every one, made them gospel, and assumed to know exactly who he was, when in truth no one knew him at all.

He carried a full glass to the window and stared out at the street, his expression flat, unreadable, looking not so much dangerous now as resigned. And she found herself looking back at the books, wondering about his wife—what her name was, what she'd looked like, what kind of husband he'd been, whether or not they'd been happy.

Not that she was a sucker for men with scars. The horror stories on his shelf paled in comparison to the ones she'd heard in the tearoom. Like poor Debby Miller who bet everything on a rebound man and lost. And lovely Anna Sarov who honestly believed she would be the last wife of a serial husband. The list went on and on, and was enough to make any thinking woman swear off hurtin' men for life.

Yet she couldn't deny the tug around her heart when he turned and looked straight at her. He wasn't the Beast of Brighton after all. Just a man with deep sadness, and he was hiding as much as she was.

"You need to know that I'm not looking for anything permanent," he said softly. "If you stay the night, we won't be a couple in the morning."

Sunny took a breath while Sonja unclipped the second earring and laid it beside the other on the Queen Anne secretary's desk. "You forget. I'll be gone by morning anyway."

"All the way to New Jersey," he murmured, his eyes following her across the room.

She switched out a lamp. "We're just a moment of madness, you and I," she said, and was ridiculously pleased when he smiled. She studied him a moment, then turned off a floor lamp. The man had a wonderful smile. Too bad he didn't use it half enough.

"If we can find each other in the dark," he said, laughing when she turned yet another switch.

"I found you," she whispered, coming to stand in front of him. Close enough to feel the warmth of his chest on her breasts and to watch desire build in his eyes. "Almost like fate, wouldn't you say?"

"If you believe that kind of thing."

"What do you believe?"

He traced the sparkling wings of the mask around her eyes. "That I need to kiss you."

He reached for her quite frankly, cupping her face in his hands and kissing her, gently, tenderly, his lips warm and moist and tasting of wine.

He touched his tongue to her lips, seeking entry. Sunny's arms hung at her side, weak and useless as her mind raced and her blood hummed. *This isn't you,* her mind whispered, and her body whispered back, *Thank God,* as her hands found their way to his shoulders and her mouth opened of its own accord.

She shivered at the first stroke of his tongue, every sense heightened and aware, waiting. And still he kept kissing her, slowly, thoroughly, until her legs were shaky, her heart pounding and her fingers clutching at his shirt.

He drew his head back, brushed a thumb across her lips.

"You're sure about this?" he asked, giving her an out, letting her choose. And for the first time, Sunny didn't need Sonja to help her decide.

"I've never been more sure in my life," she murmured, holding on to the Irish lilt because it didn't matter who was in charge on her end. It was still Sonja those hungry eyes were looking at, and she wasn't about to disappoint either of them.

He walked her backward to the sofa, lowered her down into the pillows, and Sunny held her breath when he knelt in front of her and reached under her gown. Only to sigh when she felt his hands on her feet, slipping her shoes off one by one.

Michael rose so they were face-to-face and put a hand on either side of her. The room was dark, colorless, with only the light from the window falling across the sofa. Her skin was very white against the pillows, almost translucent, and he could see her watching him, her eyes wide and bright, nervous again behind that strange mask that hid her so well.

He started to lift it but she stopped him with a small shake of her head. "Please don't," she whispered.

Michael nodded; it made no difference to him. He even liked the idea. He brushed a curl from her forehead. "Are you scared of me?"

"No. Yes." She gave him a small, crooked smile and reached out, laying her hands on his chest, her touch light, tentative, almost shy. "Just kiss me."

He felt an odd jolt as he bent to her, a sense that something was wrong that made him hesitate, think twice—not something he normally did at this stage of the evening. But he couldn't shake the feeling that she wasn't an experienced woman, accustomed to one-night stands and the seduction of strangers.

But with his mouth on hers and her fingers in his hair, it was easy enough to push the thought aside, to tell himself he was imagining things, that she was probably playing coy. And he should simply do what his body was urging him to do.

He kissed his way down her throat to the hollow where her pulse beat strong and fast. He lingered there a moment, a hand on her breast, feeling her rise against his palm, and letting her excitement push his own up another notch before moving farther down.

The cut of the dress was such that it didn't take much to push the bodice down, get it out of the way, so he could run his tongue over her nipples, and feel her rise to his touch when he closed his mouth around her.

He lifted her legs up onto the sofa and ran a hand up under the gown, not content this time to stop at her feet.

Sunny jumped when his fingers grazed her calf, her knee, her thigh all the way up to her hip, only to lock into the elastic of her panties and wait for her to help.

She felt herself blush and was glad the room was dark so he wouldn't see. She closed her eyes and lifted her hips, felt the silk slide down, and couldn't breathe when he started to push the dress up.

But he took his time, kissing her knees, stroking her thighs, in no hurry to satisfy his own need while he built hers higher and higher. He took such time, such care with her, and as he touched his lips to her thighs, all Sunny could think was that he must have been a wonderful husband.

Michael watched her face while he lifted her gown higher and higher. It had been a while since a woman trembled at every touch, sighed at every kiss, and while it excited him more than he would have believed possible, he had that same feeling, the one that told him she hadn't done anything like this in a long time. And he made up his mind to go slow, to make it last all night if he could.

The gown was bunched at her waist now and Sunny opened her eyes wide as he slid a hand down her leg to her foot again. She wasn't sure what he intended until he lifted her foot and rested it on the back of the sofa. Her mouth fell open, but she didn't bring that foot back. She could see his face in the pale light, tell by the set of his mouth, the rhythm of his breath that he wanted her, needed her.

Sunny felt bold and brash, wanton and beautiful. And when he loved her with his hands and his mouth, she held nothing back. She wasn't as skilled as he was, had no experience beyond teenage passion with Brad, and the sad, sorry gropings of Vince. But she knew enough to give him honesty in this at least, to let him know that she loved what he was doing, and he could keep it up forever.

Michael smiled with pure male satisfaction and came up to kiss her lips, her eyes, the tip of her nose. He was hard and full, wanting nothing more than to be inside this woman, to watch her face while he filled her, hear her say his name again and feel the sweetness of her response. He fumbled with the buttons on his shirt, the zipper on his pants, and was sure he'd burst when her fingers closed around him.

He buried his face in her neck as he settled between her thighs. "Sonja," he whispered against her throat and she groaned, but not with pleasure. With something else entirely, something he couldn't name, and if he was smart, he wouldn't try to. Whoever she was in New Jersey tomorrow, she was his now, and she wanted him. Who was he to argue?

But the truth was that he couldn't just take her like this. Not while she had her face turned away.

"Sonja," he said again, but fell silent when he heard a card being slipped into the lock on the front door. And he sat upright when the handle turned.

"Mr. Wolfe?"

She scrambled out from under him and rolled onto the floor, pushing the dress down and pulling it up at the same time. Michael stood up, blocking her from view and wondering when his body would realize the party was over so he could do up his pants, as the pot lights in the ceiling flicked on.

"Mr. Wolfe, are you—" Duane's hand froze on the switch. His lips moved but no words came out. Then he snapped around smartly to face the door. "I'm so sorry, sir."

Michael watched her squeeze her lips together as she tried to untangle her panties. "Just turn out the lights, Nugent."

"I only came to—"

"The lights, Nugent."

The room went dark. She was on her knees now, feeling around for her shoes and muttering something about listening to her feet.

"They need you downstairs," Duane said. "They're making some announcements and Mrs. Hill will be mentioning your name, and—"

"Get out," Michael said.

Duane nodded and started for the door. "Can I tell them you're on your way?"

"Tell them anything you like." Michael sat down beside her while she shoved her feet into the shoes. "Sonja, I'm sorry—"

"Don't be." She rose, patted her hair, squared her shoulders, and was careful to avoid looking at him. "It must be midnight anyway."

"Not yet." He touched a hand to her arm but she pulled away.

"Good-bye, Michael," she said, moving past him with the same regal grace that had caught his eye in the ballroom.

"Where can I reach you?" he called.

"You can't."

"Then call me," he said, tearing a piece of paper from the pad on his desk and scrawling his number as he crossed the room. He held the scrap out to her. "It's my private line. I'm the only one who answers."

She took the paper and ducked her head as she passed Duane. When she opened the door, light from the hall flooded the foyer, turning her into a silhouette in the doorway a second before the door closed behind her.

Michael sighed and turned on a lamp. Two perfect women in one day. That had to be a record.

"Sir?"

"Why are you still here?" Michael glanced over. "And why don't you turn on the damn lights?"

Duane hit the switch, bringing the pot lights to life. "I

just need to be sure you'll go back to the ballroom. Ms. Hill was very clear on this, sir."

From the corner of his eye, Michael saw the flash of an emerald on the secretary's desk. "Nugent, get out," he said, heading for the desk and the earrings she'd left behind.

"You'll come down then?"

Michael looked over at Duane's solemn face. "I'll be there. Now get out."

Duane gave a quick nod before heading into the hall. "And, Mr. Wolfe"—he stuck his head into the room—"you'll need a jacket."

"One more word and I'll stay right here," Michael said.

He walked to the window as the door finally shut and saw her getting into a cab. A beautiful woman escaping into the night. He looked down at the earrings in his hand, and knew exactly how Cinderella's prince had felt.

# Five

Sunny grabbed another bundle of boxes and cut the string. Lifting the first white flat from the pile, she laid it on the cash desk and folded and flipped until she had a perfect four-by-eight baker's box. With a yawn, she set it on the shelf behind her and lifted another flat from the stack. At the rate she was going, she'd have every box in the tearoom ready before Jess woke up and Moyra was on her way down the stairs.

She glanced up as Hugh's pickup pulled into the curb outside the front door. The streetlight was still on and the sun hadn't even started to rise. In a few hours, Sean would be at the tearoom too and the three of them would take over for the day while Moyra and Jack went to celebrate the renewal of Dave and Hazel's vows. But for now it was just Hugh and Sunny and a fresh pot of tea, just as it had been for more mornings than she could remember.

He'd been sleeping when she called his apartment, but he'd come without asking any questions and was at the door now with her favorite contraband biscotti, to be eaten in secret while Moyra still slept.

Hugh had always been the soft touch, the one who taught her to kick a ball, kept her from running like a girl, and never once pulled the heads off her dolls.

While Sean had stood by her since Jessie was born, threatening to beat up anyone who looked askance at his baby sister or the precious wee one she'd brought into the home, it was Hugh who had listened to her talk, and held her when she cried, because Hugh understood what it was to have a broken heart.

"Chocolate and almond," he whispered, glancing at the stairs as he held the bag out. "If we're caught, I'll say it was your fault."

Sunny laughed and headed to a table in the corner.

Her face was scrubbed, her nails her own, and the only hair on her head was red and frizzy again. All traces of Sonja had been bagged and gagged, and stowed in a closet where they couldn't do any more damage. As if they hadn't done enough already.

Hugh dropped into the chair across from her and passed her the bag. "So tell me what's wrong. And it better be good."

"The Brighton Hotel wants another mural." She reached inside and pulled out one of the biscotti. "Judith Hill left a message on my answering machine last night."

Hugh poured the tea. "Sounds like good news to me."

"It would be if she wanted it for the lobby or the spa or even the bathroom." She sighed and dipped the biscotti into her tea. "But no, they've decided they need one in the penthouse. 'Original art, top to bottom,' was the way she put it."

"And this is bad because . . . ?"

"Because that's where Michael lives."

"Back up. Who's Michael?"

Who's Michael? Sunny watched the chocolate on the biscuit soften and warm. Only a man with the darkest eyes and the sweetest touch she'd ever known. A touch that had turned her inside out so quickly, so easily. Left her weak-kneed and gasping, wanting things she hadn't thought about in so long it made her blush to think about them now.

"Michael was my moment of madness."

"Ah," was all Hugh said, but Sunny could already feel the guilt pushing down on her.

She set the biscotti down and walked to the window. "Why do I listen to you?"

"Because I have more fun than you do. Although from the sound of it, I'd say you did just fine last night. And there is nothing wrong with that."

She stared at her reflection in the glass, hardly recognizing her own face. "Hugh, I was a slut."

He laughed. "I doubt that."

"You weren't there."

"Okay, let's do this scientifically. Did you have sex?"

"Technically, no."

"There you go, then. A slut would have had very technical sex, so you're fine."

She turned her back on her reflection and wandered back to the table. "You don't understand. If we hadn't been interrupted, I would have done it. Right there on the sofa."

Hugh dunked his biscotti into his tea. "Sunny, believe me, the sofa is not one of the stranger locations for sex."

"For me it is." She sat down and dragged her teacup closer. "It was just that damn dress. The thing is possessed, I swear. And now I've lost the earrings too."

The next mouthful froze halfway to Hugh's lips. "Now, that is serious. Val needs that costume back by five."

"I'm not worried. He gave me his private number, so I'll call as Sonja—"

"You called yourself Sonja? Have I taught you nothing?"

"I was under stress, all right? Anyway, I'll call as her, tell him to leave the earrings at the front desk, then pick them up when I go over this morning."

"You've already got an appointment?"

"Michael left a message after Judith." And just the sound of his voice on her answering machine had been enough to make her silly heart race. Not that he'd said anything suggestive, or even alluded to the night before. Why would he when he thought he was leaving a message for the painter, never dreaming the lover would be the one to pick it up?

"He told me to meet him at the penthouse at nine A.M.

Being Michael, he didn't even add 'if it's convenient,' or 'if you can make it,' which I can't because I have to be here. But did it occur to him that I might have a life? Something else to do? Of course not. He just issues orders and expects people to jump."

She grabbed the last bite of biscotti from Hugh's hand and stuffed it into her mouth. "He is the most irritating man I have ever met."

Hugh sat back with a smile on his face. "You like this Michael, don't you?"

"You only say that because you've never met him. Michael Wolfe could never be my type. He's too intense, too driven." She stopped and stared at Mary, Queen of Scots' dour face. "Except last night he was different. Considerate, funny . . . But then anyone can have an off night, and that doesn't change the fact that he's still too . . . male."

"You prefer a more feminine man, then."

Sunny whacked him with a napkin. "What I prefer is a man who doesn't make me feel out of control. One who doesn't kiss me until I can't think anymore, or tell right from wrong, or up from down."

"And he does all this for you?"

"And more." Sunny slumped back. "Which is why I can't go to the penthouse, because I will be in big trouble if he recognizes me."

Hugh leaned over and covered her hands with his. "I don't know, Sunny. If he had as much fun as you did, he'd probably love to see you again."

"But that's the problem. It wasn't me he was seeing last night, it was Sonja. He doesn't know *me* from Adam. As far as he's concerned, I'm just a cute kid with a weird name. Called me Stormy, of all things. He won't have a clue it was me there on that sofa last night. But I will. And as soon as I have those earrings, I'm going to tell Judith thanks but no thanks and refer her to the gallery. A different style mural would probably be better anyway—"

"You can't afford to be so magnanimous. Not if you ever want to get out of the tearoom."

"But what'll I do about Michael?"

"What do you want to do?"

"I haven't the slightest idea."

"Then play it by ear. But if I had that much fun the first time, I'd definitely go for it again." He glanced up when he heard Moyra's slippers on the stairs. "Gotta run. But remember what I said."

Sunny rose and followed him to the door. "I already listened to you once and look what it got me."

He stopped with his hand on the knob. "A moment of madness with a man you like, something you haven't had in far too long, kiddo."

"That's not true. There was Vince. . . . Okay that doesn't count."

"And before Vince, who was there? Just Brad and he's been gone for six years." Hugh reached out, brushed the hair from her face. "Sunny, listen to me. You've been so goddamn good since Jess was born, trying to atone for some imagined sin. But you have to believe that last night was nothing you should feel guilty about, and nothing you should regret. You're young and beautiful, and you have a right to have fun, to get it on now and then with a man you like."

He shook his head when she started to protest. "Don't try and tell me you don't like him, because I am an expert when it comes to moony eyes. In fact, I invented them." He cast a quick glance at the stairs and lowered his voice. "Look, I know men can be jerks. God knows I've had my heart broken by enough of them. While this Michael may be all wrong for you, I know he couldn't have gotten you down on that sofa if he hadn't sparked something inside you. So before you jump back into a life of celibacy, take a good long look at him. Because you just might find that he's looking back."

Sunny bowed her head, toyed with the tie on her robe. "What's the point when he's leaving in a few weeks? And even if he wasn't, he's made it more than clear that he's not looking for anything permanent."

He raised her chin, gave her a small smile. "Does every relationship have to have a point, a goal? Can't you simply enjoy him, and yourself, for a while? See what you've been missing all these years?"

Sunny narrowed her eyes, put on her best Scottish burr. "You're a very bad influence, Hugh Anderson."

His smile stretched to a grin. "I try."

"But even if I did listen to you, there's still the tiny matter of my not being the man's type. You should see the women he dates. They're all like Sonja."

Hugh leaned closer. "But Sonja's not coming back. And if this man is too blind to see you're the better of the two, then he doesn't deserve to have you."

"Hugh?" Moyra called. "Are you there?"

"Just leaving, Mom," he called.

Sunny dashed back for the biscotti bag and brushed the crumbs from the table. "You'll be back, won't you?" She stuffed the bag in his hand. "They're going to Dave and Hazel's, remember?"

"The reaffirming of the vows. How could I forget?" He pushed the door and whispered, "Hold on to the job. And go get Michael," before he jogged across the sidewalk to his truck.

Go get Michael. Enjoy the man. Sunny sighed as the door closed in front of her. Sure. Piece of cake.

She caught a glimpse of herself in the glass again. Young and beautiful? Only Hugh would think so. Her lips were too thin, too pale to be sensuous like Sonja's. And the eyes she'd always considered to be her best feature seemed ordinary now without the dress to give them life and the butterfly mask to give them mystery. As for her hair? She'd need a live-in hairdresser if she wanted to keep it sleek.

Sunny turned from the glass, knowing too that if she let herself believe, for even a moment, that Michael could want her over Sonja, she'd be a bigger fool now than she had been last night.

She glanced back as Hugh tooted the horn and pulled away. Then again, Hugh was right about one thing: Sonja wasn't coming back. And for all the good it did her, she had to admit that she liked Michael Wolfe. Liked the way he held her, kissed her. Liked his sense of humor and the way he thought that Cinderella would have been just fine if she'd stayed at the ball a little longer.

But could she do it? Could she let a moment of madness turn into a week of insanity? Just enjoy the man with no thought of tomorrow or where it might lead? And come away knowing exactly what she'd be missing when he was gone?

Moyra padded through the tearoom in her slippers, and picked up the cups from Sunny's table. "Why was Hugh here so early?"

"He stopped by for breakfast," she said, Michael's kiss still stuck in her mind as she turned and smiled at her mother.

Moyra set the cups down hard. "He brought more of those doorstop cookies in here, didn't he?" She brushed more crumbs into her hand. "He'll be the death of me, that one." She dusted her hands over a teacup. "Thank God for you and Jess. I don't know what I'd do without the two of you around."

"Build a pub?" Sunny suggested.

"Don't even joke about it." Moyra carried the cups through to the kitchen. "Who's Michael, by the way?"

Sunny wasn't surprised. Moyra's hearing had always been legendary. "A client," she said. "I did the ballroom mural for him, and now they want another. I'm meeting him at the Brighton this morning." She walked to the stairs. "I'll be leaving in about forty minutes. Hopefully Jess will be awake by then, but if she's not, can you make sure she gets ready for dance class? Sean will be here to get her at eight. Can I bring anything back from the market?"

"Maybe some ham from the deli. Sunny, wait."

Sunny turned back. Moyra stood at the bottom of the stairs, her mouth set, her eyes searching Sunny's face.

When Sunny was growing up, Moyra used to say that all

she had to do was look at her to know what she'd been up to. At twenty-five, Sunny still wasn't sure that she'd lied.

"This client," Moyra said, stretching out the word, giving it weight. "You're not involved with him in some way, are you? Not that it's my business. You're a grown woman now, you can make your own choices. But I worry about you. And Jess. You have to be careful. You have to use good judgment when it comes to men."

She stopped and folded her arms. There was no need to explain further. They both knew what she meant.

"You don't have to worry." Sunny turned and continued up the stairs. "There's nothing going on between Michael and *me.*"


The elevator opened in front of him, and Michael straightened with the newspaper. The painter was early. "I thought we said nine."

Her head snapped up and her eyes widened. But his shirt was all the way back at his desk and there was no way he could do up the top button of his jeans without dropping both the coffee and the newspaper. So he leaned a shoulder against the door frame and waited for her to either say something or ride back downstairs when the elevator closed again.

She thrust out a foot and caught the door midslide. "You're the one who agreed on nine, not me. And since I have plans for the rest of the day, it's either now or Monday."

"Then I suppose it's now," he said, pleased that he wasn't going to have a mouse with a paintbrush creeping around his office for the next few days.

He still didn't understand Judith's pressing need for another mural, or why she wouldn't talk to the interior designer first. But as long as the painter didn't get in his way, they could have a hotel full of murals for all he cared. The only thing that made the idea palatable at all was knowing they'd called on this particular painter to do the work.

"Come in," he said, standing back as she walked across the hall and into the penthouse.

Had he known her hair was red? Not that he could recall, yet it made sense. With those freckles, she would hardly be blond. He followed her inside and closed the door. "It's Sunny, isn't it?"

"I'm surprised you remembered. Considering we've only met once."

"Hard to forget after last night."

She dropped her binder on the coffee table and turned abruptly, her smile bright, expectant. "Last night?"

He couldn't help smiling back. She really was cute with that big wonky grin, a short tartan skirt, and a T-shirt with some kind of emblem on it. Like a cheerleader, all fresh faced and wholesome. Although she wasn't really a kid at all, he realized. Those curves were anything but childish.

He sipped at his coffee and motioned her to follow him to his desk. "I assumed Judith would have told you. Your mural caused quite a stir at the ball."

"She did say a few people had noticed."

"A few?" He laughed and set the coffee and paper on the desk. "Trust me. You were a hit with everyone. Including me."

"I'm flattered."

"Don't be. I'm just being honest." He pulled on the shirt that he'd left on the back of the chair and fastened the buttons as he sat down. "And since the interior designer has not been called in, as project manager and penthouse sitter, I'm giving you creative control. Judith's only specification was that it has to be original—"

"Blend with what's here and no signature," she finished for him, and smiled as she drew up to the desk. "She mentioned that in the message." She perched on the corner and looked at him over her shoulder. "So you have no ideas about what you'd like to see on the wall?"

"Not one." He clicked on his e-mail. "But I figure you do, which makes my job easier. Just come up with something, I'll okay it, and you can get started right away." He glanced up and she moistened her lips. He motioned to the coffeemaker on the bar. "Would you like a coffee?"

"No, thanks," she said and lowered her chin. "But you'll be taking quite a risk. How do you know you won't be disappointed?"

He went back to his computer. "Because I had a good look at the work you did in the ballroom last night. And a woman who knows a thing or two about art showed me what I'd been missing."

She shifted, slowly crossing one leg over the other so her skirt rode a little higher on her thighs. "And what was that?"

"Cinderella." He glanced up. "I had no idea she was there."

"You never know what you'll find when you look closely." She swung around a little more, put a hand on the desk, and leaned toward him. "So, who was this woman who knew so much about art?"

He tapped a key, smiled at the screen. "A guest at the ball. Sonja. She became a real fan of yours last night. I'm surprised she hasn't called you. She seemed very keen on getting a mural herself."

"Who knows?" Sunny said, trying on a sexy voice as well. "Maybe she'll call you first. Have you checked your messages?"

"When I got up."

"Maybe you should check again." She shrugged a shoulder when he raised a brow. "Well, your hair is damp, and you never know what you might have missed when you were in the shower."

"I suppose." His eyes skimmed up the length of Sunny's legs to the tip of that skirt, which was moving up higher even as he watched. "You're on my phone," he said and was oddly relieved when she leaped off the desk.

He motioned to the sofa. "I'm sorry. I should have invited you to have a seat."

She sighed and headed over to the bar. "I think I'll have that coffee instead."

He turned his attention to the screen and pushed his cup toward her. "Could you warm this up for me while you're there? Black, no sugar. Thanks," he said, aware that the cup had been snapped up while he scanned his e-mail.

A note from Judith—*Everyone in the Lobby at 10:00!*—and an *Oh, Come On, Be A Sport* message from his brother. He deleted one, saved the other, and turned off the screen until later.

"Anything else I should know about this fan?" she asked. "What she looks like, what color her eyes are? Any distinguishing features? Just in case she does call. I wouldn't want to sit down with the wrong stranger."

He looked over at her. "The wrong stranger?"

"Well, you only met her the once. And it was a masquerade, which means she could be anyone, couldn't she? A thief, an ax murderer." She smiled at him over her shoulder. "Even me."

Michael laughed. She really was a funny little thing. "Sonja is beautiful, her eyes are green and gold, kind of hard to describe, and she has no distinguishing marks that I can remember. And believe me, I'd know if she was an ax murderer."

"I see." She came back with the coffee, and a wry smile. "I hope that's how you like it," she said, her arm brushing his as she set the cup in front of him.

"No sugar, right?"

She lowered her voice. "Only if you want it."

He blinked and turned away. "This should be fine," he said, flipping the newspaper over to get at the notebook underneath. "We should talk about price and how long the job will take. The quicker the better, of course, so I can have my office . . ." Michael drew the paper closer, forgetting all about the mural as he studied the picture on the bottom half of the front page: a full-color shot of himself and the Grant Hall team lined up and smiling at the camera. And there behind them, faint but beautiful as she pointed to the ceiling, was Sonja.

"What an interesting picture," Sunny whispered.

Michael stilled, hearing echoes of another voice. One that was soft and musical, with a subtle touch of Ireland. He gave his head a shake and looked over at Sunny, clearing the impression as quickly as it had come. Brooklyn was a long way from Ireland, after all. And as sweet as she was, she was no Sonja.

Michel tipped the paper up for her. "This is Sonja."

"I know," she said, and gave him a funny half smile. "It says so in the caption." She held his gaze a moment longer, then turned and walked toward the coffee table. "I have something to show you. Something that might make this whole thing easier for both of us."

"Great," Michael said, sitting back and taking Sonja with him. Even now, if he closed his eyes, he could taste her, smell her, hear her saying his name over and over, like a soft, sweet chant while he kissed her, touched her, and slowly drove both of them mad.

He opened the drawer and the emeralds winked at him, as though they knew something he didn't. Like where she was, or what she was doing. He smiled and picked them up, held them in his palm. A moment of madness, she'd called them. And he didn't think he'd ever forgive Duane for turning on that light.

"Are you sure there's nothing specific you'd want to see in the mural?" she called.

"I'm sure," he said and glanced over to see her standing alone in the middle of the room, looking up at the ceiling.

Michael winced. "I'm sorry. I should have told you this mural goes on the wall behind the desk, not the ceiling." He laid the earrings on his desk. "What was it you wanted to show me?"

Sunny lowered her chin, smiled at her feet. "My portfolio, but there's no need to apologize. I should have known this wouldn't be so easy."

And she should never have listened to Hugh. No one should listen to Hugh. For all that he was built like a linebacker, the man was an incurable romantic. The kind who believed in the power of love, and "one day my prince will come." He still cried every time he watched *Pretty Woman,* for heaven's sake. And she always shared his box of tissue.

She sighed as Michael folded the paper, Sonja-side up, and laid it to one side. They were quite a pair, she and Hugh. Real suckers for a happy ending, even though neither of them had ever found one. Of course he'd assume Michael would see her, want her, somehow recognize her as the woman he had all but made love to just the night before. And she'd followed right along, wanting to believe it too. Ready to jump into a meaningless relationship with a man she hardly knew.

Or at least think about it.

But what difference did it make? The man in question was not making it an option. Even though she couldn't stand near the sofa without remembering the warmth of his hands, the brush of his lips, and the soft, silky whisper that had carried her over the edge, Michael just sat there—feeling nothing for her at all, and dreaming of a woman who didn't exist.

"I'd like to see your book," he said. "Although I imagine you already have some idea of what you'd want to see in this room."

Him. Naked. Tied to the chair while she smacked him upside the head with Sonja's wig.

"Something that incorporates the view," she said, forcing herself to think, to picture scenes, because Hugh was right about one thing at least—she needed this job.

So she kept her mind on the money, her eyes on the wall, and hoped Michael would check those damn messages so she could walk out of there with Val's earrings in her hands.

She picked up her book and carried it to the desk, taking pleasure in the weight and texture of the leather, on solid ground for the first time since she stepped through the door.

Inside were photographs of every mural and finish she'd ever done, including the grape arbor at Justa' Pasta, the Loch Ness monster at the tearoom, and the clouds in Jess's bedroom. Like her brushes and sponges, the book was a tool, used to show the client what she'd done before in order to help him decide what she would do next. And the way things were going, a client was all that Michael Wolfe would ever be.

She laid the book in front of him, watched while he flipped through the pages. "Because windows and the city are so much a part of the room, I think we should continue that theme with another one looking out into a fantasy world."

"Sounds good," he said absently, and paused at the Loch Ness monster. "Where's the secret?"

"You'll have to find it for your—" Sunny's voice trailed away as she leaned across the desk, eyes fixed on the earrings. "Aren't those lovely?" she said. "Are they antiques?"

Michael looked down. "I think they're paste." Michael scooped the earrings up. "They belong to Sonja. She left them here last night."

"Can I see them?" she said, and gave a quick laugh when he raised a brow. "Can't resist an interesting shape. And those earrings have an interesting shape, don't you think?"

"It's just a standard oblong."

"Which is exactly the cut of the stone that Prince Albert gave to Queen Victoria for their wedding."

She smiled prettily and kept her hand out there like some kind of cross-gender Oliver Twist, making him feel like Mr. Bumble and worse for keeping the things from her.

"Of course, it's not as large as Victoria's," she continued, holding one up as she walked to the window. "That was a brooch, as you probably know. A sapphire. But other than that, they're very similar."

He didn't see how that was possible, but he definitely found her fascinating to watch, standing there in the sunlight, her hair a riot of red and gold, spilling across her shoulders as she went on and on about diamonds and lace and a symbol of love that would endure forever. Her rapt expression would have been hokey on anyone else, but for some reason it suited her.

She launched into the story of the wedding and Michael turned the pages of her book, letting her words and her voice wash over him, and stopping when he reached a painting of an African plain.

Everything he'd expect from such a picture was there: purple mountains, a shimmering landscape, baobab trees, and of course a watering hole with animals coming and going. Yet, while the subject matter and colors blended with the decorating scheme of what was obviously an up-scale family room, Sunny's mural wasn't just another pretty picture. There was tension on that plain, something about to happen, just as Sonja had said there should be.

"In short, it's beautiful." Sunny lowered her hand and smiled. "Thus ends the history lesson for today."

Michael glanced up. She was such an odd girl. Plain and natural, with round green eyes and a talent for painting that astounded him.

He closed her book and stood up, heading to the bar with his cold coffee. "How is it you know so much about Albert and Victoria?"

"You'd be surprised what you learn when you grow up in a genuine Scottish tearoom."

He dumped the coffee into the sink and spotted his cell phone. A tiny envelope on the screen told him he had a message.

He pressed SEND and carried the cell phone back to the desk. "Is that what happened to you?"

She pointed to the emblem on her T-shirt. He hadn't taken a good look at it before, but as he walked toward her he saw that it was a tree with the words *Stand Sure* arching above, and *Lord of the Isles* written below.

"Ever hear of the Isles Tearoom?"

"Sorry."

She blew out her breath in a huff. "Where have you been? People in Manhattan cross the bridge for our butter tarts alone."

"I'll remember that. And you were right, by the way, there is a message." He put the phone to his ear and nodded. "It's from Sonja."

"Well, what do you know?" Sunny said, her fingers closing tighter around the earrings while he listened to the message she'd left earlier.

He smiled slowly, and she figured he'd reached the part where she told him she'd had a wonderful time, wished it could have lasted longer. Then his expression turned serious and he grabbed a pen and started to jot down a note.

Sunny blew out an exasperated breath and picked up her binder. It wasn't all that difficult to remember—leave earrings at front desk. Friends in New Jersey will come and get them. Simple really.

"She didn't mention you," he said, as he hung up, "but I'm sure she'll call." He took an envelope from his drawer, held out a hand. "I'll need the earrings back. She's sending someone over to get them."

She dropped them into his palm. "Well, I have to be back at the tearoom shortly anyway. Why don't I take them down with me? Save you the trip."

"Fine with me." He slipped the earrings into the envelope and handed it to her as Duane stepped into the penthouse.

He wore a red Grant Hall windbreaker, and had another just like it slung over his arm. "Mr. Wolfe, I brought along—" He stopped, shoulders rounding even more as his gaze moved from Michael to Sunny. "I could come back—"

"Nugent, it's fine, come in," Michael said and gestured to Sunny, who was trying to hide behind her binder for some reason. "Have you two met?"

"I feel I have, sir." Duane's eyes went soft. "I love what you did in the ballroom, Miss Anderson, and look forward to seeing a second mural here in the penthouse."

She studied Duane as she slowly lowered the binder, then shot him one of those grins and said, "Glad you liked it."

Michael shook his head. She was indeed a strange one.

"See you on Monday," she said.

Michael followed her across the hall to the elevator. "I thought you'd start tomorrow."

"I don't work Sundays."

"But we haven't settled on a price or a time line."

She pushed the button for the elevator. "I'll bring an estimate on Monday, and I'm guessing two weeks."

"But you were so fast with the ballroom."

"And I won't make that mistake again." She stepped into the waiting car. "It's summer. I intend to enjoy some of it."

"Three days and we have a deal."

She jabbed the button. "Two weeks, or we don't."

"You drive a hard bargain."

"Stand sure," she said, and twiddled her fingers at him as the door closed.

And only then did it occur to him that he should have put a note in the envelope. "Sunny, the earrings—"

"Don't worry," she called, her voice fading slowly away. "I'll drop them off."

Michael walked back into the penthouse and straight to the phone.

Duane held out the red jacket as he went by. "Mrs. Hill sent this up for you. It's the official retreat jacket. Everyone will be getting one, and she'd like to see us wearing it today." He pulled a page from his pocket. "I printed out the agenda. The Empire State Building is first—"

"Figures." Michael picked up the receiver, dialed the front desk. "What else?"

"Statue of Liberty."

Michael sighed. "And they'll want to climb to the top—" He broke off and straightened. "Yes, this is Michael Wolfe. Sunny Anderson will be dropping off an envelope in a minute. If a driver comes for it, tell him to wait. I want to put—" He paused. "What do you mean she's not stopping . . . ? Well, call her back, for God's sake. Okay, thanks."

He pushed a hand through his hair, looked over at Duane. "She forgot to leave the envelope."

"I beg your pardon, sir?"

A smile eased across Michael's face. "She forgot to leave the envelope," he said again, and walked over to the windows. "Which means I'll have to miss Judith's field trip."

"Where are you going, sir?"

"Brooklyn." Michael watched her cross the road and disappear into the subway. He smiled and turned to Duane, feeling lighter than he had in days. "You like butter tarts, Nugent?"

# Six

"We're off, then," Moyra said, but still hovered in the kitchen doorway, purse in one hand and a neatly wrapped gift in the other, stalling like a nervous mother afraid to leave her baby with the sitter. "Vows will be said at ten and there's a lunch after. Then I expect the old fools will need a nap." She glanced at the round of pastry dough on the counter in front of Sunny. "Everything all right?"

"Couldn't be better." Sunny smiled and patted the dough. "And that dress is even lovelier than the last, isn't it, Hugh?"

"Absolutely stunning," Hugh said, glancing over while he spooned coconut filling into the last tart on his tray. "But then blue was always your color. And it's nice to see you have legs."

"Fabulous legs," Jack called through the order window. "That's why I married her."

"You married me for my cooking," she called back, and grimaced when Sunny pushed the rolling pin into the dough. "Gently, gently."

Sunny consciously relaxed her grip and started to roll again. Without the useless nails, there had been no excuse to leave the pastry in the fridge. Certainly not when it was the first time Moyra and Jack had gone out the door together in months, and Sunny was determined to see her mother leave with a smile on her face. Although the more she rolled, the less Moyra smiled.

Moyra started to set her purse down. "I should stay. Help you master that once and for all—"

"God forbid," Hugh said, and motioned to Sunny as he slid the tarts into the oven. "Dave and Hazel will never forgive any of us if you're late."

"I suppose," Moyra said as the two of them herded her along to the cash desk where Jack waited, jingling his keys and whistling, and making Sunny instantly suspicious.

She grabbed his tie and pretended to straighten it. "Promise me, no talk of pubs or satellite dishes," she whispered.

"Promise," he said so easily Sunny knew he had something else up his sleeve. But before she could ask why or what, Hugh was hustling them both to the door.

"Why don't you make a day of it?" he said. "Have dinner, take in a movie."

"A movie?" Moyra looked over at Jack. "What movie would we see?"

Jack shrugged. "As long as there's no Kleenex needed, I don't much care."

"And as long as there's no car chase, I don't care either." She pointed to Hugh's duffel bag by the door. "You'll get that out of the way before customers start arriving?" She cast a quick glance back at him. "And no doorstopper cookies."

"You have my word," he said, giving them one more nudge to get them moving.

Moyra waved through the front window. "I'll call whenever I get the chance."

"You do that," Hugh said, smiling and waving back while he muttered, "Thank God she won't get a cell phone."

Sunny went back to the kitchen. She sighed at the pastry, rolled the whole mess into a ball, and prepared for a flank attack. "What are the odds that they'll see a movie?"

"Slim to none, as usual."

Sunny nodded and shaped the pastry as her mother had shown her a thousand times, pressing the side of her hand into it three times up, then three times across, before picking up the rolling pin. "It's a good thing we know they love each other, or I'd be starting to worry."

"They are the most happily dysfunctional couple I know. And may I never find such bliss." Hugh hauled his duffel bag into the kitchen.

"No biscotti," Sunny warned.

He had the audacity to look hurt. "I promised, didn't I? Which is why I brought . . ." He reached into his bag and pulled out a box. "My cappuccino maker."

Sunny groaned. "Even worse."

"Not at all. This is strictly a scientific experiment." He cleared a spot on the counter and pulled the machine from the box. "Do people want to see cappuccino in a tearoom or not?"

Sunny pushed at the dough. "I swear you and Dad have a death wish."

"Or a view to the future." He held up a sign. NEW! ESPRESSO, LATTÉ, AND CAPPUCCINO. "Where do you think it will look best? In the window or on the sandwich board?"

"In your bag," she said, rolling a bigger tear this time.

Hugh put a hand over the pastry. "She's gone. You can stop now." He took the rolling pin from her, set it out of reach. "When are you going to tell her you don't want the tearoom?"

"I've been dropping hints."

He tore a page from the pad on the fridge. "I assure you, she's not picking them up."

Sunny leaned closer, watching him draw three lines down the page. "This just doesn't seem like a good time, I guess."

"With Moyra, there will never be a good time." He labeled the columns *Espresso, Latté, Cappuccino,* and *Tea,* then scribbled *Satellite TV* on the bottom, stuck the page to the cupboard above the coffeemaker, and pulled the dough toward him. "And I will never understand why she resists the idea of change so much."

"Because the Isles is about tradition," Sunny said, the

smell of the maid of honor tarts in the oven filling her head as her gaze moved around the room, lighting on a baking sheet, a spoon, the kettles above the stove. Everything friendly and familiar, and as much a part of the Isles as the recipes Moyra guarded so jealously. Family treasures passed down from mother to daughter for generations, and living on at the Isles: chocolate whiskey cake, lemon curd, and pastry so thin and flaky it melted in your mouth.

Sunny knew the Isles was a labor of love for Moyra, an extension of her parlor where customers were treated like guests, and the part of her that still longed to be in Scotland could relax and feel at home. The tearoom was her legacy to her daughter and her granddaughter after her, and Sunny only hoped she could find a way to break her mother's heart gently.

"If you ask me," Hugh said, and reached for the rolling pin, "there's a fine line between tradition and stagnation. And this place is dangerously close to crossing over." He too looked around while he rolled the dough thinner and thinner. "Wouldn't take much to give it a little spark though. A few changes to the menu, less fringes on the lamps, a new mural." He shot Sunny a grin. "Something with nudes perhaps?"

Sunny laughed. "Mom would choke, but the Glasgow ladies would love it."

"So start tomorrow," he said, touching the edges of the pastry with the rolling pin, taking it out that extra inch just as Moyra would have. "Shake things up a bit and she'll kick you out for sure. Best thing that could ever happen, trust me."

"I'll take it a little slower, thanks," Sunny said, staring at the dough her brother was shaping. No holes, no bumps, just a smooth stretch of pastry that would make her mother sigh.

The timer pinged. Sunny picked up a pot holder and went to the oven for the tarts. "You know, you're the one she should be after to take over the tearoom."

Hugh snorted and took down the cup they always used

to cut the rounds, dipped it in flour. "Can you picture that? Guess what, Dad, I'm trading in my service truck for an apron."

Sunny set the hot pan on a rack. "He might not mind if you went for the satellite dish as well."

"Aye, bring on the lads," Hugh said with a growl, but there was an edge to his smile, his laughter, because as fiercely close as the family was, some things were never discussed in the Anderson house. Like change, and Sunny moving out, and the fact that Hugh was gay.

He lifted his sign and handed it to her. "If you won't paint nudes, at least put this up, for the sake of experiment. Speaking of which, how'd it go at the penthouse?"

"Good and bad." She took the sign, letting him change the subject because it was easier than trying to make sense of the Andersons. "Michael is still thinking about Sonja and can't see that we're one and the same, but I got the earrings back."

"Val will be pleased. As for Michael, why don't you just level with him? Tell him you're Sonja and take it from there."

"Take it where? The man is not interested in me as me. Do you know what he did when I showed him a bit of leg? Told me I was sitting on his phone."

If she let herself, she could still feel the sting of that one. But what had she expected? Seduction had never been her strong point, and one night as Sonja hadn't changed a thing.

The phone started to ring. Sunny stuck the sign in the window, told herself she was not a traitor, merely a scientist, and dashed over to the cash desk. "I just want to forget last night ever happened, and get on with my celibate life."

Hugh laughed. "Coward."

"And proud of it," she said, hearing the hiss of Hugh's coffeemaker, and hoping it wasn't Moyra on the line. "Lord of the Isles," she said, and jerked around as the front door swung back.

Val grinned and held the newspaper above her head. "Was that a success story last night or what?"

Sunny gave her a thumbs-up. "Yes, this is Sunny," she said to the person on the phone.

Val's smile drooped until she spotted Hugh. "Did you hear?" she whispered, hurrying across to the kitchen. "A half bath in the Hamptons already, and I must have given out a hundred cards. She was a definite hit. We should go into the makeover business, you and I."

"Another You by Val and Hugh." He gave a thoughtful nod. "I like it."

Sunny waved a hand to get their attention and pointed at the phone. "You'd like an interview."

Val and Hugh came out of the kitchen. "Who is it?" Val asked.

Sunny put a hand over the mouthpiece. "The newspaper."

Val grabbed Hugh's arm. "This could be big. Very big." She waved at Sunny and whispered, "Is it the *Times*?"

Sunny shook her head. "Tomorrow would be fine. No, I don't mind a photographer."

Val laid her head on Hugh's shoulder. "Oh honey, our little girl is going to be a star." She straightened. "So what paper is it?"

"The *Brooklyn Banner*," Sunny whispered.

Val looked at Hugh. "Isn't that the new local paper? The one with a circulation of ten?"

"It's probably fifteen by now. Either way, I don't think our little girl is a star just yet."

Sunny put a finger in her ear and ignored them. "At the Brighton Hotel. Eight A.M. . . . in the penthouse, yes."

Val turned. "Penthouse? What penthouse?"

"Michael Wolfe's," Hugh said. "She was there last night. And this morning."

"Sunny was with Michael Wolfe?" Val screwed up her nose. "Why?"

Sunny waved a hand at Hugh. Mouthed "no, no, no" and dropped her head back to stare at the ceiling when he put an arm around Val and said, "Honey, our little girl grew up last night."

Sunny pushed at the furrow between her brows while Hugh gave Val a quick rundown of the evening's events, including the loss of the earrings. And decided she wouldn't wait for her mother to do the job, she would kill him herself.

She hung up the phone. Val's mouth was closed again. Pinched was the word that came to Sunny's mind.

"Why didn't you tell me?" she demanded.

"There's nothing to tell."

Val arched a brow. "Another mural at the Brighton is nothing?"

Sunny fought a smile. She should have known. "I was going to tell you." She reached under the cash desk for the envelope, walked back into the kitchen, and handed it to Val. "And I have the earrings."

"You're lucky there." Val tore open the envelope, shook the earrings into her hand, and dropped them in her shirt pocket. "As for Michael Wolfe, I admit I did not see *that* coming, but I'm glad all the same. It's time you had a man in your life. Time I did too, but that's beside the point."

"Well, don't feel left out just yet, because Michael Wolfe is not in my life." Sunny pulled a clip from the drawer and knotted her hair on top of her head. "The man is not interested in me."

"I see." Val squinted, moved closer to the order window. "Then why is he here?"

Sunny froze with the clip halfway to her head.

Hugh squeezed in beside Val. "Which one?"

"Tall, dark—"

"Got him." Hugh nodded at Sunny. "Very nice. Although that line between his brows makes him a little mean looking. Which is not necessarily a bad thing—"

"Will you move," Sunny muttered and shoved him out of the way.

She peered through the window. Sure enough, he was

standing by the door, studying the plates on the baker's rack. And he didn't look mean at all.

"Who's with him?" Hugh winced. "And what is he wearing?"

"That's Duane," Sunny said. "He has an eclectic taste in clothes."

Val shook her head. "The poor thing really needs someone to take him under her wing."

"A Brand-New Duane—We're in Business Again," Hugh said and the two of them high-fived before turning back to the window. "Now what do you suppose brought Mr. Wolfe all the way out here?" Hugh asked.

"Butter tarts." Sunny scowled when Hugh laughed. "And you be quiet."

It was her hair that drew Michael's eye to the little window in the kitchen. She was moving around, coming into view only to disappear again, all that glorious red knotted up on top of her head instead of falling around her shoulders the way he preferred it. Not that he had a preference, it was more of an opinion. Just as he had an opinion about Duane's choice of footwear, and Judith's taste in jackets. Just an unbiased opinion and a vague hope that Sunny didn't wear that clip when she was painting.

No, he remembered, she wore a baseball cap, which was worse.

"I have an idea where we can go next," Duane said.

"Next?" Michael said absently.

Duane pulled a brochure from his pocket. "I picked this up when we left the hotel. Apparently there's a walking tour . . ."

Michael watched him unfold the flyer and wished he'd left the kid at home.

Weak moment, he thought, and stepped back as two old women came through the door arm in arm, and sailed past him and Duane.

"Just us," one of them called. They paused outside the

kitchen door. "Oh, Sunny, did you hear about Lilli Kwan? She and André are getting married. Big wedding planned. Won't last, of course, but it should be fun." They glided on. "We'll find our own table, dear. And we'll try your cappuccino." They both giggled and disappeared around the corner. "Moyra will have something to say about that."

Michael wondered who Moyra was, and why the marriage wouldn't last as a big guy came toward them with menus.

His grin wasn't as wide as Sunny's but his hair was every bit as red, and since he was wearing a "Stand Sure" T-shirt like Sunny, Michael could only conclude that he too, was of the clan Anderson.

"Welcome to the Isles. My name is Hugh. And you are?"

It wasn't the usual line for a café host, but then this wasn't a usual café. Not with birthday cards taped behind the cash desk, pictures of children on the walls, and the Loch Ness monster lurking in the distance.

So Michael introduced himself and Duane, and followed Hugh deeper into the tearoom, already searching the misty greens and grays of Sunny's Loch Ness mural for a secret.

As they rounded the corner, his eye was drawn to the fireplace and the line of pictures on the mantel: two boys in soccer outfits, a young, smiling couple pushing a baby carriage, and a little girl in a kilt with a big wonky grin and two swords crossed at her feet.

Michael smiled as Hugh led them to a table by the window, knowing the little redhead in the picture had to be Sunny.

"We're conducting a survey today," Hugh said as they sat down. "Would you like tea, latté, cappuccino, or espresso? And would you like to see a soccer match with your lunch?"

Duane picked up a dainty teacup. "I don't know about soccer, but maybe some mugs."

"Mugs," Hugh wrote.

"And something decaf?" Duane asked.

It was still early and the tearoom was empty except for the two women who had passed them at the door earlier.

So while Hugh rhymed off a list of herbal teas for Duane, Michael rose and prowled the room, searching for more shots of Sunny, and watching her grow up all around him: laughing at the beach, nervous behind the wheel, and solemn, almost sad, at her high school graduation.

He moved closer to the picture on the wall. Roses in her arms, a background of books, but no trace of that wonderful grin, and no light in her eyes, as though the future held nothing for her.

"Scones as usual, Mr. Gardner?"

Sunny's voice drew him around. She was behind the cash desk, packing up a box for a customer, smiling, chatting, more like the Sunny he knew. And still wearing that skirt, he noticed. Her legs smooth and firm, leading all the way up to—

"See something you'd like, Michael?" Hugh asked.

Michael blinked, glanced over. Why was the guy smiling at him that way? "Butter tarts. I was told they're the best."

"Everything here is the best." Hugh pointed a pencil at him. "But you don't look like an herbal tea man to me. More like the kind who'd go for something small and hot." He smiled and headed off to the kitchen. "One espresso coming up."

Michael stared after him a moment, wondering what he'd missed, when Duane waved at him from the table. "About the walking tour, sir—"

"Forget it, Nugent—"

"He's absolutely right," a woman said, and Michael wasn't at all surprised when Valerie Conan-Smythe emerged from the kitchen and sidled up to the table. This was the Anderson's tearoom, after all, and strange was the order of the day.

"Hello, Mr. Wolfe," she said, and in a voice that was pure silk added, "Duane."

She put a finger on Duane's brochure, slid it to one side. "Organized tours are fine. But I can put one together that you will never forget." Her eyes moved slowly over Duane.

"And if you like, I can even arrange some fabulous shopping."

"You haven't lived until you've done Midnight Madness with Val," Hugh said, as he showed another couple to a table.

She smiled. "So, what do you say?"

"I haven't been shopping in a long time," he said wistfully, then looked over at Michael. "Sir?"

Michael held up a hand. "I'll pass, but you go ahead."

"You are going to love this." Val pulled out a chair. "Do you have a pen?"

Duane whipped out a ballpoint, Val nodded her approval, and Michael smiled. With any luck, she'd keep him busy for days.

"Thanks again," Sunny said as her customer went out the door. "See you tomorrow."

She rounded the cash desk and headed straight into the kitchen without seeing him. So Michael walked the few steps to the door on the tearoom side of the kitchen and stood watching her. Hugh's back was to him, marking something on a list as the cappuccino maker hissed and gurgled, and Sunny was at the counter, slicing scones and arranging them on a plate. She spooned tea into a pot and poured on boiling water, her movements quick and efficient. And when she turned, Michael didn't think he'd ever seen anyone suck in so much oxygen at one time.

"She'll get you for that," Hugh said, and handed Michael an espresso in a teacup. "That's how we serve it in Scotland," he assured him, and carried off the tray Sunny had prepared.

Michael peered into the cup. "Is this really how they serve it?"

"No, he just forgot to bring the right ones. And you scared me half to death." She grabbed a cloth, wiped the counter. "You could have said something, or at least coughed."

"You were busy."

And he'd enjoyed watching her.

"I still am," she said, taking the lid off a soup that smelled wonderful. "So what brings you here?"

"You have something I need."

Sunny's hand stilled on the ladle, and she told her heart to settle down and be quiet. There had to be plenty of logical explanations, lots of reasons he was there. But only one came to mind.

Michael inhaled deeply and came to stand beside her. "What is that?"

"Mulligatawny, and if you're here for the estimate—"

"I wasn't but now that you mention it, have you given it any thought?"

She stirred and sprinkled salt. "No."

He bent over the pot, sniffed again. "Can you?"

She dropped the lid, narrowly missing his nose, and went to the fridge. "Let's see, on a Saturday morning, when I'm working another job, I'd say you're looking in the neighborhood of one million dollars."

Michael blinked. "That's an awfully expensive neighborhood."

She smiled. "Then why don't you wait until Monday? The price is bound to be better." She opened the fridge, poked around inside for the black forest ham that should have been right there in the plastic container . . .

Sunny sighed. She forgot to stop at the deli. Which meant the lunch special would have to be something else.

She rummaged around a little more. "So if it's not the estimate you're after, what is it?"

"Hmmm?"

She glanced over as she reached for a tin of salmon at the back of the fridge. "What is it you need?"

"Need?" Michael gave his head a shake. "You know, you really shouldn't bend over in a skirt like that."

She snapped to attention, brushed her skirt down with the tin of salmon, and blushed in a way that told him she'd had no idea of the picture she made. And when he sipped at his coffee, he was confident she had no idea she was the reason his mouth was so dry all of a sudden.

The woman was one of a kind, that much was clear. Just not his kind. Which brought him round to Sonja, and the reason he was there.

"You've got—" he started, but was cut short by a child hollering "Mommy, mommy," at the front door.

Sunny slapped the salmon on the counter. "Hold that thought," she said, and dashed away.

Michael stood by the stove, watching as a little girl of five or six dressed in a kilt and dance slippers launched herself into Sunny's arms. Sunny swung her up and hugged her hard. "How was dance class?"

"She was the best," a man said and came to stand beside them.

He was tall, dark haired.

Michael ran a hand over his mouth. Why hadn't it occurred to him that she might be married, have children? Probably because she seemed so young, wore no ring.

The little girl's eyes widened as Hugh came toward them. "Uncle Sean says you brought your cappuccino maker."

Both her brothers, Michael realized. Not that it mattered, not that he cared. It was just a fact. Like red hair and freckles, and the way her daughter looked so much like her when she smiled.

"Nana will be soooo mad," the girl said.

"But the coffee is soooo good," Hugh said, taking her from Sunny and setting her giggling as he lifted her up and carted her off to the baker's rack, with Sunny and Sean close behind.

"I made special tarts for you," Hugh said, and Michael backed away, suddenly feeling awkward, knowing he didn't belong.

In the tearoom, he glanced over at Duane and Val, who were now deep in conversation with the old ladies and the other couple—all of them offering opinions on the best spots for bargains.

Having nothing to add, Michael wandered back to the mural of Nessie, determined to locate the secret. But instead found himself listening to Sunny and her daughter by the cash desk—the two of them laughing, talking, while the child munched on a carrot stick and the promised tart waited on a plate by the till. She called the girl Jess, and ran a hand unconsciously over her hair as she bent down, hearing a secret meant only for mom.

And Michael couldn't help wondering where the father was. If he would be by in a while. And why there were no pictures of Sunny with a man to be found anywhere.

# Seven

"I'm telling you, Sunny," Hugh whispered. "The man's tongue is on the ground."

Sunny turned the soup down. "I'm not listening."

"Some guy bugging you, Sunny?" Sean asked.

Jess was instantly alert. "What guy?"

"No one," Sunny said, but Sean was already checking out the tearoom, ready to protect his baby sister, as usual. "Point him out," he said to Hugh.

"Don't do it," Sunny muttered and wondered why she bothered as he went to join Sean in the doorway.

"The one studying the mural," Hugh said.

Jess tried to squeeze between them. "Which one?"

"No one," Sunny said, hauling her back.

Sean screwed up his nose. "Does he always frown that way?"

"Val says he's intense," Hugh explained.

Jess broke away. "Who's in tents?"

"No one." Sunny brought her back. "Can we get to work here?"

"She likes him but he's not interested," Hugh said.

"You want me to beat him up?" Sean asked.

Sunny had to laugh. "Not yet." She held Jess with one hand and arranged two scones on a plate with the other. "Let's see what he wants first."

Jess threw her hands up in frustration. "What *who* wants?"

"No one," they said in unison, and went back to their posts.

Hugh held up the salmon. "I thought the special was ham."

"It is," Sunny said, "But I forgot to buy it on the way home." She frowned at their raised eyebrows. "Don't worry, I'm going."

"You certainly are." Hugh shoved the salmon into the fridge without ceremony and shot a knowing look at Sean. "She was with Michael this morning. Strictly business, of course."

"Of course." Sean glanced over at her. "Just say the word and he's toast, kiddo. Anytime."

"Thanks." Sunny turned to Jess. "Now go on upstairs and change. And no tarts until you finish the carrot."

Sunny saw the protest coming in the thrust of her lower lip, the tilt of her shoulders, and was about to cut it short when Mrs. Dempster called, "Where's our darlin'?" and Jess perked up right away.

"I learned a new step," she called, and was gone, heading for the Glasgow ladies' table and casting a quick glance at the mural along the way.

But if she saw Michael she gave no sign as she hugged each of the ladies in turn.

"Wait till you see," she said, and went into position right there beside the table. Head high, arms up, fingers just so.

"If there's a medal for guts, she'd win it," Sean said, his eyes warm, his smile tender as he and Hugh came to stand beside Sunny in the kitchen doorway.

Sunny nodded, her throat suddenly tight as Mrs. Fitzhenry made appropriate bagpipe noises, Mrs. Dempster clapped, and Jess danced. Toes pointed and feet moving between imaginary swords, while the Glasgow ladies beamed and people she had never met looked on and smiled.

She had no fear, that child. Not a moment's doubt that she was loved and accepted. And Sunny swallowed hard when the dance ended, hoping no one would ever come along and snatch that confidence out from under her.

A burst of applause, a lovely curtsy, and Jess's moment dissolved into conversations and the clink of china.

"Let her sit with us," Mrs. Dempster said when Sunny came to claim her daughter.

Ever alert to an opportunity, Jess leaped into a chair and sat neatly. Hands folded, ankles crossed. The very picture of decorum, which wouldn't last two minutes.

"Just long enough to have a snack," Mrs. Fitzhenry said, setting half of her own scone in front of Jess.

"Fine," Sunny said, "but then it's upstairs to change. And no more dancing."

"Fine," Jess said, already reaching for jam.

"She's very much like you," Michael said, drawing Sunny around.

He still stood by the mural with Hugh's illegal espresso, his eyes dark and unreadable, just as they had been last night when he'd first touched her.

*Touched Sonja,* she reminded herself, but her skin remembered all the same, and her heart was pushing hard to find out what he wanted.

He smiled as he came toward her. "Were you the best too?" he asked, and gestured to the picture on the mantel.

"Not even close," she said, focusing on the photographs so she wouldn't be tempted to read anything into his smile, or think about what Hugh had said. "They only let me use the swords in pictures because they were afraid I'd lose a toe when I danced." He laughed in that low, sexy way she liked too much and she looked over, meeting his gaze at last. "How was the coffee?"

"Good." His smile faded as his eyes moved over her face. "Just not what I expected in a tearoom."

Sunny moistened her lips. "Oh, there are plenty of unexpected things to be found around here."

"So I'm discovering." His eyes narrowed at the mural. "But I'll be damned if I can find the secret."

"That's because there isn't one." She glanced over at

Nessie. "What you have here is a fine example of an early Anderson. Completed during her baby-in-diapers stage. Unsophisticated and simple in technique, but showing promise all the same." She directed his gaze to the front door. "If you were to venture next door to Justa' Pasta, on the other hand, you would see a refining of the work, the first hint of something deeper, a sure sign that the artist had entered her toddler-in-nursery-school period. And if you were to travel as far as D'Amici's Bakery, you would see the emergence of the first secret, a little something to fill the time of the customer standing on line."

"So the street is like your own private gallery."

"Somewhat. Although the collection comes to an abrupt end when the artist entered a more commercial period."

"Why is that?"

"I started to charge."

He studied her a moment, then motioned to a table. "Can you take a break?"

Sunny glanced over at the kitchen. Her brothers turned away quickly and made themselves busy, rattling teapots and spoons, trying hard to make her believe they hadn't been eavesdropping.

She sighed, knowing exactly how fish in a bowl felt.

"To be honest," she said, "I'm just on my way to the deli." She took a breath, shot him a smile. "Would you like to come along?"

He glanced at Duane, then set the cup down. "Why not?"

Sunny tried not to smile too much. Tried not to let her heart leap ahead, or jump to conclusions. It was only a trip to the deli.

"I'll just see if Jess wants to come, and get my purse. By the way, what do I have that you need?"

Michael stared as though not understanding the question, then gave his head a small shake. "Sonja's earrings," he said. "You forgot to leave them at the desk."

Sunny's heart not only quieted, it almost shut down.

"I didn't leave them?" she asked, hoping her face wasn't as red as it was hot. "Are you sure?"

"Positive. I called the front desk just after you left. I wanted to put a note into the envelope and they said you walked right past."

"A note." Sunny gave a short laugh, waved a hand. "Well, don't I feel silly. I must have been so caught up in the mural that the earrings went right out my mind."

"Understandable," Michael said.

"You know, I could bring them with me tomorrow morning. Leave them with Val, save you the bother."

"I'd rather take them with me today. In case Sonja's friends come tonight."

"Of course." Sunny gestured to the stairs. "So, I guess you'd like me to get them now."

"That would be best."

"Uh-huh." She took a few steps, glad that Val and those earrings were still in the building. "Well, I'll just go upstairs and have a look."

Hugh had joined Val and Duane, and the three of them were now hunched over butter tarts and a sheet of paper. "Val," Sunny said as she drew up to the table. "Can I have a word with you?"

"Sure." She fell into step behind Sunny. "You know, that Duane is an interesting guy. A little strange, but interesting."

"I'm sure he is," Sunny said, smiling at the Glasgow ladies, and sending Jess a quick wink on her way to the stairs.

Then she ducked around the corner, took the stairs two at a time, and didn't look back until she reached the third floor.

Val eyed her suspiciously as she stepped onto the landing. "What's going on?"

Sunny pulled her farther along, away from the stairs. "I need the earrings back," she whispered.

"What?"

Sunny shushed her. "He knows I didn't leave them. He wanted to put a note into the envelope for Sonja, and

found out it wasn't at the front desk. That's why he's here."
Sunny pushed that particular disappointment aside and
focused on the business at hand. "So give me back the
earrings and he can leave."

"Mommy?"

Both women turned as Jess came up the stairs. "What
are you doing?"

"Talking," Sunny said, and latched on to Val's arm when
she would have crept away. "You go and change, and then
we'll go for a walk to the deli, okay?"

"Can I call on Natalie?"

"Yes."

"Can we come back here to play?"

"Yes."

"Can we—"

"Just go," Sunny said, and Jess looked from one to the
other before closing the door to her room.

Sunny took a breath, faced Val again. "I need those earrings."

"Sunny, you don't understand. If I don't have that costume back on time, my name will be mud. Do you have
any idea what happens to a concierge whose name is mud?
Tickets dry up. Restaurants don't call back." She shuddered. "It's not pretty, believe me."

Sunny's eyes locked on Val's pocket. "I won't need them
long. Michael just has to go back to the hotel, write his
note, and leave the earrings at the desk again." She moved
a step closer. "I guarantee I'll have them back in time."

Val laid a hand over her pocket. "I can't risk it."

"What am I supposed to tell him?"

"Tell him you lost them, or better yet, tell him you were
mugged."

"I can't tell him that now. He'll think I'm trying to steal
the damn things."

"So tell him the truth."

Sunny thought about it. Thought about marching downstairs, plunking herself in front of him, and saying, "Michael, that was me lying naked on your sofa last night. So

whatever you wanted to say in a note, you just go ahead and tell me." But the heat in her face was too real to deny this time, and getting those earrings back suddenly seemed the easier task.

"Val," she said, solemnly. "Give me the earrings."

Val shook her head, backed up a step.

"Give me the damn—" Sunny grabbed Val's hands away from her pocket and shoved her fingers inside.

"Are you crazy?" Val slapped at her hands. "Cut that out."

But Sunny's fingers were small and quick.

She held the prize close to her chest and backed up to the sitting room. "I promise I'll have them back in time. But right now, I need an envelope." She grabbed one from her desk, dropped the earrings inside, and sealed it on her way to the stairs.

Val glared at her from the top step. "What if you can't get them back?"

"I'll get them back." Sunny headed down at a run, slowed halfway, and entered the tearoom with grace and aplomb, and a fine line of sweat on her upper lip.

She gave her lip a discreet swipe and carried the envelope to Michael's table. "You were right, of course." She laughed lightly. "I still can't believe I did that."

"No harm done," Michael said.

"I guess you'll be in a hurry to get back to the hotel now," she said.

"Not really." He picked up a butter tart. "I haven't tried one of these yet."

"I could always box it for you—"

"Oh, Sunny," Val called from the stairway. Sunny turned and Val smiled too sweetly. She held out Sunny's cell phone. "Call for you. Someone named Sonja."

Sunny could only stare, and wish she'd hidden her phone.

But it was too late. Hugh's head snapped up and Michael was already on his feet.

"Sonja's on the line?" He glanced over at Sunny. "I told you she'd call."

"And you were right." Sunny shot Val a significant look. "Get a number and I'll call her back."

"Can't do that." Val held the phone out as she walked toward her. "She's on a plane to Wisconsin and wants to make an appointment to see you now." She drew up in front of Sunny, thrust the phone out a little farther. "Better hurry, you know how expensive those air-to-land calls are."

Sunny smiled at Michael, motioned to the phone. "I'll just take this in the kitchen."

She plucked the phone from Val's fingers and strolled into the kitchen. "Now what am I supposed to do?"

"Make an appointment," Val said through clenched teeth.

"For when?"

"Who cares?" Val muttered and looked over at the door. "Michael, hi."

Sunny put the phone to her ear, said, "Sonja?" into the dead air, then smiled. "I have heard so much about you."

Michael gestured from the doorway. "Say hello for me."

"Michael Wolfe says hi. Yes, he's here." She put a hand over the mouthpiece. "Sonja says, what a small world."

He held out a hand. "Let me talk to her."

"Sonja? Michael would like to talk to you." She started to pull the phone from her ear, then stopped. "What's that? Uh-huh . . . oh, I see."

She watched his face fall. "She doesn't want to talk to me?"

He looked so hurt Sunny instinctively shook her head. "Of course she does." Sunny laughed into the phone. "Michael thinks you don't want to talk to him." Sunny wrinkled her nose at him. "Sonja says, don't be silly. She just needs to make the appointment first."

Val whispered, "Oh my God," Hugh just grinned and Sunny heard Sean ask, "What's going on?" as she turned to the calendar on the fridge.

"When's a good day for you?" she said into the phone

while she hunted around for a pen. She mouthed "thanks" when Michael offered her one, and turned her attention back to the calendar. "Sorry, Sonja, I'm tied up then. But Tuesday is good . . . Lunch? At the Plaza?" Sunny laughed and waved a hand. "I'd love it."

Val stood slightly behind Michael now, tugging on her earlobe.

"Your earrings are here, yes," Sunny said, then glanced over at Michael. "Sonja says, don't bother leaving the earrings with the front desk. Just give them to me."

"Sure, fine," Michael said. "Just let me talk to her."

Sunny nodded with the phone. "Okay, Sonja. Nice talking to you, too. Here's Michael . . . What's that? They're serving drinks now and want you to hang up?" She shrugged at Michael. "You know how that phone cord gets in the way on a plane."

He took a step closer. "Just find out where she's staying. Someone get me a piece of paper."

Hugh handed him one from the pad on the fridge. Val got him another pen. Sunny tried to think faster.

"Michael wants to know . . ." She gave him a helpless look. "She doesn't know where she's staying."

"Then get a number."

"A number? . . . Sonja? . . . you're breaking up. . . ."

Michael eyed the phone openly. "How about the name of the gallery? Her friends in New Jersey? There has to be a way to reach her. Doesn't she have a cell phone, for God's sake?"

"Yes," Sunny said, and blurted out her own cell phone number.

Michael jotted down the number, then glanced up. "That's a New York area code."

"Because she's in art," Val said quickly. "And what city is the capital of the art world?"

"Right," Michael said and shoved the number into his pocket. "Is she still there?"

Sunny pushed END. "Nope, she's gone."

Val piped right up. "But the good news is that Sunny

will see her on Tuesday, right? And that means . . ." She gave Sunny an encouraging nod.

"Another mural," Michael said, visibly relaxed now, and smiling. "Congratulations."

"Thanks," Sunny said, earning a poke from Val. "And it also means that you don't have to take the earrings." She set the phone on the counter and led him back to the table where Duane, the Glasgow ladies, and a couple no one had noticed come in, all sat staring at her.

Sunny grinned. "Just got another mural."

Duane smiled, the Glasgow ladies seemed pleased, and the couple in the corner snuck out quietly.

"We have cappuccino," Hugh called after them, and there was no question in Sunny's mind anymore. Moyra was definitely going to kill them all.

Michael sat down and Sunny picked up the envelope. "I'll take— What are you doing?"

He had his own phone out of his pocket. "Phoning Sonja."

"You can't do that yet."

"I beg your pardon?"

"Because she's on a plane. You can't use a cell phone on a plane."

"I'll leave a message."

He started to punch in numbers and Sunny jostled his arm. "Oops," she said, and sent Hugh a "save me" look.

"So, Michael," he said, jostling him again as he pulled a chair in beside him. "What did you think of my espresso? And be honest."

Sunny dashed back into the kitchen and picked up her phone.

"What are you going to do?" Val asked

Sunny dropped the envelope on the counter. "What do you care, you've got the earrings."

"Look, I'm sorry about the phone call, but I couldn't think of what else to do. And I didn't tell you to give him your number. What were you thinking about anyway?"

Sunny slumped against the fridge with the phone. "I

don't know. It all happened so fast, and he looked so sad when he thought she wouldn't talk to him." She leaned her head back. "There was no way Sonja would have refused to give him her number."

"What are you talking about?"

"She liked him," Sunny said. "And I couldn't let him walk out of here thinking she didn't. Thinking she was the kind of bitch who would throw him over through someone else. Can you imagine how hurt you'd be, if you got the message that someone didn't want to talk to you, through someone else? It's all so junior high. And Sonja is not like that."

Val put a hand on her arm. "Sunny . . . Sonja is not real."

Sunny looked up at her. "But Michael is, and I couldn't hurt him that way."

Val drew her head back.

Sunny pointed the cell phone at her. "It means nothing. I couldn't hurt *anyone*, okay. I'm a nice person."

Val laughed. "A nice person with a cell phone that is going to go off any minute."

"So I won't answer it."

"And when it goes to voice mail, and he hears your message?"

Sunny pursed her lips. "I need a new message."

"Generic, and fast."

Sunny glanced into the tearoom. Michael was eating the butter tart and nodding while Hugh rabbited on about something, bless his heart. But that phone was still right there, with her number on a paper beside it.

Sunny sighed and dialed her own number. Why didn't the man just go home? Hadn't he done enough for one day?

At the prompt, she changed her message. "The cellular customer"—Sunny recited her number into the phone—"is not available . . ."

She hung up. "God, I hate those messages," she said, but the only consolation was that no one but her family had the number. And now Michael too, of course.

"There," she said to Val. "Now he can call all he likes and I will never, ever answer."

Jess appeared in the doorway. "Are we still going out?"

"I was wondering the same thing," Michael said, as he drew up behind Jess. "And I wanted to thank you for getting Sonja's number."

"No problem," she said, setting the phone down on the counter.

"Can we go now?" Jess asked.

"I think—" Sunny started, but broke off as Moyra's voice floated into the tearoom.

"I'm not bringing in offtrack betting and that's . . . What's all this?"

"I think we're in big trouble," Sunny said, taking Jess's hand as Moyra hollered, "What is going on in here?"

Sunny and Jess swung around the corner into the tearoom.

Hugh just smiled, Sean strolled into the kitchen with cups, and the Glasgow ladies sat back for the show.

"What's happening?" Michael asked.

"We're going for that walk right now," Sunny said as she hustled Jess up the stairs. "Care to join us?"

# Eight

Jack was outside the tearoom, rocking back and forth on his heels and whistling, when Sunny emerged from the apartment door on the other side of the picture window. Hugh's sign was gone, but his voice and Moyra's could still be heard out on the street.

"Dad," Sunny said softly. "Dad."

Jack shot her a grin as he ambled toward her. "Got out, did you? Well, you always were the smart one." He glanced over at the door. "Where's Jess?"

"She's coming," Sunny said. "Then we're off to the deli. Shouldn't be long."

"It was cappuccino two to one," Hugh shouted.

Sunny glanced over as Hugh's duffel bag slid out to the street. "Then again, it could take a while."

Jack laughed. "Take your time, I'll cover for you. And don't worry about Hugh. He loves this."

True enough, Sunny thought. Where Sean would simply leave and Sunny would try to placate, Hugh had always been the one who would stand up and fight.

Jess came through the door followed by Michael.

"Grandpa," she called and ran to give him a hug.

Jack got down on one knee to greet her, but kept one eye on Michael. "Who do we have here?" he said as Michael ambled toward them.

Jess sucked in a breath. "This is—"

"Michael Wolfe," Sunny cut in, meeting her daughter's

frown head-on and making a mental note to speak to Jess later about what she'd heard in the kitchen. There was no point in the child's having wrong notions about things. "I'll be doing another mural for him at the Brighton."

Jack held out a hand. "Well, this is a rare pleasure. Sunny's customers don't usually come to the house." He cocked his head. "Had some business to discuss, did you?"

Sunny wondered what she had done to deserve three meddling men in her life.

"I had to pick up something," Michael said, shaking her father's hand and graciously enduring a frank once-over.

"And now we're going to the deli," Jess said.

Jack raised an eyebrow, and Michael smiled. "It makes more sense when you're under the influence of butter tarts."

Sunny was half afraid her father would offer to tag along with them, for the exercise, or the fresh air, or some other excuse. But instead he gave Michael a grin and stepped back, a sign that he found him acceptable company for Sunny and Jess—in public at any rate.

"That's Moyra's baking for you," Jack said and glanced back at the tearoom. "Although you might want to come another time and tell her what you thought."

"I'll do that," Michael said.

"Let's go," Jess said.

"I want to talk to Grandpa a minute," Sunny said and took Jack a step away. "Were you trying to talk Moyra into offtrack betting during Dave and Hazel's vows?"

"Of course not," he said, the very soul of indignation. "I waited until we were on the way out. But of course, she wouldn't listen. And it's not like it takes up a lot of space. Just a blackboard, a small booth—"

"Dad," Sunny said. "Forget it."

"I know. But I want to find something we can do together. I did think a comedy club—"

"Why don't you help her in the kitchen?" Sunny said. "Learn how the tearoom works as it is. Be part of it with her."

*And let me off the hook,* she thought.

"Mommy, pleeease," Jess whined.

"You go on, now," Jack said to Sunny. "As long as your mother doesn't throw anything else out, we'll be fine."

Michael looked over at Sunny. "I forgot Nugent."

Jack squinted up at him. "Gawky fellow? Odd clothes?" Michael nodded.

"He'll be all right. He's not family," Jack said.

She glanced over at Michael as Jack headed back to the tearoom. "I apologize for the third degree. My family tends to be overprotective sometimes."

"I can't blame them," he said. "After all, they wouldn't want you out here with the wrong stranger."

Sunny smiled and strolled, enjoying the sun on her face, the breeze on her skin, in no hurry to get back to her meddling family or to try and figure out why Michael was walking beside her.

She was simply going to enjoy herself. And if he called Sonja later, she'd deal with that then.

" 'Scuse me," Jess said, darting between them and racing ahead, skillfully dodging shoppers and sidewalk displays, and skidding to a stop when she reached the Lucky Koin Laundry half a dozen stores down. She turned, signaling to Sunny that she'd only be a minute, then dashed inside.

Michael raised a brow. "She has a little laundry to do?"

Sunny laughed. "She's hoping to catch the latest update on Lilli and André's engagement. She loves to one-up the Glasgow ladies."

Michael smiled. "She's an interesting kid."

Sunny tried not to preen. "I'm proud of her," she said, and paused to check out the specials on the sandwich board at the restaurant next door.

"Number three looks good, Frank," she said to the man taking a cigarette break on the front step.

He tossed the butt as a smile lit his face. "Sunny, bella. When you going to run away with me, eh? You break my heart all the time." He cast a curious glance at Michael. "Who's this? My competition?"

"Michael's a client," she said, glad to be able to say it again, to hear the words herself and hope that maybe this time, they'd sink in. "And this is Frank," she continued. "The man who makes the world's best arrabiata sauce."

"She flatters me. But I take good care of the arbor she did for me, because this girl is gonna be famous one day."

"If I ever need an agent, Frank, I am calling you," Sunny said lightly as she strolled away.

"At last I'd be near you," he called, and Sunny laughed.

"He seems to like you," Michael said.

She slowed at a table outside the dollar store. "Frank is all talk. He has five kids and a wife he adores. If I ever said let's go, he'd faint on the spot."

"In other words he thinks you're safe."

"I guess he does," she said absently, her gaze moving past the half-price Christmas ornaments and calendars already six months old to a deep wire bin beside the table marked ALL TOYS HALF PRICE.

She crouched down in front of the bin, then shot back up and smiled. "I have seen the chalk. And it is mine."

She reached a hand into the toys, her brow furrowed, as she pushed through coloring books and markers, yo-yos and water guns. "Who's idea was it to use a bin?" She bent lower and dug deeper, her skirt rising awfully high in the back.

Michael took hold of her arm, hauling her out before she could cause an accident. "I'll get it."

"Are you always so pushy?" she asked as he dug.

"I believe the word is overbearing." His fingers closed on the chalk and he slowly maneuvered it past the other toys to the top. He held the box out to her. "Why is this so important anyway?"

"Because next to dancing, sidewalk chalk is Jess's favorite thing. She draws these wonderfully intricate hopscotch patterns outside the tearoom, then sits like a troll and tells people they can't come in unless they do it." Her smile was decidedly wicked. "Drives my mother crazy."

Michael walked with her to the cashier. "There's a very twisted side to you, isn't there?"

She grinned. "Comes from having brothers."

"I understand," Michael said, remembering how he and Andy went to great lengths to get a rise out of their mother. Frogs in the linen closet. Worms on their spoons. He wondered what his nephews did to drive Jill up the wall.

The cashier rang up the chalk. "One dollar fifty."

Michael handed him a bill. "Let me."

Sunny held out her own bill. "Sorry, but I can't do that—"

Michael took her hand, drew it back, and smiled when she looked up at him. "Because she danced so well."

Her face softened, and Michael knew that was the only thing he could have said to make Sunny put her wallet away.

"Thank you," she said, pulling her hand back and taking the bag. "I'll save it for when Jess gets home."

As though summoned, Jess leaped out of the Lucky Koin. "Going to call on Natalie. Then can we go back to our house?"

Sunny nodded and Jess was off again.

"Does she ever walk anywhere?" Michael asked.

Sunny smiled and continued on. "Only when it's time for bed. Then you'd think her feet were made of lead."

Michael looked over at her. "I know it's none of my business, but is her father around?"

"Nope," Sunny said, too accustomed to the question by now to be offended. "Jess has never met him."

"What kind of fool is he?"

"Just a regular one," she said, watching her daughter slow again as she passed by the wedding cakes at D'Amici's Bakery.

She remembered seeing Brad that last day, sitting in the backseat of his parents' car, the place where they had made love more than a few times. Being careful not to look up, to see Sunny there at the window above the tearoom while his mother and father sat in the next room, explaining to

Sunny's parents all the reasons why their son couldn't possibly marry their daughter. And why a cash settlement, accompanied by mutual agreement to release Brad from any future claim or financial obligations, would be in everyone's best interest.

"I can't imagine a man not wanting to see his own child," Michael said.

"Neither could I," she said softly, letting the image fade as Jess and her best friend Natalie did their high-five, bump hips, stick-out-your-tongue greeting that always embarrassed Natalie's mom—pleased that she finally felt nothing at all for the boy who had broken her heart.

"But to be fair," she said, "we were very young. I was only eighteen when Jess was born, and if we'd married, we'd probably have divorced by now."

"I'm not sure I could be so understanding," Michael said, sounding so much like her brothers Sunny had to smile.

"I wasn't always." She paused to peek into the florist's front door, and ask how her husband was doing.

Michael hung back, remembering the graduation picture in the tearoom and finally understanding why she'd looked somber and sad, and more than a little scared—a far cry from the confident and vibrant woman she'd become. He could only imagine what it had taken her to get there, and wonder if Jess's father had any idea what he'd lost.

Jess and Natalie came toward them at a run. And Jess's feet had barely stopped when her mouth started.

"Lilli and André are fighting about the wedding gown," she said. "Her grandmother says red, but his mother says white. Lilli's crying at the counter and André's walking back and forth, back and forth. So I told her to wear electric blue and tell them all to go suck an egg."

"Jess," Sunny snapped.

Her daughter's brow furrowed. "Well, it's not fair. They're in love and they should get married if they want to. Right, Nat? Nat?"

But Natalie was too busy giving Michael a wide-eyed once-over. And when she grabbed Jess and spun her around, it wasn't hard to figure out what had been said when the two of them giggled and wedding-marched along the street ahead of Sunny.

"It's nice to see they're still optimistic about Lilli's wedding," Michael said, and Sunny breathed a sigh of relief that he was as blessedly oblivious as ever.

But Jess's romantic notions were her own fault really. Hadn't she read fairy tales to the child without altering the endings? Hadn't she been happy to let Snow White play the domestic for seven men, and sighed when Beauty fell for the Beast?

And had she even once mentioned that in reality Beauty was a hostage suffering from Helsinki syndrome? Of course not, and now she was reaping what she'd sown—a daughter who believed in impossible relationships and happily ever after, while Sunny herself had been seriously considering the merits of a meaningless relationship. One based strictly on enjoyment and buffing up the sexual skills. And as she walked beside Michael, Sunny wondered which one of them was wrong.

"Can we go now?" Jess asked. "I want to show Natalie my new video games."

"I still have to go to the deli, so I'll watch you down," Sunny said, and the two girls took off at a run, heading back toward the Isles.

"It's funny," Michael said when Jess waved from the front of the tearoom. "I've lived in Manhattan for almost a year, and never ventured over the bridge until today."

Sunny headed for the deli. "It's a different world."

"And you're part of it, aren't you."

"I love it here," she said matter-of-factly. "I know some people long for the quiet of the country, and others want the lawns of the suburbs, but I can't imagine living anywhere else." She paused with a hand on the door, her gaze moving past him to the curb. "Although I could be persuaded to move as far as the next block."

She stepped back from the deli and shaded her eyes with a hand. "And if that white car belongs to who I think it does, then I am about to make a quick detour." She glanced over at him. "This was only supposed to be a quick trip to the deli and I know Duane is waiting, so if you want to head back, I'll understand."

Michael pursed his lips, thought about detours and Duane, and the work waiting for him at the hotel. "What's at the end of the detour?"

"Brownstones," she said, as though the word was a prayer.

Michael looked into those clear green eyes. "I've always liked those."

"Then you are about to be delighted," she said, drawing him along with a smile.

They turned onto a shade-dappled street lined with stately brownstones, and there on the front stoop six doors down was an OPEN HOUSE sign.

"I knew it," Sunny said, taking the stairs two at a time. "I have a nose for these things." She pressed the buzzer as he came up behind her. "And as an added bonus, I know the real estate agent."

The door opened and a woman with defiantly dark hair and the weight of middle age smiled broadly. "I haven't see you in ages," she said and waved Sunny in. "How's your mom?"

"Still getting used to having my dad around all day."

"Tell her I sympathize. Never mind, I'll go and reward myself for losing ten pounds with one of her lemon tarts." She gave Michael a considering glance as he came in behind Sunny. "The apartment is on the third floor. It's vacant so you'll see it needs work. Which isn't so bad if you're handy." Her eyes narrowed as she took a feature sheet from the hall table and handed it to Michael. "Are you handy?"

"He's a client," Sunny said, taking the feature sheet from Michael and heading for the stairs.

"I'll wait here. Those stairs will be the death of me."

"Who is that?" Michael whispered as they rounded the landing on the second floor.

"Rona McCloskey. She and my mother go way back. She knows I can't buy, but she indulges my fantasies and lets me into her open houses anyway. And she always views men as potential husbands."

He laughed. "I hadn't noticed."

She sent him a bland look. "Why am I not surprised?"

The apartment was airy and open, with high ceilings, tall windows, and a working fireplace. It made no difference that the floors were watermarked where plants had sat, and the walls gray where pictures hadn't. The apartment was everything Sunny wanted and couldn't have. A little like Michael, she thought.

He strolled through the empty room, his expression neutral as he ran a toe over the stains, glanced up at a section of peeling paint on the ceiling that she hadn't noticed, then crouched down in front of a radiator, seeing the apartment with the critical eye of a professional, not a dreamer.

"I'm curious," he asked, dusting his hands as he straightened. "After all you've been through, you still want to get married?"

"Yes," she said, and turned her back on reality to walk the length of the room with her imagination instead. "Just because Brad was an idiot doesn't mean I've branded all men with the same label. I haven't dated in a while, but to be honest, I can see myself being quite the happy homemaker one day. With an easel there and a rocking chair there and a new brother or sister for Jess playing on an afghan I knitted myself right there."

"You'd stop painting?"

"Of course not." She paused at the screen door to the roof deck, picturing potted roses and flowering trees where there was only gravel and dried leaves. And closing the main door quickly before he could explain to her about weight loads or heat gain, or anything else she didn't need to know about right now, when it was all just a pipe dream.

"I'll always paint," she said, and wandered over to peer

into a bedroom. "I'd just work nights so my husband could baby-sit."

"Sounds like you've got it all planned out," he said, but his tone made her turn, look over at him.

He was leaning back against the window frame, studying her with the same mild interest he'd shown the radiator, as though breaking her down into costs and work involved as well.

"I know what I want," she said.

He gave her a wry smile. "I like your confidence."

He pushed away from the window, looked around. "And if you insist on dreaming, you could start with worse places than this. It's a good size, has plenty of charm and character." He glanced over. "An awful lot of stairs, though."

"I'm used to it," she said. "Keeps me in shape."

That much was true, he thought, watching her hips sway as she came back across the room.

"Besides, what more do I need?" she continued. "This apartment is close to the park, the school, and the tearoom. In short, it's perfect."

Michael shook his head. The woman was a bonafide Annie. A big-eyed redhead with romantic notions and a firm belief in tomorrow. He wouldn't have been surprised if she burst into song right there on the spot. But what did he need with a dreamer?

He'd learned the hard way that even the best-laid plans can slide right out from under you without a moment's notice, shattering all those carefully nurtured dreams so fast it takes your breath away, and leaving you groping and fumbling for a foothold again.

He turned away, hoping Sunny's fall would be an easy one. And that her landing would be soft.

He opened a door and pulled a string. "Closets, of course, are always an issue."

"Which is exactly why God created armoires."

Michael glanced over. She might not be his type, but she did make him smile.

He strolled over to where she stood. "You know, I used

to be in the house-building business, and my favorite part was figuring out what a person needed as opposed to what they thought they wanted."

She folded her arms, leaned back against the frame. "How very overbearing of you."

He laughed. "Not at all. It's just a matter of making the house fit the family, not the other way around." He studied her in that way again. "Take you, for instance. If I was going to build a house for you, I'd start by asking if you cook or eat out most of the time."

"I cook. And Jess helps."

"Gourmet or simple?"

"Simple. One pot if I can manage."

"Do you eat at the table or in front of the television?"

"Table. And inevitably there are a couple of six-year-old guests as well. So what does all of this tell you?"

"There are a lot more questions, but already I know that you'll need durable surfaces, an eating area, not a breakfast bar, and a preparation area with minimal steps between appliances because you get your exercise on the stairs. You find out how a family lives, and you build the house around them."

His face was animated, his eyes bright, as he strolled back to the window. "All right, so now it's my turn. What kind of house would be perfect for you?"

"Small," he said without hesitation. "With a fireplace in the kitchen, a wraparound porch, and not a useless room in the place."

"Sounds like you've already designed it."

"I've already built it," he said, and turned to look out the window.

"And where is the house?"

"Maine," he said, and Sunny added the house to the picture she'd created last night, and wondered if he were seeing it himself as he stared out at the street.

She took a step toward him. "Where in Maine?"

"A fishing town called Hailey."

"Yet you live in Manhattan."

He shrugged. "That's where the job is, and the house was never home. It was the place we ran to, the reward for making it through another week."

She chose her words carefully because only Sonja knew of his wife. "We?"

He looked over at her, his eyes dark, unreadable. "I was married, and I built the house in Maine for my wife."

Sunny held his gaze. "What was her name?"

"Kate," he said softly. "Katherine at the office."

"What happened to her?"

"She died in a car accident three years ago."

"You must miss her very much," Sunny said gently.

His eyes narrowed "There isn't a day goes by that I don't think of her. And that house is all I have left."

"Do you go back often?"

He turned back to the window. "I haven't seen the place since."

"Why not?"

"Too many memories. Too many things she loved. I didn't move anything out, couldn't to be honest. So I gave away the plants in her greenhouse and left everything else where it was."

Not everything, Sunny thought, remembering the book on the shelf, the one beside the cartoons that were meant to lighten him up, make him laugh.

"I pay someone to cut the grass," he continued, "and look in on the place, make sure the raccoons haven't set up house. Unfortunately, the guy's wife is in real estate and she always seems to have buyers who are panting to buy the house."

"But you're not interested."

"I don't even read her e-mails anymore, and I have never returned her calls. Some day I'll have to decide what I'm going to do with it, but not yet." He turned from the window, looking down at the floor. "I don't know why I'm telling you all this. I don't usually talk so much."

"You can talk to me anytime," Sunny said. "I'm a good listener." He raised his head and she managed a smile. "I think I was a bartender in a former life. Either that or a priest."

His face visibly relaxed. "I like the bartender better."

"Me too," she said, her voice no more than a whisper as he came toward her. "Like they say, the bartender is everybody's pal for a while."

He stopped in front of her, so close that she could feel his warmth through her T-shirt.

"Is that what you are? My pal?"

"I could be," she said, and Michael found himself reaching for her, needing to kiss her, to find out what that sweet mouth tasted like, to feel the softness of her breasts against his chest. To lift her skirt and bring her hard against him.

It was a routine as familiar to him as breathing since Kate died. Bury himself in another woman to drive away the loneliness, the ache, the constant goddamn emptiness.

Sunny saw it the instant before he slipped an arm around her waist and drew her closer—something akin to anger, only darker, sadder. He bent to her and she laid her hands on his chest, feeling the beat of his heart against her palms, his breath against her lips. She waited, barely breathing, certain he was going to kiss her. But then he was pulling away, backing up, apologizing, for God's sake, and she had no idea what she had done wrong.

"I'm sorry," he said again, cursing himself for a fool and worse.

He glanced up, saw her standing where he'd left her, those green eyes wide and confused. What the hell had he been thinking? She wasn't Sonja or Trish. Wasn't the kind of woman who would be interested in what he had to offer.

She was the kind of woman who could be hurt, and he had no right to put his hands on her.

Better to think about Sonja, to place that call. See if she'd have dinner with him after her meeting with Sunny. A few hours together before her next appointment.

A good time was all he had to offer. And he couldn't see that ever being enough for Sunny.

"Buddies then," he said, flashing her a quick, nervous smile as he headed for the door.

Sunny watched him head for the stairs, pause and look back.

"Buddies," she said, as she walked toward him.

For now.

# Nine

Michael saw the front door open just enough to allow a head with a frizzy red ponytail to poke through. Sunny glanced around, and flashed him a grin when she spotted him under his desk. "You're dressed."

"And you're late," he said, as he crawled out.

He knew because he'd been watching the clock since he put his feet over the side of the bed earlier that morning. Waiting for the slide of her card, the first glimpse of her smile while he shoved his desk across the living room, found a new spot for the drafting table, and hunted down a plug and a phone connection for his computer. Making room for her in his office, his life, and wondering what it was going to be like having a buddy around all day.

"Couldn't be helped," she said lightly, then swung the door back and propped it with a toolbox that rivaled any Michael had seen a contractor haul in. "First day of summer camp always marks the beginning of the sunscreen wars with Jess." She ducked back into the hall. "Okay, take everything over there."

Michael stared as a young man with a shaved head, a ghetto blaster, and a stepladder came through the door, followed by a wiry older woman lugging a camera bag and an armload of drop cloths. And bringing up the rear was Sunny, carrying a plastic bin filled with pictures, sponges, brushes, muffin pans, tubes of paint, yogurt containers of various sizes and brands, and a roll of paper towels.

"I know what you mean," the older woman said. "My daughter has to bribe her kids to keep the stuff on. A dollar every time they reapply."

"I only got fifty cents when I was a kid," the young man said solemnly.

"You're still a kid," the woman said. "And slower than molasses," she added, giving him a nudge with the drop cloths to hurry him along.

Noisy, Michael thought as the parade passed by. It was going to be noisy. And crowded, he added as they began to unload and spread out.

"Here's the estimate, as promised," Sunny said, taking an envelope from the box and walking it over to him. "And I also brought you this." She pulled a folded piece of paper from the bib of her overalls. "From Jess." She motioned to her companions. "You did remember that the reporters from the *Banner* would be here?"

Oddly enough, he did, and said as much as he set the envelope on the desk and unfolded the note. An intricate hopscotch took up most of the page, and inside she had printed very neatly *Thanks for the chalk. My nana says, yeah thanks a lot, too. Jess.*

He smiled and tucked the note into his daytimer. "I take it you have hopscotch outside the tearoom."

"And a troll on the step." Sunny looked down as she pulled her baseball cap out of her pocket. "I thought about calling to see if you wanted to come and see. But I figured you'd be working."

"I was," he said. Or at least he'd tried.

He'd sat at his desk with the bills from the contractors stacked next to the maintenance reports from the grand opening, knowing he had less than two weeks to clean everything up before the job in California began.

But he'd caught himself staring out the window more often than at the pages, watching the comings and goings at the park, and wondering what she was doing. Imagining her and Jess out somewhere, laughing, talking, and having a helluva lot more fun than he was—an odd thought for a man who could lose himself for hours in his work.

He'd given his head more than a few shakes, told himself to focus, yet still he'd been restless and edgy. Jumping every time the phone rang, thinking it might be her, the first woman who ever wanted to be his buddy, inviting him to come out and play.

Of course she hadn't, and when he'd finally given up on the paperwork, he'd picked up the phone and dialed the tearoom, only to hang up before the first ring, because he had no idea what he'd say when he heard her voice. So he'd returned Sonja's call instead, knowing exactly what to say when her answering machine kicked in.

"We're ready," the reporter called.

"Coming," Sunny said, then yanked on her cap and peered at him from under the bill. "I've heard rumors that you work too hard."

He had to smile. "And what do you think?"

She considered a moment, then turned and sauntered away. "I think that next time, maybe I'll call you anyway."

Michael felt himself nod. "Okay then," he said, and knew his smile was slowly turning into an idiot grin. And there wasn't a damn thing he could do about it . . .

"Duane, what a great tie," Sunny called.

. . . until now.

"You don't think it's too loud?" Duane asked, stroking a hand down the length of his tie as he ambled toward them.

"Not at all," the reporter said, and the photographer gave him two thumbs-ups.

Michael had to admit it was an interesting tie. Tasteful even. While *great* was pushing it, the colors went well with the red Grant Hall jacket, and would probably be a big hit at the meeting as well. Now if he could just remember where he put his own jacket—

"Sir, can I have a word with you?"

"If you're going to remind me about the meeting—"

"No, sir." Duane pulled a manila envelope from inside

his jacket and lowered his voice. "I came to talk to you about the Carillon."

Michael should have known. He had slid the envelope with Judith's drawings under Duane's door after calling Sonja had failed to take away the restlessness last night. He'd needed a walk and Nugent had needed to see them in case the project came up at the meeting. He might not want him as an assistant, but Michael wasn't about to let the kid be the only one there who didn't know what was going on. And he could tell by the set of his mouth that the changes had not sat well with the boy architect.

"Okay," the reporter said to Sunny, "let's begin with how you got started as a muralist." He held up a small tape recorder. "Do you mind if I use this?"

"Not at all," Sunny said, and sat down on the drop cloth, which prompted the reporter to join her while the photographer walked slowly around them, snapping pictures.

"I always painted," Sunny began, "but I didn't attempt my first mural until after my daughter was born."

Michael wondered idly if Jess knew she'd been the inspiration for the Loch Ness monster as he motioned Duane into the hall. "What did you want to know?"

"I have to say, sir, that I am extremely disappointed with the Carillon proposal. The brief clearly put an emphasis on restoration—"

"You're talking about the old brief," Michael said, glancing back as laughter drifted into the hallway.

"Of course, that was when I believed in lucky brushes," Sunny said brightly, but the rest was lost as she tossed her cap aside and got to her feet.

Michael watched her a moment, wondering about lucky brushes and what she was looking for as she rummaged around in one of the boxes, before consciously shifting his attention back to Duane. "I wasn't given the new brief," he said, "but I'd hazard a guess that it said something like *needs waterslides*. And taken in that light, I'd say they did a fine job."

Be sure to visit our website at www.kensingtonbooks.com.

To start your membership, simply complete and return the Free Book Certificate. You'll receive your Introductory Shipment of 2 FREE Zebra Contemporary Romances. Then, each month as long as your account is in good standing, you will receive the 2 newest Zebra Contemporary Romances. Each shipment will be yours to examine for 10 days. If you decide to keep the books, you'll pay the preferred book club member price of $10.75 – a savings of over 20% off the cover price! (plus $1.50 to offset the cost of shipping and handling.) If you want us to stop sending books, just say the word… it's that simple.

# BOOK CERTIFICATE

## Yes! Please send me 2 FREE Zebra Contemporary romance novels. I understand I am under no obligation to purchase any books, as explained on this card.

Name _____

Address _____ Apt. _____

City _____ State _____ Zip _____

Telephone (____) _____

Signature _____

(If under 18, parent or guardian must sign)

Offer limited to one per household and not valid to current subscribers.
All orders subject to approval. Terms, offer, and price subject to change. Offer valid only in the U.S.

*Thank You!*

CN021A

## THE BENEFITS OF BOOK CLUB MEMBERSHIP

- You'll get your books hot off the press, usually before they appear in bookstores.

- You'll ALWAYS save more than 20% off the cover price.

- You'll get our FREE monthly newsletter filled with author interviews, book previews, special offers, and MORE!

- There's no obligation — you can cancel at any time and you have no minimum number of books to buy.

- And — if you decide you don't like the books you receive, you can return them. (You always have ten days to decide.)

PLACE
STAMP
HERE

"You can't honestly believe that, sir. I saw your original assessment—"

"And Judith rejected it. So all that matters is what she wants *now.*"

"But it's not right."

Michael smiled. "Your nobility has been duly noted, Nugent."

From the corner of his eye, he saw Sunny on the move, walking back and forth in front of the blank wall, her hands lifted, making broad sweeping gestures as she spoke. He could only catch bits of what she was saying, but every now and then she would turn to the reporter on the floor, or the photographer who had forgotten she was supposed to be taking pictures, and it didn't matter what the words were because everything he needed to know was right there in her face.

"Sir, perhaps if we talk to Judith together—"

Michael turned on him. *"We* are not talking to Judith about anything. *I* am going to do my job, and if you're smart, you'll do your best to hold on to yours."

The elevator opened beside them, and Judith looked from one to the other. She too was wearing the Grant Hall jacket, and somehow it managed to look more masculine on her than it did on Duane.

"Twenty minutes to the meeting, gentlemen," she said as she stepped out of the car. "Nice tie, Duane. And, Michael, you won't forget the jacket, will you?" She snapped her head up at the sound of voices inside the penthouse. "Is the painter here?"

Michael nodded. "She's being interviewed by the newspaper."

"The *Times?*"

"The *Banner,*" he said, and left her to wonder as he headed into the sitting room, staying back from the circle, but near enough that he could hear Sunny's voice and see her face.

"I'll start with a frame the same size as the windows across the front of the penthouse. . . ."

Her skin was flushed, her eyes bright and clear, and he suddenly realized how striking she was as she painted the picture with words.

"The frame is actually a stone archway leading into a formal rose garden enclosed by a tall hedge. A white stone path encircles a planting of boxwood and roses, and in the distance, there's a small gazebo with a domed roof."

She moved closer to the wall, her voice rising and falling like music, a pied piper's tune leading him into a garden that existed only in her mind. Making it so real she took his breath away, because he remembered in that instant what it was to feel that way.

Remembered himself and Kate sitting in front of the banker years ago, so bold and sure of themselves, neither one smart enough to realize they were asking the impossible. Knowing only that they had a vision, and it was right there on paper, and if that banker would only look twice, he'd see just how damn brilliant it was.

Michael had talked and talked until his throat went dry and his tongue was like rubber. Then he'd sat back and waited, feeling Kate reach for his hand under the edge of the desk, her fingers cool and smooth, and not minding at all that his were hot and sweating. They both leaned forward when the banker reached for the proposal, turned the page. And Michael remembered to this day the way her fingers had tightened on his when the banker nodded, just once, and smiled.

Michael sucked in a breath just as he had that afternoon, when all of their dreams were right there within their grasp, and he'd known what it was to feel alive and completely indestructible.

The photographer snapped a picture, bringing Michael back to the room, the moment, and Sunny, who was looking straight at him, into him. As though she could see where he'd been, what he'd been doing. He realized then that it wasn't the noise or the crowds that were going to be a problem. It was Sunny herself.

He almost laughed. Who would have thought that Sunny

of the baggy overalls would turn out to be dangerous? The kind who could make a man wonder, make him feel, make him start dreaming all over again. If anyone knew the folly of dreams, it was Michael.

"She's very good at this," Judith said. "Not much to look at, but she's quite the little promoter."

"You're wrong," Michael said quietly. "She's beautiful."

But it was Duane who murmured, "Yes, she is," because Judith was already halfway across the room.

Michael watched Sunny take Judith's hand, her smile bright and confident, so sure of her future it made Michael ache for her. Or perhaps for himself.

"You must be Sunny Anderson. I'm Judith Hill, and I have to say that you impressed me just now. I'm looking forward to seeing the finished mural." Sunny managed to squeeze in a thank-you before Judith turned to the reporter.

"What paper are you with again?"

"The *Brooklyn Banner.* Small but growing," the reporter said and held out his tape recorder. "What made you decide on another mural for the Brighton?"

Judith checked her watch, obviously not finding him worthy of her time. "A whim really. Spur-of-the-moment decision based on what I saw at the ball. I don't do that often, believe me, but the criteria are simple enough. Make it blend, no signature, and if I don't like how it comes out, I can always roll it over." She glanced at Sunny. "Nothing personal, of course."

"Of course," Sunny said as Judith turned and headed for the door.

"Michael, Duane, I'll see you downstairs."

She hustled out and the photographer rubbed a hand over her chest as if she'd been wounded. "Now that was harsh."

Sunny shrugged and picked up her cap. "I hear it all the time. People are nervous because they're buying sight unseen. But I've never had anyone roll one over yet." Her smile was quick and genuine. "And Judith Hill will not be the first."

A dangerous woman, Michael reminded himself. A real Annie, with her head in the clouds and a smile that never failed to move him. And it was going to be a very long two weeks.

She yanked on her hat and herded the crew to the door. "If you want any pictures in the ballroom, we'd better go now because there's going to be a meeting there in twenty minutes."

Michael turned away, walked to the desk, searching for something real, something solid, and landing on Sonja's phone number. Sonja: sexy and distant, and not a red hair on her head. Truly the perfect woman.

"What time is it in Wisconsin?" he asked Duane.

"Around seven. But, sir, the meeting . . ."

"Lots of time," Michael said, plucking his cell phone from the charger as he walked away.

The elevator opened and the three of them trooped into the car. Sunny pressed the button, then leaped out before the door closed. "You go on down," she said when they started to follow. "I just want to call and make sure Jess took the sunscreen to day camp."

"Understood," the reporter said.

"Meet you there," the photographer added as the elevator whisked them away.

Sunny dashed back into the penthouse only to find Duane kneeling in front of a box of photographs.

"Where's Michael?" she asked as she came up beside him.

He nodded at the bedroom. "Calling Sonja." He looked decidedly sheepish as he faced her. "I hope you don't mind me poking around. I've been curious about how you work ever since I got here."

"It's fine," she said, glancing at the bedroom while deep inside the box filled with sponges and brushes, her cell phone started to chirp.

Once, twice.

Duane motioned to the box. "Aren't you going to answer that?"

"I make it a point never to take calls when I'm on a job. I just forgot to turn it off." Sunny crouched down beside him and lifted the phone out gingerly, as though it might go off in her hand. She kept it turned away from Duane as she raised it higher. Sure enough, there on the display was Michael's cell phone number.

Three, four.

Idiot, she thought and lowered the phone gently into her pocket while she drew Duane's attention back to the photographs. "All the pictures are arranged according to subject, so if I want to know what a yew looks like, I go to *Bushes,* and then to *Yew.*" She held a snapshot out to him. "See?"

Five, six.

Duane stared at her pocket. "What if it's a client?" he asked, obviously appalled that she would ignore the urgent summons of the cell phone—a result of working too closely with Michael.

"I'll call back," she said, and tried not to be obvious about letting out her breath when at last the phone fell silent. "Voice mail," she said. "Don't you love it?"

The low rumble of Michael's voice drifted through the bedroom door. Sunny tried not to wonder about what he might be saying, and busied herself with the pictures instead. "I only brought what I need for this mural, but I have boxes of them in the truck."

"This is fine," Duane said, a hint of a smile coming to him slowly, easing the tension around his mouth. "I always wanted to paint. Spent years taking courses and workshops, but I was never a real artist, more of a technician." He flipped through the photographs slowly. "Which is why I went into architecture. I am hell with a straightedge."

Sunny laughed and sat down beside him. "You know, you're a lot different when Michael's not around."

"That's exactly what Val said when we went shopping." Duane smoothed a hand over the tie. "She picked this out for me. Hugh suggested something a little more daring, but Val seemed to know what I need." A trace of a smile touched his lips as he went back to the pictures. "I'm looking forward to seeing where she takes me for shoes tonight."

"Nobody knows leather like Val," Sunny said. "You'll be in good hands."

"I know." He glanced over at the bedroom door. "As for Michael, he's not so bad, really, and I knew what I was getting into when I took the job with Concord. His reputation as a son of a bitch is well established in the field. But if he ever lets me be his assistant, I know I'll learn a lot from him." He checked his watch as he got to his feet. "The only thing I don't know, is why a man of his caliber stayed when Grant Hall took over."

Sunny rose and followed him to the desk. "Is he really that good?"

"Michael is what they call a master architect. A visionary." Duane stopped at the desk. "What he's done for Concord is good, fabulous even, but it was his early work that really shone. He was a pioneer, a revolutionary. When everyone else was hollering *build it bigger, build it faster,* he was the lone voice saying *make it smaller, make it better.*"

"No compromises," Sunny said softly.

"Exactly. Only the best materials, the finest craftsmen, and small-home designs that were truly unique." Duane opened an envelope on the desk and slid the pages out. "He used to speak at architectural colleges, and I honestly believe his lecture and his book were part of what kept me going."

"Michael wrote a book?"

*"Dream Small.* It's still considered subversive material in some circles."

Sunny laughed, picturing Michael on that rocky coast again, spitting into the wind. "Why am I not surprised?"

"I'll bring in my copy, let you have a look. I know it changed the way I see things." He leafed through the sketches on the desk. "Which is why I know he can't honestly agree with what Grant Hall has planned for Sundridge."

Sunny moved closer. "What's in Sundridge?"

"Our next project. A beautiful old estate, a castle by anyone's definition, with a ballroom of gold and mirrors, like something out of a fairy tale. Michael's idea was to restore it back to its original state." He handed the pages to Sunny. "But this is what head office wants to do with it."

Sunny flipped through the sketches, finding nothing objectionable at all. The Carillon looked like any other Grant Hall hotel: identical rooms, waterslides, mini-golf. She paused, realizing then what Duane meant. While Michael had turned the Brighton into a tiny jewel with charm and personality, the hotel in the sketches had been stripped of all identity, all sparkle, even the fairy tale ballroom. And knowing what she did of Michael, it was hard to imagine him going along peacefully.

She set the sketches on the desk. "Why is he doing it?"

"Tell her why, Nugent," Michael said.

Both Sunny and Duane turned as he came toward them, his steps slow and deliberate, his expression disturbingly neutral.

"Go ahead," he said to Duane. "Give her all the reasons."

Duane looked down at the floor. "Because it's your job."

"He can be taught," Michael said and clapped him on the shoulder. "Why don't you go down and save us a couple of seats at the meeting. I'll be down in a few minutes." His eyes were still cold as Duane headed for the door. "And, Nugent, pick me up a coffee along the way. You know how I like it."

Michael turned that icy stare on Sunny. "If you're ever curious about what I do, just ask, all right? You can get into trouble listening to hearsay."

She folded her arms, refusing to be intimidated. "All right, I'm asking. Why are you so horrible to Duane?"

He raised a brow as he came toward her. "That's all you want to know?"

Of course not. She wanted to know what he'd said to Sonja, and what he'd written in his book, and whether or not there was a way to take a step back without letting him think he'd won.

Figuring there wasn't, Sunny stood her ground as he came to a stop directly in front of her, his body angled slightly forward, not quite touching but close enough to make the fine hairs on her arms stand up as a shiver moved through her.

He seemed not to notice, however. His eyes were focused on her mouth, which seemed odd since she hadn't spoken a word, a situation she immediately remedied by tipping her head back a little farther and saying, "It's not all I want to know, but it's a start. So why are you mean to a man who only wants to learn from you?"

"Maybe because I have nothing to teach," he said and tipped her cap back a little farther on her head, his eyes moving slowly over her face, feature by feature, as though he was counting her freckles.

She frowned and pushed his hand away. "Or maybe you don't want to."

He sighed and was the first to step back, to give way, but somehow Sunny didn't feel as though she'd won anything as he turned to his desk.

"I've already told Duane what he needs to know," Michael said. "But it's not what he wants to hear. The kid is under the impression that architecture is some sort of crusade, a moral high ground."

"And where would he ever get an idea like that?"

"No idea. Architecture is a business. Dollars and cents, and keeping the client happy." He held up the sketches. "In this case, the client is Judith Hill. And if this is what makes her happy, then who am I to argue?" He slid the pages back into the envelope. "Unlike Duane, I just go with the flow. Roll with the punches. Dance to the piper—"

"Lie like a trooper?"

He laughed and dropped the envelope into the tray, catching sight of the red jacket on the floor behind the rack of blueprints. "On the contrary," he said and rounded the desk. "While their view for the Carillon isn't mine, to be honest, I don't give a damn. You, on the other hand, care too much."

"What are you talking about?"

"The mural." He picked up the jacket, gave it a shake. "Painting isn't just a job to you, and that makes you vulnerable. You've already invested so much of yourself in a garden that doesn't exist, that if Judith does come in here with a can of paint and a roller, you'll be devastated." He smiled at her over his shoulder. "But she already took a steamroller to my idea, and I'm just fine."

Sunny pursed her lips as he dusted off the jacket. He had a point. The murals were definitely more than just a job. Why else would she have dressed up like Sonja, crashed the ball, and ended up naked on his sofa? If she'd been able to treat the work casually, she'd never have known the taste of his kiss, the touch of his hands, or the sweet, sexy sound of his voice in the dark. Which would have made life a whole lot easier, come to think of it. But she couldn't imagine working at something day in and day out that didn't matter.

While she suspected that he didn't belong at Grant Hall any more than she belonged at the tearoom, he certainly had indifference down to an art. The careless shrug, the wry half smile, the words that fell off his tongue just a little too easily. As though he'd rehearsed them so many times he'd almost convinced himself. But there was a weariness around his eyes, a sadness that didn't fit the apathy, and told her he hadn't succeeded after all.

She strolled toward him. "So you've invested nothing in the Brighton, nothing in your proposal for the Carillon?"

"Not a thing," he said, holding the jacket up.

"And you're happy to be a Grant Hall man?"

"Absolutely." He looked directly at her as he shrugged the jacket up over his shoulders and gave it a sharp snap in the front. "See what I mean? Perfect fit."

She lowered the bill of her cap and gave him her sexiest look. "I always did love a man in uniform."

Michael figured that if her tongue was any farther into her cheek, she wouldn't be able to talk at all. Which would suit him fine.

He reached out, pulled her toward him, delighting in the shocked look in her eyes, the way she drew in a quick breath as he tipped up her baseball cap and let it tumble to the floor.

He bent her back over his arm. "I'm going in, shweet-heart," he said, smiling when she squealed and grabbed his shoulders for support. "If I don't make it back, tell Duane I really did like his tie."

"That will mean the world to him," she said, smiling back as she ran her fingers across his shoulders, looped her arms around his neck.

His gaze dipped lower, moving over her lips, her throat, the soft swell of her breasts beneath the overalls. Her breath was warm on his lips, her breasts soft against his chest, and something about the scent of her skin, her hair was haunting and familiar. There was no denying that this was wrong. No denying he should step away, give himself space to think, to breathe. And he would have if she hadn't moved her fingers into his hair, or looked into his eyes as if she knew him better than he knew himself.

His arms tightened around her, his eyes darkened almost imperceptibly, and Sunny felt her heart pound a little harder, certain that this time he was going to kiss her. And if he did, then maybe she could be honest with him, tell him about Sonja and the ball. Then again, maybe not. And who cared anyway as long as he stopped driving her crazy and just kissed her?

She cupped his face in her hands. "Any other messages?" she whispered, and watched him nod mutely, moisten his lips.

"If you hear from Sonja," he managed, "give her my office number too."

"Right," she said, as he lifted her up, set her on her feet, and left her wondering what it was about her that scared him off as he all but ran to the door. "Good luck with the mural," he called over his shoulder.

"Thanks," she called back and plunked her hat back on her head, so she wouldn't be tempted to tear out her hair.

# Ten

Val paused at the penthouse door, took a quick look around. "Are you alone?"

"For now," Sunny said, holding the level steady as she dragged a blue watercolor pencil down the wall, finishing the frame of the mural. "Michael and Duane are at the meeting and the reporters just left." She propped the level against the wall and stepped back to check the size of her window against the others. "By the way, that was a great tie you picked out for Duane."

"I like it." Val sauntered across the penthouse. "I like him too. Duane is a rare man. Articulate, interesting, and so easy to fit. Tonight Hugh and I plan to introduce him to the joy of Italian leather." She put her pager on the table. "If that goes off, I have to run. I'm trying to get Yankee Stadium for a few hours so one of the guests can practice his pitch, and right now, it's still iffy." She sank down on the sofa and kicked off her shoes. "So tell me how the interview went."

"I'd say it was a success." Satisfied with the window frame, Sunny shoved the pencil behind her ear and crossed to the coffee table, where she'd stacked her photographs. "So much so, in fact, that they're putting me on the front page on Saturday." She glanced over. "You'll have to pick up a copy, if you can find one."

"I'll not only find one, I'll get the neighborhood newsstands to carry a few copies as well." She pulled a foot into her lap and rubbed her toes. "And what about bookings? Is your phone ringing off the hook yet?"

"Not exactly." Sunny selected three shots of a formal garden and one of a gazebo, and carried them back to the stepladder. "But the half bath in the Hamptons came through before I left this morning. Other than that, the only calls have been for Sonja. Michael left her a brief but touching message asking why she bothered to carry a cell phone if she never intended to answer it."

"Getting frustrated, is he?"

Sunny stood the photographs up and glanced over at the wall, choosing the starting point for the mural. "He's not the only one. One minute I think he's interested in me, and the next he's backing up so fast, I'm amazed he doesn't break something. It's as though the idea of being anywhere near me scares the heck out of him."

"Scared can be good." Val said. "One of the best relationships I ever had was with the guy from Venezuela, remember him? Used to jump every time I touched him in the dark." A smile softened her mouth. "Those were good times."

"Well, the way things are going," Sunny said, "I won't be having a good time with Michael in the dark or anywhere else for that matter. Sonja, on the other hand, has an open invitation to come right over as soon as she gets back."

"So what are you going to do?"

"Give up." Sunny plucked a yogurt container from the box and headed for the bathroom. "The next move is definitely his."

Val sighed and pushed herself off the sofa. "You are such a backslider." She came up behind Sunny, peered at her in the mirror. "What is the most important thing you learned as Sonja?"

Sunny turned on the tap. "That beautiful women have it easy?"

Val shook her head in disgust. "I was thinking more along the lines of taking risks, making things happen."

Sunny filled the container, turned off the water. "And how do you suggest I make things happen with Michael?"

"For starters, you eliminate the competition."

"You want me to kill Sonja?"

"No, I want you to turn her into an ally. Every time you leave Michael a message, have Sonja bring your name into the conversation, talk you up a little." She shrugged, leaned her back against the door. "And if that doesn't work, then we kill her."

Sunny laughed and went past her to the hall. "I think she'll cooperate with the phone calls. Besides, I'm beginning to think that the real competition isn't Sonja. I think it's his wife."

Val was right behind her. "Michael has a wife?"

"Had." Sunny set the water on the stepladder and as she walked over to the bookshelf, she gave Val a quick rundown of everything she knew. But the greenhouse book was gone, leaving her no clues at all about the woman he had loved.

She turned back to Val. "So now the question is, how do I compete with a memory?"

"You start by getting close enough to give him something else to think about."

"That's just the problem. When I was Sonja, he couldn't get enough of me, but now?" Sunny sighed and pulled the blue pencil from behind her ear. "Now he won't even kiss me."

"And where is it written that you have to wait for him to decide?" Val cocked a brow. "Would Sonja have waited?"

"No, but—"

"But what? You couldn't do it? Come on, Sunny, you *were* Sonja once. The next time you're with him, why not let a little bit of her out again? Show him what he's missing. Give him something new to think about."

Sunny tried to imagine herself as a vixen in overalls, a siren in painter's drill. But she still felt like Sunny in workwear. "Okay, so what if I throw myself at him—"

"You're not throwing. You're *inviting*."

"All right, so what if I invite myself at him, and he still doesn't want me?"

"Then he's a fool and he'll deserve it when you stomp on his instep. But if you think and act like Sonja, then I guarantee you won't have to." Val's pager chose that moment to beep. She swept it off the table and headed for the door. "Wish me luck."

"Good luck." Sunny moistened her lips, took a step forward. "Val?"

She stopped, turned back, and Sunny felt ridiculous all of a sudden. "Just tell me straight. Am I doing the right thing?"

"I'd have to see you in action to say for sure—"

"No, I mean am I right in pursuing Michael?"

Val's brow scrunched. "Where did this come from?"

"I don't know. It's just that I can't help thinking maybe there's a reason this isn't going well. That maybe the cosmos is trying to tell me something, like 'be honest with the man, tell him about Sonja.' "

"Don't be silly. Sonja is thousands of miles away and not due back anytime soon. If you do this right, he will lose her number and not even care. And twenty years from now, when you run into him at the opening of your European show, you can tell him all about it, and the two of you will laugh." Val started to leave. "Trust me, it'll be great."

"But what if that's not it?" Sunny asked quickly. "What if this really is a warning, a way to get me to back off before I do something stupid again—"

"Sunny, stop beating on yourself. There is nothing stupid or careless or in any way wrong with what you're doing. In fact, there is nothing in this life that is more natural, more honest than simple lust. And if the cosmos has any opinion at all, which I doubt, then it is merely shaking its head and saying 'What took you so long?' " Val stepped away from the door. "But there are two things you need to remember in a relationship like this. One, always wear great underwear. And two, never fall in love."

"Great underwear, no love."

Val frowned as her pager went off again. "I have to go, but I'll drop by later. And I'll bring Sonja's makeup bag."

Sunny tapped her pencil against her palm as the door closed. Maybe Val was right. Why muddy the water now when it would be so much easier in a decade or two?

As for rule number two, love had never entered the equation. She'd known from the start that Michael wasn't available for anything permanent, and she wasn't about to start kidding herself now. All she wanted was to get her feet wet, experience a little of what Sonja had on the sofa that night—and leave celibacy behind once and for all.

Which left only one burning question.

"Where do I get great underwear?" she whispered, and was smiling as she turned back to the wall.


Judith held up a hand and leaned closer to the microphone. "As everyone knows, Grant Hall takes fun seriously. And that's exactly what we're going to have today."

She stood in front of the fireplace at the end of the ballroom with the head office staff of Grant Hall grouped before her: marketing at table one, sales at table two, followed by communications, public relations, finance, legal, and finally the in-house design group, with Duane slotted between interior design and landscape, while Michael sat next to their chief architect—a move undoubtedly meant to foster the team spirit that Judith valued so highly.

Michael remembered them from the ball, and knew that the architect was Doug, the interior designer was Agnes, and if he could just keep from calling the landscaper Attila, things might work out fine.

"I'm going to turn the meeting over to our facilitator." Judith paused and gestured to a young man sporting a goatee and a T-shirt that read *There Are No Stupid Ideas*—a theory Michael might have questioned under different circumstances. "Let's hear it for Rob McLean."

Loud rock music started and the young man stepped up to the microphone. Attila leaned close to Michael as they clapped. "If this guy mentions anything about the paper clip game, I say we make a run for it."

"Or the business trip game," Agnes whispered.

The landscaper nodded at Michael. "That too."

Doug let out a weary sigh. "And if it's corporate trivia?"

Both the landscaper and the designer looked over at Michael. "It's every man for himself."

Michael laughed. He had no idea what the paper clip game or any of the others were, but since he'd already pegged his teammates as reasonable people, he figured he'd follow along when the time came.

"All right, people," the facilitator called, "I want everyone on their feet."

The three of them had made a point of seeking out Michael and Duane while coffee was being served, quietly apologizing for not getting back to them on Sunday, admitting they'd taken the day off, done some sightseeing—had some real fun on Grant Hall's time. Then they'd welcomed both Michael and Duane to the team, said how much they were looking forward to working with them, and asked how they found the company so far.

"Efficient," Michael had said, congratulating himself on achieving a new level of diplomacy and ignoring Duane's snort of derision as he left the group, and sat down to brood over his coffee.

"On your feet," the facilitator called again. "Everybody this time. Up, up."

Michael rose and glanced over at Duane, who was still grim-faced and tight-lipped. Probably spent the last half hour composing his resignation, Michael thought. And good for him. Maybe the kid would find a white knight out there after all. Someone to take up the cause of good taste and sensitivity in building, because he certainly hadn't found one in Michael.

Contrary to what Sunny or anyone else might think, Michael was perfectly content with the way things were. He'd finish up at the Brighton and move on to the Carillon, where he'd give them water slides and mini-putt, and anything else they decided to squeeze in. And if it hurt when he walked into the ballroom, it would only be because he hadn't worn his safety boots.

"We'll start by limbering up." The facilitator put his hands on his hips. "Let's roll our heads around and around. That's right. Limbering up, letting go of the tension. Getting ready for the Grant Hall Olympics."

The landscaper glanced over as he rolled. "Chair races, guaranteed."

Doug slid his chair in. "Pager just went off. Got to find a phone."

Michael watched him cross the room, wondering if the page was real or if he'd just witnessed a well-executed getaway.

". . . and the other way now. Roll back and to the side . . ."

Michael took a quick look around. The redcoats were rolling, even Duane was rolling. The only one standing still was Judith, who was watching him closely. Michael smiled, feeling like the kid who opens his eyes during prayer and catches the preacher looking at him. Which one of them was wrong?

But it was evident by the way she raised a brow that his were not the actions of a team player. So he rolled and smiled at the ceiling as he went by, pleased that he spotted Cinderella right away.

He rolled again, slower this time, letting his gaze move across the faces of the dancers, and pausing when he reached the gangster. There was something familiar about that one, but Michael couldn't put a finger on it. Probably someone who worked at the hotel. The sous chef? Michael frowned and rolled on. It would come to him later. Probably in the middle of the night, when he'd wake up hollering "It's the bellboy!" Although that wasn't right either.

"Okay," Rob said, "let's raise those shoulders and relax. Raise and relax. Higher now, really squeeeeeze."

Michael squeeeezed and dropped his head back, focusing on the flapper this time. Noticing the way Sunny had captured the motion of the fringes, the flash of the sequins, and worked *S.A. Anderson* neatly along the flapper's thigh.

So she'd signed it anyway. Thumbed her nose at all of them, right above their heads. The woman had more nerve than anyone he'd ever met. And knowing Sunny, her name would be somewhere in the new one as well—a symbol of pride in her work.

He understood that need. His name had once been everywhere: on blueprints, lawn signs, contracts—*Another Capitol Design by Michael Wolfe and Katherine Shaw.*

Even at Concord, he'd been pleased to have his name on the designs, his stamp on the blueprints. Now, however, he was more than happy to be anonymous. The unknown face behind the water slide. Just doing his job and being well paid for it.

". . . now twist to the left, and to the right . . ."

Michael twisted just as Sunny went by with the reporters. She glanced through the door as she passed and slowed when she spotted him, a smile easing across her face.

"Okay, people, now lift your arms up over your head. Really stretch, higher and higher. Feel the tension leave your body."

Sunny was staring openly now. Michael ignored her and stretched with new determination, discovering a knot in his back that he hadn't realized was there.

He couldn't hear her but he knew she was laughing at him. But what did he care? He was a Grant Hall man and proud of it.

"Okay, everyone, take your seats, and I'll be around with a box of paper clips for each team."

The architect returned to the table and leaned his head between the designer and Attila. "Major problems in Arizona. They've already booked our flights."

Michael watched the three of them pack up. "It's the paper clips, right?"

Doug turned to him, his voice low, confidential. "We didn't get the zoning approvals." He motioned to Judith. "This is really going to set us back."

Attila and the interior designer were already on their way to the door when Judith drew Doug away from the table.

". . . okay, everyone," Rob said, "You have five minutes to attach all one hundred paper clips in a creative fashion. And . . . go!"

Judith leaned close to Doug, listening, nodding, saying nothing until Doug left and she sat down next to Michael.

"Doug is going to be tied up for a while," she said quietly. "So I want you to pick up the ball on the Carillon job."

Michael nodded. "How?"

"Doug was going to schedule a site check with the water slide and mini-golf designers. I'd like you to do this instead. Get to know them, because we work with them all the time."

Michael shrugged. "Sure, no problem."

"He was also going to attend a meeting here on Wednesday." She smiled, moved her chair closer still. "I'm flying in the planners from Sundridge to show them what a Grant Hall hotel in their area will mean. Our bankers will be here as well, and I want you to come in Doug's place. I want you to sell this idea."

Michael sat back. "Sell it?"

She held his gaze. "I'll give it to you straight, Michael. Concord had financing and zoning approvals based on your proposals. Now I need those same approvals for mine." She laid a hand on his arm. "I don't just want you to sell this project, Michael. I want you to make them love it."

"Love it," he said, knowing he was echoing her, but hard put to stop.

Judith sat back. "You're well respected in the field, we all know that. I also know I have one holdout on the planning board, one die-hard restorationist who could sway the other two. I need him brought over to our side. You've already dealt with him as Concord, and I know your name will carry weight with him, and your endorsement even more so." She touched his arm. "I need you on this, Michael. I need you on my team."

Michael almost smiled. So now he really would be the Grant Hall Man, banging the drum for mini-putt in the ballroom, complete with pirate ships, lighthouses, and goddamn snapping turtles.

"Okay," Rob called. "Time's up! Put the paper clips down . . . put them down . . . you too." He started moving between the tables. "Now, where will I find our winner?"

"So, Michael, are you with me on this or not?" Judith asked.

Her eyes were cold, her mouth set. She still didn't understand that he wasn't going to fight her on anything. Because what was the point?

"When do they get here?" he asked, and watched her smile.

"I am going to enjoy working with you," she said softly.

"We have our winner," Rob called, and pointed past Michael.

He and Judith both turned to see Duane with all one hundred paper clips connected and wrapped around his wrist like a bracelet.

"You did that by yourself?" Judith asked.

Duane nodded as the applause rose.

"Well, that's the kind of team spirit I like to see," she said, and clapped him on the back.

He looked over at Michael, gave him a cold stare. "Just doing my job, ma'am."

Michael nodded and glanced over at the door, but Sunny was gone. Which was really too bad. He could have used that smile one more time.

# Eleven

Michael unlocked his front door and tossed the key card on the side table. The red jacket was slung over his shoulder and on his chest he sported the medal Duane had won for their team—a giant paper clip dangling from a red, white, and blue ribbon. Together, they'd lost all the other events by a landslide, but Judith had made a point of telling everyone how this plucky little team had risen to the challenge as she pinned the medal to their shirts.

He dropped the medal in the wastebasket on his way to the desk, pleased that Sunny wasn't around to see. But her gear was still there, stretching as far as the coffee table now, where a dozen or more photographs lay scattered across the spot usually reserved for carefully arranged art books. He threw his jacket at a sofa, wondering idly what she'd done with the books as he wandered over to have a look at the mural.

She'd started with an outline of everything she'd described that morning: the paths, the hedges, and a gazebo with a domed roof in the distance, reminding him of a blueprint of a house waiting to be brought to life. He stepped onto the drop cloth where her toolbox lay open, her stepladder stood ready, and the ghetto blaster was still turned on with a handful of CDs beside it, as though she'd only stepped away for a moment, and might come back anytime and catch him there, among her things.

But it was already after 4:00, and Michael knew she

wouldn't be anywhere near the Brighton at that hour. She had a life, after all.

He knelt down, sifted through her CDs, then pressed EJECT on the ghetto blaster, discovering she was a Maria Muldaur fan. And as he sifted through the rest of the cases, he wondered if she played Maria as often as the Celtic flutes or the Crewcuts, and hoped he would be out if she ever plugged in "All Bagpipe Friday."

He set the CDs down and turned his attention to the box beside him, giving himself permission to poke through the brushes, the sponges, the tubes of paint. For some reason, he'd half expected her to be there when he opened the door—paintbrush in hand and tongue still firmly in cheek, unable to resist asking him how the meeting went. And as he picked up a damp sponge, held it in his hand, Michael found he wanted to tell her. Or he wanted to tell someone at any rate.

He dropped the sponge back into the box and got to his feet. It was times like this that he missed Kate most. Missed sitting across the kitchen table from her at the end of the day, just the two of them, laughing at a screwup, toasting a victory, or simply listening when the other needed desperately to talk.

A grief counselor had once suggested that he talk to her anyway, and he'd tried for a while. He couldn't bring himself to sit at the table, so he'd stand in front of the kitchen sink and chat away as though she were still right there, curled up in the chair and hearing every word. But he'd stopped after only a few days, finding the sound of only one voice in that room far lonelier than any silence.

Michael pushed the memory aside and punched PLAY on the ghetto blaster. A stuttery honky-tonk intro started, and then Maria's twangy voice filled the room, warning him not to feel her leg as he wandered back to his desk and the work that would keep the past from swamping him, and driving him out of his mind.

The mailbox in the corner of his screen told him he had mail. The flashing red light on his phone said he had messages, and the stack of invoices waiting to be dealt with hadn't grown any shorter since he'd left for the meeting that morning. But it was Sunny's estimate sitting on the corner of his desk that drew his attention.

He slit the envelope, scanned the page, discovering she was not only talented but quick. The penthouse mural would be less than one third the size of the ballroom, yet the price to Grant Hall was half again as much as she'd charged Concord. Michael smiled as he signed his name, knowing she'd get that brownstone yet.

Leaving the rest of the invoices for later, he turned his attention to the phone messages instead. The first was from Doug, thanking him again for taking his place at the meeting on Wednesday. The second was a notice that the new mantel for the ballroom had been installed, and the third was the only one that interested him.

"Michael? It's Sonja. And believe me, I am as frustrated as you are with the way things are going."

Michael wondered at the edge in her voice, but put it down to overwork as she continued. "I can't say when I'll be back in New York. There is so much talent out here, it's taking me longer to make the rounds than expected. I'll let you know when I have a date. And, Michael, say hi to Sunny for me. She sounds like an interesting person."

He glanced over at Sunny's corner of the room. "Sonja says hi and she thinks you're interesting." He smiled and clicked on his e-mail. Sonja didn't know the half of it.

There were three notes in the queue this time: one from Judith, another from the real estate agent in Maine who always had someone interested in buying his house, and finally a note from Andy marked *Warning: Family Visit Imminent.*

Michael drummed his fingers on the desk. If nothing else, his brother was good with a headline.

They'd spent most of Sunday morning sending e-mails back and forth. *Please design the house?* No. *Will you at least think about it?* No. *Do you know you're pissing me off?* Yes.

And Michael had ignored the rest, knowing Andy would

chew on the issue forever if he didn't. It was a quality that had made him insufferable as a kid, and now served him well as a journalist. But as he clicked on the new message, Michael was relieved to see that his brother had finally seen the light.

> *Okay, you win. No house. But we definitely want to see you. If you don't give us a firm date for a visit, we will descend on you en masse. We're talking the dog too, understand? And as an added incentive to get you here, Jill's cousin will be in town for the next few weeks. Let me know what you think.*

Michael sighed, knowing that was one issue Andy would never let go of. Being happily married for the past ten years, he honestly believed it was time for Michael to move forward, to love again. He couldn't get it through his head that Michael was perfectly happy to be single.

As for love? He could never go through that again.

He read over Andy's e-mail again, oddly pleased that they hadn't given up on seeing him, but not at all fooled by the quick surrender on the house. Already prepared for a flank attack, Michael started his note. *I think I'll give it my best shot, but can't make any promises. Am leaving to kill the Carillon . . .*

He paused, glanced over at the red jacket on the floor. What was he thinking? This was the perfect chance to start on his presentation. To practice saying good things about the new resort before he had to meet with the planners.

He erased the last line and typed in a new one. *But do I have great news! I'm going to be working on a fabulous new Grant Hall resort!*

Michael frowned. A little forced.

He typed again. *How many ways can you spell fun! Fun, funner, funnest, fu—*

He hit DELETE. Definitely not.

He tried again—*Mini-golf Rules!* and *Water slides: does life get any better?* But he wasn't sure what mini-golf rules were, and since he'd never been on a water slide he didn't feel qualified to comment. So he finally settled on, *Will try to get up there. But no promises. And no cousins.*

He rocked the chair back, stared at the ceiling. Obviously he needed a little help with this Grant Hall thing. A consultant. Someone who knew a thing or two about fun and children. Someone who wasn't afraid to laugh out loud, or draw on the walls, or get down on the ground and play. But if he called Andy, his brother would find a way to swing the conversation around to the house. And why start the fight now when there would be plenty of time for that if they landed on his doorstep?

He looked over at the mural. Then, of course, there was Sunny. The woman who could turn a room upside down in minutes, and understood the aesthetic value of sidewalk chalk.

He pursed his lips, reached for the phone book. Wouldn't hurt to call the tearoom, ask her a few questions, maybe even talk to Jess, get her take on what was fun. And didn't he owe it to Grant Hall to start taking fun seriously?

"Good afternoon. Lord of the Isles."

Her voice was friendly and familiar, and Michael felt himself relax for the first time that afternoon. "You said you'd call."

"I said *maybe* I'd call."

Michael didn't need to see her to know she was smiling. And he couldn't help smiling himself when she added, "So, how was the meeting?"

"Funny you should ask," he said, and gave her a quick rundown of the problem in Arizona and the presentation he had to do, and ended by saying, "So I thought I'd call, talk to Jess, pick her brain about water slides and mini-golf." He paused, pushed a hand through his hair. "And maybe see if she knows what her mom is doing for fun tonight."

"Her mom? Well, last I heard, it was Girls' Night Out, which means she's doing pizza and a movie with Jess."

Michael nodded. He could do Girls' Night Out. Once anyway. "Do you think her mom would mind if a buddy tagged along? Strictly for research purposes."

"That all depends. Does the buddy like Disney?"

"It's been a while, but he thinks he used to." Michael walked as far as the phone cord would allow, then turned around and came back. "So what time are they leaving?"

"Soon."

His feet stilled and he grew serious. "Will you wait if I promise to spring for popcorn?"

Her laughter washed over him. "You do know how to tempt a girl."

"I try," he said softly.

"Then, I guess we'll wait."

Michael felt that idiot grin taking over his face again. "I'll see you in a while."

Sunny jogged in place, punched a fist in the air, then walked calmly into the kitchen and grinned at the lump of pastry on the counter.

Michael was coming to Girls' Night Out.

And he hadn't called Sonja!

"How are you doing in there?" Moyra called from the depths of the tearoom, where she was busy setting up tables for the last rush of the day.

"Have to call it quits." Sunny bid the lump good-bye and dropped it into the garbage. "Jess will be home any minute."

As though summoned, Natalie's mother pulled her car up to the curb outside the tearoom. And judging by the eye patches and the way both girls were hollering "Arrrrr, matey" at each other, Sunny figured it was pirate week at camp. And mud was just part of the costume.

"Don't let her in here like that." Moyra paused on her way to the kitchen. "I don't know why you waste your money on that camp when she could spend the day here with me."

*That's why,* Sunny thought, and waved to Natalie's mom as Jess trudged across the sidewalk with her backpack.

Sunny went out to meet her. "You have a good time?"

"Arggh," Jess said, handing her the backpack.

"Sit down and I'll get some of that mud off you before we go inside."

Jess's snarl turned into a yawn as she sank down on the step.

Sunny laughed and pulled off her sneakers, banged them against the wall. "You still up for tonight?"

"Yup," Jess said, perking up enough to growl in true pirate fashion at a couple passing by.

Sunny shot them an apologetic smile, then glanced into the tearoom, wondering if Moyra would appreciate the troll a little more once pirate week was over.

"Well, hello, darlin'," Mrs. Dempster called, and both Sunny and Jess looked up as the Glasgow ladies strolled toward them.

"Aren't you looking fierce today," Mrs. Fitzhenry said, winning a very convincing growl from Jess.

"Pay her no mind," Moyra said.

But Mrs. Dempster smiled at Jess all the same. "We're planning a shower for Lilli and André."

The grumpy pirate disappeared behind wide eyes and an even wider grin. "Can I come?"

"Of course," Mrs. Fitzhenry said. "You'll be in charge of handing her the presents."

"If there's a wedding," Mrs. Dempster put in. "I heard Lilli bought an electric-blue dress, if you can imagine. Don't know where she got such an idea."

Jess preened and gave Sunny a high five as the ladies went into the tearoom.

"Where's Jack?" Mrs. Dempster asked.

"God knows, and I hope he keeps him there." Moyra glanced down at Sunny. "Who was on the phone, by the way?"

"A friend." Sunny signaled Jess to follow her to the apartment door. "And you and I are going to have company for pizza night."

"Who?" Jess asked.

"Remember Michael?"

Jess nodded, Moyra scowled, and the Glasgow ladies stopped dead.

"Wasn't he the nice-looking one who sat by the window with the odd fellow?" Mrs. Fitzhenry asked.

Mrs. Dempster gave Sunny a smug little smile. "I knew he was after you the moment he walked through the door."

Mrs. Fitzhenry's mouth dropped open. "You knew nothing of the sort. I'm the one who said 'Look at the way he looks at her,' and you said 'My God, Trudy, how long has it been since anyone looked at us that way?' Remember?" She turned a smile on Sunny. "So, dear, when will he be here?"

"Soon," Sunny said and opened the door for Jess. "You don't mind, do you?"

"Why would I? He bought me chalk." Jess went through to the hall. "So, is this like a date or something?"

Sunny nodded to the ladies and Moyra and followed Jess inside. "No, this is not a date. He's just a friend."

"Aye, and he was just a client before that," Moyra muttered. "What will he be tomorrow, do you think?"

"You'll be the last to know," Sunny murmured, and raced Jess up the stairs.

# Twelve

Sunny swung her purse over her shoulder and paused in front of the dresser to inspect her makeup again. A touch of sable on her eyelids. A hint of mocha on her lips. A brush of sienna across her cheeks . . . and naked eyelashes.

She blew out an exasperated breath and dug through Val's makeup bag. Hugh was so much better at this.

She opened her eyes wide, dabbed mascara on her lashes, worked out the clumps with a fingernail, and stood back. Hair down and almost straight, tank top suggestive but not blatant, and jeans nicely tight.

She nodded, brushed a stray hair from her forehead. Not exactly Sonja, but no longer one of the boys either.

And perfect for a nondate.

Sunny put a hand to her chest, told herself to breathe, to think like Sonja. No expectations and no disappointments. Just take the evening as it came. And when the time was right, be bold and kiss the man. Just pucker up, buttercup, and see what happens.

And if he still didn't want her? Sunny lowered her hand, stared at her spiky lashes. At least she'd stop wondering.

She tossed the mascara into the bag and glanced over at her answering machine, making sure it was still turned on and ready to take any and all messages for murals. The light had been flashing when she came upstairs, but the caller had hung up without saying anything. With luck they'd call back. And with a little more luck, it wouldn't be someone offering her yet another great deal on carpet cleaning.

She headed out to the stairs. "Jess, are you ready?" she called, poking her head into the sitting room on the way by.

A much cleaner Jess sat on the floor in front of the television with a video game controller in her hands, bobbing and weaving as she and the princess on the screen battled the forces of evil together.

Her hair was still damp from the shower and her nose was only a little pink, assuring Sunny that she had indeed won the sunscreen war that day and leaving only another fifty-five or so days to worry about. *The joys of summer,* she thought, and stepped into the room.

"Jess, we have to leave soon."

"I just have to find one more jewel." She jerked the controller up as the princess leaped high into the air. "Then I can go back and finish off the big—" But the princess missed the mark, tumbled into the abyss, and *Game Over* flashed on the screen. Jess's shoulders slumped. "I can't believe I missed that jump."

Sunny backed out the door. "I'll call you when Michael gets here."

Jess said nothing as she hunkered down to start again.

Sunny hesitated in the doorway. "Are you sure you don't mind Michael tagging along tonight?"

"I'm sure. It's just weird, is all. I mean, Natalie's mom goes out with men all the time but you never do. Nana says it's because you're too smart, but Uncle Hugh says it's because you never met anyone you liked." She pressed PAUSE and glanced over. "Who's right?"

Jess had always been open in her questions and Sunny had made it a point to be as honest as possible about everything. And as she looked into her daughter's round, amaretto eyes, Sunny knew this wasn't the time to start hedging on her answers.

"Hugh's right," she said. "I've never liked anyone since your dad."

Jess swung her legs around, faced her. "Then that means you must like Michael."

"I suppose I do."

"And do you wish this was a real date?"

Sunny felt her face warm. "Yes, but we keep that between us, okay?"

Jess studied her a moment longer, her expression far too serious and solemn for a girl of her age. "Okay," she said at last, and turned back to her game. "I'll be down in a minute."

Sunny headed for the stairs, making up her mind to enroll her in another week of summer camp. Maybe Viking week, or better yet, outer space week. She smiled as she followed the sound of voices to the tearoom. Moyra should really enjoy having an alien on the step.

As she rounded the corner, the scene in the tearoom was familiar enough: Sean seated at a table with a cell phone and a beer in front of him while Moyra stirred a pot in the kitchen. The only surprise was that Hugh was there as well, nursing a pint with Sean.

He'd been officially stripped of his door key after the cappucino incident, and no one was ever to speak of it again. But if the *Two to One* slogan on his T-shirt was anything to go by, Sunny figured he was still claiming victory.

"Where's Jess?" Moyra asked as she came out of the kitchen. "She was going to help me with this new soup."

"She's helping the Princess conquer the underworld right now," Sunny said. "And I don't expect her to emerge for a while yet."

"Waste of time if you ask me," she said, but the usual rant was cut mercifully short as Jack strolled into the tearoom with a brand-new *Kiss Me, I'm Scottish* apron around his waist and a spoon in his hand.

Sunny smiled. "What's this?"

Moyra scowled. "His latest attempt to drive me crazy."

He smacked his lips, held up the spoon. "I don't know, Moyra. This soup doesn't have much zip."

"See what I mean?" she muttered, then glanced over at Jack. "It's Dundee broth. It's not meant to have zip."

"Says who?" Hugh asked. "Give me five minutes alone with that pot, and you could start a whole new trend."

"You pipe down over there," Moyra warned, but Jack was nodding and looking thoughtful. "The lad might be on to something," he said, heading back to the stove with the spoon.

"He's on to nothing," Moyra called after him, and turned to Sunny. "Somehow your father has got it into his head that I need his help. And in the kitchen, of all places. Can you believe that?"

"Really?" Sunny waved a hand, tried to sound casual. "Well, maybe it's not such a bad idea. The two of you working together, side by side, just like you did when you were first married." She gave her an encouraging smile. "Could be fun, Mom."

Moyra's face scrunched. "Fun for who? Since Saturday, the man has alphabetized my spice rack, rearranged my plastics cupboard, and God alone knows what system he's using in the freezer. I can't find a bloody thing, and if he so much as looks at my pastry again, I won't be held responsible." She glanced over at the kitchen. "And why would I need him anyway, when I have you?"

Sunny could have listed a dozen reasons, but Jack chose that moment to reappear with a sherry bottle.

"I was thinking your trifle could use a drop more of this, too," he said.

And Sunny knew from the way her mother's shoulders tensed that this was not the best time to pursue the matter.

"You're wrong, Dad," Hugh said and flashed Moyra a wicked grin. "It wants apricot brandy instead."

"It wants nothing of the sort," she said. "And stop putting ideas in his head." She cast a glance at Sunny as she headed back into the kitchen. "I tell you, Sunny, I am counting the days until you're finished at the Brighton and back here full time."

"But I'll be a while yet," Sunny said. "And then I have a mural in the Hamptons—"

"A half bath," Moyra called over her shoulder. "How long can that take?"

"A year?" Sunny said softly.

"It'll be longer than that if you're smart," Hugh said.

Sean slid back a chair for her. "Why don't you just come out and tell her you don't want to work here?"

"I will," Sunny said. "Once I figure out how." She dropped her purse on the floor and sank into the seat. "What brings you guys here, anyway?"

Sean passed her his beer. "I need to talk to the old man about a customer he dealt with a few years back."

"I just tagged along to bug Moyra." Hugh chuckled as Moyra went to the cash desk, grumbling something about fools and fruitcakes. "But I see Dad's beating me to it."

Sunny sighed. "And this time, it's my fault. I told him to help out, make himself indispensable." She shook her head and raised the beer to her lips. "I should have told him to take up lawn bowling."

"They just need more time," Hugh said, but even he winced when Jack called out, "Do you want me to start on the pastry?" and Moyra stomped back into the kitchen to take the rolling pin from his hands.

Hugh leaned closer to Sean. "I'm meeting Duane and Val over at QB's later. Why don't we take Jack over now, give Moyra a break?"

Sean nodded and Sunny handed him back his beer. "She'll like that," she said.

"Only because she'll think it was your idea." Hugh turned back to Sean. "You'll have to make sure the old man makes it home though, because I'll be going into Manhattan later."

"Heavy date?" Sean whispered.

Hugh leaned closer. "Yes, but he's on a diet."

Sunny laughed and Sean just rolled his eyes. Hugh's dates were rarely discussed in their parents' presence, and were *never* brought into the tearoom—something Sunny had always hoped would change.

Hugh turned to her as he got to his feet. "You look nice, by the way. What's the occasion?"

"Girls' Night Out," Sunny said.

"You and Jess planning to paint the town red?" Sean asked.

"We hope to." She couldn't hold back a smile. "With a little help from Michael Wolfe."

"Michael Wolfe? I knew it." Hugh laughed and held a hand out to Sean. "You owe me five bucks."

Sunny looked from one to the other. "I can't believe you two had a bet on this." She frowned as Sean went for his wallet. "And I can't believe you bet against me."

He gave a small, guilty shrug. "You have to admit, the man was a bit dense where you're concerned."

"He still is," Sunny admitted. "But I'm hoping things will change tonight."

Sean slapped a bill into Hugh's hand. "I take it he's off Sonja."

"He hasn't called her back yet," Sunny said. "Which I am choosing to read as a very positive sign."

Jack approached the table, his smile broad, his eyes sparkling. "You lads aren't leaving, are you? I just found this recipe for Welsh rarebit—"

"We don't serve rarebit," Moyra called.

Jack smiled at them. "But we could."

Hugh threw an arm around Jack's shoulder as Moyra steamed into the tearoom. "Actually, Dad, I was going to offer to buy you a pint over at QB's."

Sean got to his feet on the other side of Jack. "And I need to ask you a few questions about the Neilsons. Remember them?"

Jack laughed and started to undo his apron. "How could I forget? Biggest account is always the biggest pain in the—" He broke off and looked over at Moyra. "But I hate to leave your mother with all the work—"

"I'll be fine," Moyra said quickly, and shot Sunny a grateful look as the two men steered Jack toward the door. "Just be quiet when you come in because I'll be asleep. Do you hear me, Jack? I'll be asleep."

"I hear you," he said, and winked.

Moyra lowered her voice. "That's it. I'm getting a lock for my door."

Sunny smiled and went to the stairs to call Jess. "I don't know, Mom. There are a lot of women who would gladly trade places with you."

"Let them," she said. "Then maybe he'd stop bothering me."

Sunny glanced back, searching for a trace of humor in Moyra's face, and coming back a step when she found none. "You can't mean that."

"Why not? For over twenty years, your father spent twice as much time at his office than he ever did at home. Now that he's got nothing to do, I'm supposed to be grateful that he remembers where I sleep?"

"Not grateful, particularly, just . . ."

"Just what? Accommodating? Not a chance." She frowned at the sound of male laughter drifting along the hall. "To tell you the truth, I'd be happy if everything went back to the way it was, with him at work, and you, me, and Jess here on our own."

Sunny felt the tiny hairs on the back of her neck stand up, but the front door opened, Hugh called, "Michael, good to see you again," and there was no more time to think about what Moyra had said, or what it meant.

"Jess, he's here," Sunny called up the stairs, her pulse already picking up speed as she walked back to the table for her purse.

"Good to see you too," Michael said, his gaze moving past the men, his mouth relaxing into a smile when he spotted her there in the shadow of the tearoom.

Sunny's skin tingled, and her blood warmed. Tonight she would kiss his lips, run her hands through his hair, and hope to God Sonja didn't desert her when she needed her most.

"I hear you're doing Girls' Night Out," Sean said.

Michael laughed, his eyes still holding hers. "I'm sure it'll be a new experience for all concerned."

Hugh sent her a thumbs-up behind his back, Sean gave her a nod of encouragement, and Jack said solemnly, "We'll have a pint for you, lad."

"I'll hurry Jess up," Sunny called and turned, almost running over Moyra.

Her mother stood back from the corner, arms folded tightly across her chest. "That's Michael, is it?"

"That's him," Sunny said, and immediatly tempered her smile. "I could introduce—"

"There's no need. I saw what he is. Handsome, well off from the looks of him. Must be plenty of women out there who'd gladly trade places with *you*."

Sunny sighed. "We're just friends."

"So you've said. But I've never known you to fall all over yourself this way just to get to a friend."

Sunny moved past her. "I don't know what you're talking about."

Moyra followed close behind. "Fool yourself if you want to, but you can't fool me. I know you too well, and I've seen this before." She grabbed Sunny's arm, waiting for her to turn. "I'm telling you now to be careful of this one. Just like I told you to be careful of Brad, if you remember."

Sunny almost smiled. "How can I forget when I have you to remind me?" She jerked away, leaned up the stairs. "Jess," she called, more sharply than intended. Finding herself suddenly impatient, anxious to put the tearoom and Moyra behind her while she could still hear Michael's voice, still know what she wanted.

She put on a smile as Jess came down the stairs. "Did you beat the monster?" she asked.

"Yup," Jess said, taking her hand.

"Well, that makes one of us," she said, and lifted her chin as she swept past her mother.

\* \* \*

Danté's Pizzeria was the kind of place tourists never found and locals loved. Tucked in between a skateboard shop and a beauty parlor well off the beaten path, Danté's carried only soft drinks and the menu could fit comfortably on one side of a playing card. You placed your order at the counter and they delivered the pizza to your table. To pass the time until then, the place mats were blank and each table came equipped with a cup of crayons. And in case that wasn't enough, every kid under the age of twelve could reach into the treasure chest on their way in and pluck out a surprise. It wasn't fine dining, but as far as Sunny and Jess were concerned, the pizza was the best in Brooklyn. And the treasure chest even better.

Sunny handed Michael the playing card menu. "I'll eat anything but anchovies," she said. "Jess won't eat anything but cheese. So pick out what you like and we'll take it from there." She passed the crayons to Jess, who waved them away and opened the tiny deck of cards she'd scored from the chest.

"Every meal includes cheesy bread and a trip to the sundae bar," Sunny continued, "but I usually pass. We do, however, order a salad, which Jess pretends to eat, and I pretend not to know." Sunny glanced over at him. "And I'm going to hazard a guess that you haven't been in a place like this for a while, have you?"

He started to protest, then set the menu down. "What gave me away?"

"Little things. Like the way you keep turning the menu over, and the way your eyebrows rose when I said cheesy bread. Just out of curiosity, what do you normally have on your pizza?"

"The hotel serves up a very good one with goat cheese and sun-dried tomato."

Jess's head snapped up. "Oh, gross." Sunny shot her a warning glance. "Well, it is," she muttered, and went back to her game.

"We tend to be pizza purists," Sunny said to Michael, then she lowered her voice, leaned closer. "And if you let me order for you, I guarantee we'll have you back in the fold before the night is over."

Michael held out his hands. "Take me home, sister."

Sunny laughed. "Somebody say Amen."

"Amen," the cashier called, and Michael knew this was what he had come for. The laughter, the teasing—all the things that were part of a night out with a buddy. Although he could honestly say he'd never had a buddy who was anything like Sunny. He leaned closer, watching her frown at the menu while she went over the differences between the Deluxe and the Super for him. ". . . to really appreciate the Super, you have to love hot peppers . . ."

Peppers he could take or leave, but he did love the way her hair was fighting whatever she'd done to it, the curls slowly coming back, brushing her bare shoulders and framing her face.

She raised a brow, looked directly at him. "So are you game?"

"Definitely," he said, wanting nothing more than to lean across the table and kiss her now, while a smile still played on her lips and her eyes shone.

And her daughter watched his every move.

Jess lowered her gaze, flipped another card, but Michael wasn't fooled. Ever since they left the tearoom, he'd had the distinct impression that he was being sized up, judged. And as she laid the card down, he wondered what his score was so far.

"All right then," Sunny said, and got to her feet. "One Danté's Deluxe coming up."

Michael sat back, reminded himself she was off-limits, and went for his wallet instead. "Let me get this."

"We can fight about that when they bring the bill," she said, and looked over at Jess. "Coming, kiddo?"

Jess glanced up, flipped another card. "Can't I stay here?"

Sunny hesitated. "I don't think—"

"It's okay with me," Michael said. "As long as she moves that red seven before it makes me crazy."

Jess raised her chin in a gesture so like her mother Michael had to smile. "I saw it," she said as she slid the card across. "I was just seeing if anyone else would."

"Uh-huh." He rested his elbows on the table, studied the cards. "So I guess you also see—"

"The red queen," Jess cut in and shot him a smug glance as she moved the card. "I'm very good at this game."

Michael nodded, picked up a two. "I can tell."

Sunny stepped away from the table. "You two play nice."

"We will," Jess said, but once Sunny was safely in line, she gathered up the cards and smiled at Michael.

"You want to play a game?" She shuffled like a dealer, dealt like a shark. "Five-card stud with a ten-cent limit—"

"Jess," Sunny called, and she picked the cards back up. "Or we could do something else." She held the deck out to him. "Know any tricks?"

The moment of truth. Would he measure up? Michael picked up his place mat. "Not with cards, but I can do a little magic with paper."

He tore the place mat into a perfect square and tried to remember the steps. He hadn't done this since Ben was two. He folded and turned, folded and turned, seeing Ben sitting on his lap, so wide-eyed as he watched his Uncle Mike do magic. And Kate crouched in front of them, snapping pictures, always snapping pictures. *Practicing for when we have kids of our own,* she'd say, and kiss the top of Ben's head.

Michael swept the image aside and after only three screwups, produced a decent bird, which he set in front of Jess with a flourish. "Swan," he said.

She picked the bird up, gave it a quick once-over, then lifted her own place mat. "Just give me a moment."

Michael sat back while Jess too folded and turned, folded and turned, and in less time than it had taken him to create a half-assed swan, she set an intricate bird in front of him.

"Pterodactyl." She leaned closer. "And it will eat your swan."

He snatched the poor thing out of the way. "Did I say

swan?" He put it on his head. "I meant *hat.*" He and the bird sat back. "So," he said casually. "What do you recommend at the sundae bar?"

Jess opened her mouth, and closed it; then a grin spread across her face as she put her own bird on her head. "I always start with a layer of sprinkles."

Sunny smiled as the two of them discussed the need for whipped cream and the thorny issue of whether or not green maraschino cherries were acceptable, while the birds teetered back and forth on their heads.

The girl behind the counter laughed. "That is seriously weird."

"Yes indeed," Sunny said, watching Michael catch his swan as it started to slide down his forehead, only to put it right back up again, much to Jess's delight and the amusement of the people at the other tables.

Sunny shook her head in amazement. There was something undeniably appealing about a man who didn't take himself too seriously. Who could let himself look ridiculous in a roomful of strangers just to make a child laugh. And who would have ever dreamed that Michael Wolfe would be one of them?

"He yours?" the girl asked.

Sunny felt herself smile when he reached over and repositioned Jess's pterodactyl. "Not yet. But I'm working on it."

The girl nodded, scribbled on an order pad. "So you'll want an extra-large Deluxe then."

Sunny nodded and reached for a tray. "With double sauce."


By the time the order was placed and Sunny was juggling glasses and a pitcher of root beer back to the table, the swan and the pterodactyl were sitting side by side in front of the salt and pepper shakers and Michael and Jess were bent over a game of hangman.

"Who's winning?" Sunny asked.

"I am," Jess announced, giving the little man dangling from the noose a smiley face.

"I demand a rematch," Michael said. "And next time, the topic will be foreign films. No more of this Saturday morning cartoon stuff."

Jess grinned. "Sorry, rules say that only the winner can pick the topic. And I think it will be"—she shot him a sideways glance—"Barbie."

Michael looked up at Sunny. "Your daughter is ruthless."

"That's my girl." She poured root beer into a glass and handed it to him. "I hope this is all right with you. It's a tradition on Girls' Night Out."

He pulled the glass toward him. "Who am I to argue with tradition?"

"Don't pour mine yet," Jess said, already climbing down from her seat. "I want to put ice cream in first." She signaled her intentions to the girl behind the counter, grinned when the girl waved her on, then turned back to Michael. "You want to make yours into a float too?"

"I'll pass this time. But make sure they've got red cherries over there."

"They better," she said solemnly, and headed for the sundae bar with her glass.

Sunny sat down across from Michael and filled her own glass from the pitcher. "So, are you having fun yet?"

"Definitely," he said, his smile warm and a little wry, as though he was surprised to hear it. "Although I'd like to talk about a name change. Girls' Night Out could give me a complex."

Sunny smiled, keeping it light as she walked straight through the door he'd opened. "So whenever you're along, we'll call it Pizza Night. How's that?"

"Perfect. And it will make it easier if my brother descends with his crew. He threatened to make the trip with the dog, so I know he's serious."

Sunny laughed and sat back, taking her glass with her. "And how many are in his crew?"

"Four. Andrew, his wife Jill, and the boys, Nicholas and Ben. Nick is about Jess's age, Ben is eight."

"Do you see much of them?"

"I used to," he said absently. "We'd alternate holidays, Christmas in Toronto, Easter down here, always a week or two at the cottage in the summer. But all that stopped when I started to work for Concord. Too much traveling, too little time off. To be honest, I haven't seen more than pictures of the boys for a couple of years now."

"As difficult as they can be sometimes, I can't imagine not seeing my family for that long."

"You get used to it. And sometimes it's easier. Tight deadlines and construction headaches make it hard to think about anything else, harder still to commit to weekends and holidays, and be good company when you get there." He sighed, reached for his glass. "I just hope the boys remember me. Two years is a long time for a kid."

*It's a long time for anyone,* she thought, watching him raise the glass and drain it, and seeing him as she had that night at the hotel, roaming the halls alone, tense and restless. A restlessness not born of ambition, she realized now, but of being lost and lonely, and having nowhere else to go. And she knew it had nothing to do with deadlines and building projects, and everything to do with losing Kate.

"Do you think you'll see more of them now that you're with Grant Hall?"

"Hard to say." His voice took on an edge as he set the empty glass down, reached for the jug. "Apparently they've got big plans for me."

"Like selling the Carillon project," she said quietly.

"The first of many, I'm sure."

He topped up his glass and sat back, shutting her out again, his expression flat, resigned. A man without hope is how she would have described him. One who had turned his back on everything he loved—family, home, even his work. One who told himself that nothing mattered, nothing was worth caring about, and merely lived day to day, or job to job in his case. And she couldn't help thinking about Duane and the book he carried around with him. The one written when Michael had still hoped, still dreamed, and had taken on the world and won. And she couldn't help wishing she'd known him then, before the sadness and the sorrow had taken it all away.

Sunny sighed, knowing she couldn't change a thing or take away the pain. But she could give him something else to think about. And maybe she could make him smile again.

"Well, if you ask me," she said, "you don't have a hope in hell of selling that project to anyone, because you don't have a clue what you're talking about."

His eyes lifted. "I beg your pardon?"

"Come on, Michael, they'll know you're a phony the minute you sit down."

Jess came back to the table, looked from one to the other. "Who's a phony?"

"Michael is," Sunny said.

The fire came slowly to his eyes. "And on what do you base this absurd opinion?"

"Observation," she said and leaned closer. "Now, I want you to be absolutely honest. How long has it been since you played mini-golf?"

"A few years." He shrugged. "All right, twenty."

"And have you ever been on a water slide?"

"No."

"Have you ever tried laser tag?"

He shook his head.

"Video games?"

"Sorry."

Jess's eyes widened. "Glow-in-the-dark mini-golf?"

"Never."

Jess looked over at Sunny. "That is so sad."

Sunny nodded. "I think the movie will have to wait, don't you?"

Jess smiled. "La Dome?"

Sunny smiled back. "La Dome."

Michael looked wonderfully confused. "What are you talking about?"

Sunny propped her elbows on the table, gave him her most enigmatic smile. "Only the most exciting night of your life."

# Thirteen

La Dome had once been Harry's Discount Appliances, a fine if somewhat dusty example of what one man could achieve with door-crasher specials, free delivery, and the hungriest sales staff this side of a used car lot. But when Harry's wife decided she wanted a mayor for a husband, Harry sold off his assets, spruced up his image, and disappeared from the appliance world.

As far as anyone knew, Harry had yet to hold office anywhere, but the building had gone on to bigger and better things, emerging from the sell-off to become a family entertainment center where the staff was friendly and door crashers were dealt with privately in small, poorly lit rooms in the back.

Michael had allowed himself to be led through the cavernous lobby where video screens, air hockey, and pinball machines guaranteed that conversation was not only unnecessary, but close to impossible. But Sunny's reassuring smile and Jess's endless bouncing up and down had told him that this was not a madhouse, but rather a modern-day fun house. And he would get the hang of it yet.

So he had stood quietly while a young girl strapped a bracelet on his wrist, stamped something illegible on his hand, and explained that his All-Night Adventure band included admission to the Most Amazing Video Arcade on the third floor, the Fabulous Laser Tag game in the basement, and of course, the World's Greatest Glow-in-the-Dark Mini-Golf, which was right through the door on the left.

It was there that Michael waited now, on the fifth tee, his putter dangling at his side while Sunny and Jess decided the fate of his ball.

The golf course itself was a cheery underwater world of dolphin calls, flourescent paint, and black lights, where wispy green seaweed climbed the walls, schools of brightly colored fish hung from the ceiling, and corals and rocks were strategically placed to make shots difficult.

There were small sand traps and fake water hazards, but it was the fifth tee that truly separated the men from the boys, or in this case, the girls.

In the middle of the green sat a giant clamshell that took up most of the space. When struck by a ball, it would open, swallow the ball whole, and emit a huge belch before sending it sputtering back to the player, much to the amusement of those who had made it to the sixth green.

Jess had made it around the shell in five shots, Sunny in six. Michael's ball, however, had lodged under a piece of coral on his third shot, and it was impossible to get a good whack at the thing where it lay.

The shell waited, the players on the fourth tee waited, and Jess just kept grinning.

"Two-stroke penalty if he picks it up," she said. "That's the rule."

Michael glanced over at Sunny. "She's making this up as she goes along, isn't she?"

"Pretty much," Sunny said. "But she must like you because if it was Hugh, she'd call three strokes at least, and make him dance the horn pipe."

"And if the situation was reversed?"

Sunny didn't hesitate. "Two strokes and she'd have to sing 'I'm a Little Teapot,' with actions."

"You guys are merciless," Michael murmured.

"It's one of the Anderson charms." Sunny raised the score card. "So I'll put you down for two strokes and you can go get the ball."

Jess strutted on to the sixth green singing, "In the lead, in the lead."

"Not so fast," Michael said, gaining her full attention and a raised brow from Sunny. "I haven't given up yet."

They moved closer as he approached the coral. He eyed the clam and the cup beyond, then flexed his fingers, snapped his wrists, and lay down on his stomach with his putter.

Sunny moved a step closer, pleased that he was not only smiling, but grinning broadly as the weight of the past lightened for the moment.

"What are you doing?" Jess asked him.

"Holding on to my lead." He closed one eye, propped his fingers on the green, and using his putter like a pool cue, he lined up the shot. "Golf ball in the corner pocket," he said, and gave the ball a sharp tap. It whizzed past the clam, hit the far wall, and came rolling back to drop with a satisfying *thunk* into the cup.

"Four shots," he said, retrieving his ball to a round of applause from the people waiting. "And I believe I am still first."

Jess stared as he did the strut to the sixth hole, singing her song under his breath.

"Can he do that?" she asked.

Sunny laughed and marked down his score. "I believe he just did."

But Jess still won after Michael convincingly missed the cup on the eighteenth hole six times, and Sunny was still shaking her head as they slid their putters into the rack.

"You didn't have to do that," she said. "Jess knows she can't win all the time."

"Maybe," Michael said, watching Jess give the attendant at the door a whirlwind version of her last-second victory. "But I didn't see you cleaning up in there either."

Sunny put a hand to her chest. "I am honestly bad at mini-golf. You, on the other hand, gave it away."

Michael laughed and followed Jess out into the lobby. "I'll try to do better at laser tag."

She watched him go, knowing he would do no such thing.

"Mommy, look. The picture machine is working."

"Wonderful," Sunny said, following her daughter's gaze to the instant-photo machine by the escalators.

Jess grabbed Sunny's hand, and looked up at Michael. "It was broken last time we were here, so we couldn't get a picture, and we always get a picture, right?"

Sunny gave him a small nod. "We always get a picture."

"Then you'd better get over there," Michael said. "While there's no lineup."

"You have to come too," Jess said, taking his hand as though she'd been doing it for years. "Everybody who plays is in the picture, right?"

"Right," Sunny said. "But if he doesn't want to—"

"Hey," Michael said. "Like I said before, who am I to buck tradition?"

Jess hauled them both along to the booth, and slid back the black curtain. "Okay, Michael, you sit on the stool, and, Mommy, you sit in front of him, and I'll kneel down in front, and that way we'll all be in the picture at the same time."

"Sounds like she knows what she's doing," Michael said as he sat down.

"She knows these machines better than anyone," Sunny said, and sank down on the edge of the stool in front of him.

Her hips were warm and firm between his thighs, her hair a ticklish cloud in his face. He brushed her hair to one side, his fingers skimming her shoulders and the tender nape of her neck.

"I can tie it up," she said, opening her purse, but Michael shook his head.

"It's fine," he said, and lowered his hands to his sides, reminding himself that she was off-limits—a pal and nothing more. But when she wriggled back farther, making room for Jess in front of her, his body refused to listen to reason, knowing only that there was a beautiful woman pressed closed against him.

A beautiful woman who had not only helped him appreciate the simple joy of pepperoni and double sauce, but also the only one who could ever have put a mini-golf club in his hand and made him stay long enough to play.

While La Dome was a far cry from the concerts he and Trish went to, and nothing close to the theater nights he and Kate had loved, if he was honest, Michael had to admit that he'd enjoyed everything about the place. The noise, the crowd, even the stupid clam.

And if he had to put a reason to it, he'd have to put it down to the big-eyed redhead in front of him right now.

"Everybody ready?" she asked, and damned if she didn't wriggle those hips again.

"Oh yeah," Michael grunted and shifted slightly, moving his own hips back, out of harm's way.

"You okay back there?" she asked.

He propped his chin on her shoulder. "Just do it," he muttered in her ear, making her laugh and jerk her shoulder up, almost toppling them both off the stool.

Michael blew her hair out of his eyes and wrapped his arms around her, telling himself it was to keep them both steady, but aware of the smooth, supple muscles of her back against his chest.

"Here we go," Jess said, and fed the coins into the slot.

Michael dipped his head slightly, breathing in the fresh, sweet scent of Sunny's skin, and knowing he should have let the two of them do this alone. He wasn't part of their group, wasn't part of their lives. He was just along for the ride, and Sunny wasn't his to touch or want. But when Jess hollered "Smile" and the flash went off, Michael held her closer, heard her sigh as she leaned back, and couldn't think of anywhere else he'd rather be.


The tearoom was dark and Jess was all but asleep on Michael's shoulder when Sunny unlocked the door and motioned him to follow her inside. They'd played laser tag, foosball, and every arcade game from Heli-skiing to Combat Quints, until Jess had crawled into Michael's lap while he was driving the virtual-pro circuit, and fallen into a very real sleep with the two paper birds still clutched in her hands.

Michael carried her across the tearoom, heading for the back stairs. "Third floor, right?"

Sunny nodded and locked the door. "Just go quietly."

And God forbid Moyra should catch him on the way.

Sunny hurried up behind him, and they had just reached the top when Moyra called out, "Sunny, is that you?"

She waved Michael on and peered over the banister. "Yes, Mom."

"Is he with you?"

"No," she lied, feeling her face burn when Michael glanced back, a wry smile curving his lips.

"Do you want a cup of tea?" Moyra called.

"No, thanks. I have to get Jess to bed." She stepped away from the banister. "Good night."

"You had a call," Moyra continued. "Rona McCloskey of all people. She said she saw you on Saturday at one of those brownstones."

Sunny gave a short laugh. "You know me, can't resist an open house."

"I'd have thought you were done with that nonsense by now."

Her laughter died. "I was just looking."

"That's what I told her when she said there was another one coming up. She was planning to drop off a feature sheet, but I told her not to bother, since you're not in the market."

"Moyra?" Jack called from the living room. "Are you up?"

"Not for you," she called back, then looked up at Sunny. "I changed my mind about the lock. I'm getting a pit bull instead."

And Sunny heard the sharp snap, snap, snap of her slippers as Moyra hurried back to her room.

She turned to see Michael and Jess both watching her closely, Michael looking merely curious, Jess looking decidedly cross.

"Are we moving?" she asked, rubbing her eyes as she pushed out of Michael's arms.

"Not for a while," Sunny said, herding them both into the sitting room and closing the door behind her.

"Don't you want a place of your own?" Michael asked Jess.

"Sometimes," she said. "But mostly no."

Sunny took her hand, shot Michael a weary look. "There are days when I feel like I'll be here for life." She started for the door. "Make yourself comfortable while I put Jess to bed. But for God's sake, do it quietly."

"I'm not even here," he said, and that sexy laugh of his was still drifting through her head as she led Jess along the hall to her room.

Jess set the swan and the pterodactyl on her dresser. "I've decided I like him too," she said, with a yawn.

Sunny handed her a nightgown. "Good. Because he'd like to do it again some time."

Jess dropped her clothes in a heap and the nightgown over her head. "Would it be a real date then?"

"I'll let you know when it happens," Sunny said, hearing him roaming around the sitting room, not making any real effort to be quiet. But then, she had a hard time imagining him being afraid of Moyra's footsteps on the stairs.

And what if she did come up and catch him there? What could she do? Rant, rave, kick Sunny out?

*I should be so lucky,* she thought, and made a mental note to call Rona back in the morning, just out of curiosity. And a touch of desperation.

Jess brushed her teeth, and Sunny sang the prayer and switched on the nightlight as she pressed a kiss to Jess's cheek. "Sleep tight."

Jess sat bolt upright. "Wait," she said, tossing back covers and scrambling out of bed. She took a pair of scissors from her dresser drawer, pulled the strip of three photographs from her jeans pocket, and smoothed them on the dresser. "I forgot to give Michael his picture," she said, and started to cut them apart carefully.

She handed two to Sunny. "You can have this one, and Michael can have this one. I'm keeping the other."

In the two shots Jess had given her, all three of them were smiling nicely—Sunny looking a little more than comfortable in Michael's arms, and Jess perfectly happy to have a camera pointed at her. Nice pictures, both of them, and Sunny knew exactly why Jess had kept the third.

That was the one where Michael had closed one eye and was using a strand of Sunny's hair like a mustache. Sunny was laughing, and Jess was watching them both with a broad grin on her face.

Sunny smiled. They looked completely natural together. Relaxed and happy, almost like—

Almost like three people having fun, Sunny told herself, refusing to allow any silly ideas to creep into her thinking. They were not now, and would never be, a happy little family.

They were just a good time.

She tucked Jess back into bed. "Good night again," she said.

Jess laid her head on the pillow, her eyes closing on a yawn. "Tell him he can come to Arts Night on Friday if he wants." She opened her eyes, looked straight at Sunny. "You'd like that, wouldn't you?"

"Yes, I would," she admitted.

Jess smiled and snuggled deeper into the pillow. "I thought so."

Sunny went out to the hall, deciding she'd have to have a talk with Jess about the nature of adult relationships. And the fact that not every one ended with happily ever after.

"Don't close the door," Jess said quickly.

"I never do," Sunny said, knowing she'd probably end up with Jess in her bed later. Which precluded Michael being there, of course. And why hadn't she thought of that before?

She sighed and popped into the bathroom to fluff her hair, check her makeup. Celibacy was so much simpler for a single mom.

And so much safer, she thought, shooting a worried glance along the hall as music drifted down from the sitting room. She waited, listening for Moyra's slippers on the stairs but hearing only the faint noise of their television, because Moyra was holding herself prisoner in her own bedroom.

And the curiosity would be driving her crazy by now.

Sunny smiled. *Serves her right,* she thought, and headed along the hall to the sitting room.

Michael was at the stereo, flipping through CDs. He'd turned on Bessie Smith, who wondered aloud about the nature of love and men while Sunny stood in the doorway, suddenly awkward, unsure of her next move.

"When your mother said you had a call, I thought it might have been Sonja," Michael said and looked over. "She's not coming back on Tuesday, did you know that?"

"Yes." Sunny waved in the direction of the answering machine. "She phoned earlier. I just forgot to mention it."

"You must be disappointed. I'm sure you would have liked to get another job booked."

"More than you know." She crossed to the stereo, leaving the door open behind her.

"She said to tell you hi, by the way, and mentioned that she found you very interesting."

"I'm not surprised. We hit it off right away. Seems we have a lot in common. In fact, we're a lot alike in many ways."

"You don't seem anything alike to me."

"Just give it time," she murmured.

"What?"

"Nothing. Jess sent this for you," she said, handing him one of the pictures.

Michael smiled. "She kept the good one, I see."

"Naturally."

"Well, tell her I liked this one better anyway." He tucked it into his shirt pocket, gestured to the answering machine. "You've got another message waiting." She glanced over, saw the flashing light. "Go ahead and check it," he added, and started flipping CDs again. "I know I would."

That much was true, she thought. Business first and foremost, because that was his life now, the only thing he had to fill up the hours and the empty spaces. But she'd managed to put a smile on his face earlier, even had him laughing. And the way he'd held her in the instant photo booth had made it easy to believe that she might just get him thinking about something else before the night was over. And it all could start with a kiss.

If she didn't lose her nerve first.

Michael watched her cross to her desk, punch the button, and wait for the tape to rewind. He had to smile as she tapped her fingers, her toes, bounced her head back and forth.

She was never still. Always moving, doing, and her flat reflected her perfectly. Minimal furnishings, no knickknacks to dust, and art everywhere, both hers and Jess's: detailed ink sketches of people in the hotel bar, moody watercolor landscapes, some truly creative finger painting. And of course, a mural on the wall by the window.

Curious, he walked over for a closer look. It was a seaside village in Greece, with the ocean sparkling on one side and houses clinging to the cliff on the other. And scattered throughout were mythological figures—Sisyphus chasing his rock down a hill, Venus rising out of bed, Persephone descending to the laundry, and through a torn curtain, he could see the Fates, spinning, measuring, and cutting short a life—the unexpected twist that set her work apart, and should guarantee that no one ever rolled it over.

"Hi, Sunny, this is Val."

Michael glanced over as she zipped through her messages. "This is Jamie from Sure Clean Carpets . . ." "Your books are overdue at the library . . ." She switched off the machine. "Nothing good," she said, and turned, catching him watching her. She stilled, motioned to the kitchen at the end of the room. "Would you like coffee? A beer?"

Michael knew he should leave, just call it a night and go home. He had work to do, a presentation to prepare. But it was early by his usual standard, and for the first time in years, he was in no hurry to get back to his desk. And what harm could there be in one beer?

"Beer, thanks."

She nodded and went to the kitchen. "Jess also told me to invite you to Arts Night on Friday. She always loves a large, appreciative audience."

"Then count me in. But maybe I should meet your mother first."

Sunny grabbed a bottle from the fridge, closed the door with a hip. "It'll be better in a public place, believe me."

Michael shot her a wry smile as he took a slow tour of the rest of her work. "I gather she doesn't like you having men in your room."

"I've never had a man in my room." She unscrewed the cap, reached for a glass. "Not since Jess was born."

He paused for a second look at a watercolor of a goldfish swimming upside down, and shouldn't have been at all surprised to find the fish grinning back at him. "So where do you usually entertain your dates?"

"I don't." He glanced over and she shrugged. "Let's just say that I have led a quiet, monastic life."

He watched her come toward him, fascinated by the sway of her hips, the fullness of her breasts, and finding it hard to believe that not a single man had passed through her door in all these years.

"Were you waiting for Jess's father to come back?"

"For a while," she admitted. "But to be honest, I was too busy learning how to be a mother to think about anything else."

"And now?"

She stopped in front of him, held out the beer. "Now I'm ready to branch out a little."

He took the glass, held her gaze. "Into what?"

"That's still undecided," she said softly.

"You're leaving it to the Fates then?"

She smiled slowly. "I was."

His gaze drifted down, coming to rest on that cheeky mouth of hers. "But now?"

She moistened her lips, took a step closer. "Now I'm making my own fate."

His mouth went dry, his fingers tightened on the bottle. "You're that sure of what you want?"

"At the moment," she said, and suddenly reached up, cupping his face in her hands.

Desire hit him hard and quick, making him suck in a long ragged breath. "What are you doing?"

She rose up on her toes, drew him closer. "I'm trying to kiss you." She frowned, pulled a little harder. "But if you don't help me out here, I'll just end up sucking on your chin."

Michael laughed, the tension broken as only Sunny could manage. He set the bottle down, wrapped his arms around her. "You are the strangest woman I have ever met."

She flashed him that wonderful grin that he liked too much and leaned into him. "Is that a compliment?"

"I think it is," he said softly, dragging her closer, aware of her breasts against his chest, her fingers in his hair, and the way her smile was slowly fading.

Her moves were bold, but after six years, this had to be new and shaky ground for her. And Michael knew she wasn't half as sure of herself as she pretended. He stroked a hand down her back, marveling again at the strength, the courage of this woman in his arms. And knowing he owed her the same kind of honesty she had always shown him.

"You know that if we do this, we won't just be friends anymore."

"I have other friends." She touched her lips to his, lightly, hesitantly, and Michael found it hard to form a co-

herent thought. But he had to be sure she understood,
that she knew exactly what he had to offer.

"You also have to know that if we make love, we won't
be—"

"A couple," she said impatiently. "I know that."

He drew his head back. "How?"

"Because I listen to gossip," she whispered and pressed
her mouth to his again. Once, twice, lingering a little
longer each time.

Michael hauled her up, covered her mouth with his, and
felt his pulse jump when she opened her lips, welcomed
him inside. He broke the kiss, drew his head back. "But
what about the brownstone, the afghan, the baby in the
rocker?"

She stood, dazed for a moment, then shook her head
and looked him squarely in the eye. "I'll have all of that,
but not with you. I know that you and I are just a moment
of, of . . . magic. A good time, not a long time. And when
you're gone, I won't think of you at all."

*Liar,* her mind whispered, but she told it to be quiet as
he bent to her again, kissing her, deeply, thoroughly, as he
had before. And if he recognized anything in her kiss, he
didn't show it, didn't say a word, just went on kissing her
until her knees wobbled and her arms seemed too heavy
to hold up.

But when he swept her up, carried her to the couch,
Sunny's mind nudged her again. "Wait," she whispered,
struggling to sit up, to think.

Michael sank down beside her, brushed soft kisses across
her cheek, her throat. "Don't worry. I'll take it slow."

"No," she breathed. "It's Jess."

His hand was warm and sure on her breast. "She's probably asleep."

"I don't know," Sunny whispered, arching to his touch,
her nipples already taut and waiting.

"Mommy?"

Sunny bolted off the couch, pushed at her hair. Thank
God, Jess hadn't made it to the door.

Michael sat back, rubbed a hand over his face, wondering what it was about sex and couches—

"It can never be here," Sunny whispered.

"What?"

"Never here," she repeated. "In this house."

"Mommy?" Jess called again.

"Just a second, sweetie." Sunny hauled him to his feet. "In fact, it's time for you to go."

"Go?" He reached for her again. "Go where?"

Jess wandered to the door, rubbing her eyes. "Can I sleep in your bed?"

"Of course, go on."

Jess squinted at Michael. "Did you give him the picture?"

"She did, thank you," Michael said.

"I kept the good one," she said on a yawn, and headed across the hall to what Michael assumed was Sunny's room. The one he would never see.

She grabbed his hand, pulled him to the door. "You have to leave."

"Why?"

"Because I don't want you to." She hurried him along the hall to the stairs. "Just go quietly."

"I feel I should say good night to your parents—"

"Don't even joke," she whispered, nudging him past the second landing. "This is humiliating enough."

They went through the darkened tearoom to the front door. Sunny reached for the lock. "I'll see you tomorrow."

But she wasn't ready when he pulled her close and kissed her hard and long. And when at last he let her go, she had to catch her balance with a hand on the door frame.

They stared at each other, both itchy, frustrated, and more than a little jumpy when a key turned in the lock behind them.

Hugh opened the door and stopped cold. "Well," he said, and gestured uselessly with a hand, at a loss for words for the first time that Sunny could remember.

Through the glass she saw a figure leaning on the fender

of a car, a man waiting for someone. And it occurred to her that Hugh's date wasn't all that heavy after all.

"I'm just leaving," Michael said, moving past him through the door.

He glanced back at Sunny. "Tomorrow," he said, his eyes dark, making her skin tingle all over again.

She locked the door behind him, leaned her back against it.

"So?" Hugh asked.

She frowned. "How did you get in?"

"Jack gave me my key back after a couple of beers." He took two spice jars from his pocket, flicked on a flashlight. "And I'm about to make Dundee broth history."

"Alone?" Sunny asked.

"Not much choice." Hugh cast a quick glance out the window, then headed for the kitchen. "But it won't take long, and I'm hoping he's the patient type."

"I'll keep my fingers crossed." She groaned when he opened the first jar of spice. "I can't watch," she said, and headed for the stairs.

"Just tell me one thing. Are you all right?"

She paused, gave him a rueful smile. "Ask me tomorrow."

# Fourteen

Sam from Sam's Woodworking sent a hopeful smile across Michael's desk. "So you're happy with the new mantel?"

Michael gestured to the interior designer coming through the door. "You'll have to ask Yanka."

"Wrong trim this time," she said, and pulled a chair up to the desk. "I wanted one inch, you gave me three-quarters. Did you honestly think I wouldn't notice the difference?"

Sam held out his hands. "You wanted a fast delivery."

Michael sighed while the two of them went at it, and looked over to where Sunny was working on the mural. She'd started by laying in broad areas of color across the entire garden with a big brush, giving definition to the paths, the hedgerows, the first hint of roses. Now she was using a finer brush, adding details to the delicate domed roof of the gazebo and a couple standing inside, while her head bobbed in time to a song only she could hear behind her headphones.

She'd arrived at 8:00 A.M. followed by Judith, who had come to deliver Doug's package from head office. She was returning to head office that morning, but would be back for the meeting, and if he had any questions in the meantime, he was to call her immediately.

She was no sooner out the door when the air-conditioning guy arrived, followed by a plumber and an electrician, and now Sam and Yanka—none of which was new or unexpected. Ordinarily, he'd take it in stride, sort everything out, and even get to Doug's envelope, all before coffee break. But ordinarily, he wouldn't have Sunny Anderson there, every move, every glance reminding him of what they'd started last night. And were going to finish today.

"Yanka," the carpenter said in a most reasonable tone, "sometimes compromises are necessary."

"Agreed," she said. "But this is more than a compromise. This is an eyesore. And I'm certain Mr. Wolfe will agree. . . . Mr. Wolfe?"

Michael turned back, looked from one to the other. "I'm sorry, I missed that," he said, wishing they'd just go away and give them a few hours alone. Just long enough to touch her skin, kiss her mouth, make love to her over and over and—

"We should go downstairs and settle this," Yanka said.

"Downstairs?" Michael glanced back at Sunny, who was bending over the box, wiggling her butt to the music as she searched for a tube of paint—and smiling straight at him. There was no doubt in his mind that this time, she knew exactly what she was doing.

She blew him a kiss and turned her back, and he wondered why he'd never noticed how damn sexy those overalls were.

"That's really the only way," Yanka said.

Michael reluctantly looked over at her. "I suppose you're—"

"Sorry I'm late," Duane called, hurrying into the penthouse with four cups of coffee balanced in a cardboard tray, and a file tucked tightly under his arm. "I overslept, and then everyone in line ahead of me was ordering something with froth." He sighed heavily as he pulled the cups from the tray. "This has not been my morning."

"Don't worry about it," Michael said, noticing that the kid really did look worn out. Probably spent the night agonizing over the Carillon project while Michael had been with Sunny. And he couldn't find it in him to feel the least bit guilty. He took the coffee cup Duane handed him. "Great haircut, Nugent."

"Thank you, sir." He handed one to Yanka. "That's cream, no sugar"—and another to Sam—"double, double, right?"

"How'd you know?" the carpenter asked.

"Good contacts," Duane said absently, and put the file in front of Michael. "I found the names of four mini-golf-course designers and three water-slide contractors. I know Grant Hall usually uses the same people, but I thought we owed it to ourselves to take a look at alternatives."

Duane went off to deliver a coffee to Sunny and Michael stared at the file. The kid had definitely done an about-face on this one. Abandoned his visions, compromised his principles. Michael dropped the file on top of Judith's envelope. Given enough time, they'd make team players of themselves yet.

He shifted his attention back to the carpenter. "What kind of trim did we originally order?"

Sunny set her brush down as Duane came toward her. "One cream, one sugar"—he reached into his jacket, lowered his voice to a whisper—"and one book."

She put the cup on the stepladder while he slipped a book into her hands. *Dream Small* by Michael Wolfe—a slim hardcover with a blueprint in the background and an artist's impression of the same compact house in front.

"Thanks," she whispered back, taking her cue from Duane, although not really sure why the silence was necessary.

"Just keep it under your hat," Duane said.

Sunny couldn't understand the reason for the cloak-and-dagger routine. Surely Michael would be pleased to know that Duane owned a copy, and had carried it with him to New York—Lord knew, she would have been. But because it mattered to Duane, she said "sure" and tucked the book into her toolbox. "Great haircut, by the way."

"Hugh took me to his salon." He looked down at his feet. "Then we went for shoes."

Sunny smiled at the shiny black loafers with the jaunty tassels. "So what's next on the shopping list?"

"Val and Hugh are taking me for a suit." He gave her a small, embarrassed smile. "Can you believe I've never had a tailor-made suit before?"

Sunny's eyes drifted over his jacket to those odd pants that he had in four different colors. "I'm sure you'll enjoy it," she said. "And they both know a good cut when they see it."

"I'm counting on it," Duane said.

"Nugent," Michael called. "Can we see you over here?"

Duane turned back to Sunny. "I'll get the book from you later," he added, and was off, loping across the office to Michael's desk, passing Yanka on her way over.

Sunny put Duane and his suit on the back burner, as the designer gave her an elegant smile. "I wanted to make sure I spoke to you." She shook Sunny's hand while her gaze went to the mural. "I have to admit I was really offended when Judith didn't ask me to consult on this one, but I'm over it now. And I have a restaurant chain that wants to talk to you about doing chalkboards for every location."

Sunny smiled. "I have a lot of experience with chalk. Do they need to see a portfolio?"

"Nope. One of their executives was at the ball. He said some strange woman had them all looking up at the mural, and he was impressed by what he saw."

Another point for Sonja. And for Val for pushing her into it.

"This will be steady work, too," Yanka continued. "A couple every month, cartoon format with almost total creative freedom, and your signature can definitely be included. Plus you can do them at home and ship them out. Interested?"

"Are you kidding?" Steady work, steady income. And at only one or two a month, she wouldn't have to say no to more murals. Sunny smiled, picturing herself lining those chalkboards up beside the window in the brownstone. After blowing her first check on a night out with Val, of course. "Just say where and when."

"I'll set up a meeting and get back to you." Yanka cast another glance at the mural. "That is going to be another good one, damn it. Which is more than Judith Hill deserves."

"Don't worry," Sunny said. "I made sure I overcharged her."

Yanka laughed and headed back to Michael's desk. "I knew there was a reason I liked working with you."

"Okay, it's settled," Michael said.

"How?" Yanka asked, and Sunny watched a moment longer, seeing Michael glance over at her, and enjoying the look of true frustration on his face when Yanka and Sam started arguing again.

When he turned to address Sam, Sunny took the book out of her toolbox, and sat down on the drop cloth, facing the wall. She flipped open the cover and spotted the dedication. *For Kate, Always.*

Nothing flowery or sentimental, just a straightforward declaration of love. And her heart squeezed when she turned the page and found their picture. *Michael Wolfe and Kate Shaw at their summer home in Maine.*

The home Michael had built for Kate. A small stone cottage with a porch, a swing, and a design that was truly unique. They sat on the top step, looking straight at the camera, their smiles wide and confident, ready to take on the world.

And Kate was lovely. Dark haired, slender, a classic beauty. Michael was intense as always, but there had been no weariness around his eyes then, no line between his brows. He had been the warrior, the hero, fighting for what he believed in, and she had been his lady fair.

Sunny glanced over her shoulder and he looked up, as though he had felt her eyes on him. And she knew a moment of real and painful jealousy, because no one had ever loved her the way he had loved Kate.

Michael watched her shake off whatever it was that had

stolen the light from her eyes, the smile from her lips, leaving behind an expression so bleak and lonely he had found it hard to breathe.

But it was gone as quickly as it had come, fading behind a vampy come-hither look that made him smile in spite of himself. And when she closed her book, rose up on her knees, and put a fingertip in her mouth, Michael knew the gauntlet had been officially dropped.

"Tell you what we're going to do," he announced and got to his feet. "Nugent, I think you're ready for some real responsibility." He picked up the tray of invoices awaiting approval and held it out to him. "I want you to take these, look them over, and sign them."

Sunny's eyes widened, her finger dropped out of her mouth, and Michael felt a surge of pure masculine pleasure as she scrambled to her feet.

Duane shook his head. "But I don't have the authority, sir."

"You do now." Michael dropped the tray in his lap and reached for a pen and paper. "And to show you how serious I am about this, I'm going to put a note on the door and one with the operator, instructing the trades and maintenance to contact you for the rest of the day."

"All day?" Duane asked.

Michael cast a glance at Sunny. "And all night too."

She swallowed, looked around, then lifted her chin in that way of hers and slowly slid one overall strap over her shoulder, only to snap it back up again when Sam turned his head.

Michael's smile broadened as he scribbled his note. He would never understand her, but in the little time they had left, he was definitely going to enjoy her.

"As far as the mantel is concerned, I'm also giving Nugent final say on that issue as well."

Sam started to protest and Michael held up a hand. "Nugent is my right-hand man. I trust him completely."

Duane blinked, then shot to his feet. "I won't let you

down, sir." He motioned to Sam and Yanka. "Show me the mantel."

Michael picked up his cell phone and handed it to Duane on his way to the door. "Take that too. It'll only be business calls anyway."

"I'll guard it as if it were my own," Duane said. "But, sir, what if Sonja calls?"

"Take a message," he said, but didn't notice Sunny's little victory strut to the stepladder.

Michael held the door as the three of them trooped out into the hall. "Good luck, Nugent."

"Sir, about the mini-golf and the water slides—"

"I'll be sure to have a look at it." Michael walked over and pushed the button for the elevator, stuck his note to the penthouse door, and clapped Duane on the back as he headed back inside. "I know I can count on you, Nugent."

"I'll let you know my findings, sir."

"No rush," Michael said, then closed the door, locked it, put the dead bolt on, even slid the chain into place for the first time since he moved in, needing to be certain that today no one would come in unannounced.

He tested the door one last time and finally turned to Sunny. She was standing by the stepladder, dipping the tip of her paintbrush into a drop of paint on the palette. "I thought I'd work on this while you go over Duane's list."

"The list can wait." Michael went back to his desk, lifted the receiver.

"But you said—"

"I lied." His gaze moved over her slowly, hungrily as he spoke into the phone. "This is Michael Wolfe. Please direct all calls to Duane Nugent, room . . ." He rifled through the notes on his desk. "I don't know what number it is. Check your list, and keep sending them there until I call you back."

He hung up the phone. "Sunny, put the brush down."

Her fingers tightened involuntarily on that brush, every nerve, every cell in her body instantly aware, excited, and more than a little afraid.

This was it, then. The end of celibacy as she knew it.

Unless, of course, she could outrun him to the door.

But why think about that now? Wasn't this what she'd wanted, dreamed about, obsessed over, ever since that first night on the sofa? Wasn't this the very reason she was wearing really great, if somewhat uncomfortable, underwear?

Yes, it is, her body hollered. So what was the problem?

Rule number two, her mind said and Sunny knew in her heart it was true.

As much as she'd enjoyed playing the siren in overalls, the vixen in painter's drill, as he came toward her now, Sunny realized she didn't want this to be a moment of madness anymore. She wanted it to be real.

She wanted to be part of a couple. To be loved and cherished, to have someone build her a house so she could make it a home. And she wanted that someone to be Michael Wolfe, because in spite of all her good intentions, she was already falling for him. Slipping and sliding into an impossible relationship just like Snow White and Cinderella, and poor hapless Beauty. But unlike the fairy tales, her happy ending wasn't going to be with this particular Beast.

Yet as he drew up in front of her, she stayed put, knowing that if she turned away now, she'd regret it tomorrow and the day after, and for a long time to come. Because she hadn't been in love for years, and the feeling was too damn good to ignore.

So she handed him the paintbrush, watched him smile, and made up her mind that this would be enough. She would forget tomorrow and simply enjoy him now. And when it was over, she wouldn't cling or beg. This time she'd simply walk away with her head held high.

He set the brush down and reached for her, drawing her close against him. "I thought for a moment you were going to change your mind."

"Not me," she said, the heat already building deep inside as she looped her arms around his neck, rose up on her toes. "Of course, it is almost lunch, so if you want to go out for a sandwich or another coffee—"

"All I want is you," he said softly.

There was no preamble, no feathery-light brushing of lips across eyelids and cheeks, just his mouth on hers, hot and demanding and exactly what she needed to push away any lingering doubts or fears or rational thought.

She leaned into him, kissed him back, and Michael knew he was in trouble. His heart was racing, his blood pounding, and he was already too hard, too ready. And when she dragged him closer, rubbed her breasts against his chest, it took every ounce of willpower he possessed not to lower her to the rug and bury himself inside her right there.

But he remembered she hadn't done this in a while, and he wanted to take his time, to make it good. It didn't help a bit when she broke the kiss and started undoing his shirt.

"Why are men's buttons on the wrong side?" she asked, her fingers fumbling, impatient and so eager, so honest about what she wanted that his heart swelled with pride and longing, and something akin to pain because they didn't have long. A few days, a week at most. And he knew already that he would miss her.

Her hands were on his skin now, pushing the shirt aside so she could rub her palms across his chest. And her smile was delightfully wicked as her fingertips brushed his nipples, circling with maddening gentleness while she touched her lips to his throat, his chest, anywhere she could reach, and finally grabbed his chin between her teeth.

He howled and lifted her up. She was so light, so small that he swung her around, hearing her squeal and laugh as he hoisted her over his shoulder and carried her, kicking and thumping like a heroine from a silent movie, all the way to the bedroom.

He set her on her feet and she was on him again, pushing his shirt off once and for all and sliding her hands down his back to loop her fingers in the waistband of his jeans. Her eyes were clear and wide open as he slid the straps of her overalls down only to discover how quickly and easily they slid to the ground. If only he'd known earlier, he thought, as she kicked them aside and stood before him in nothing but a tiny T-shirt and a pair of sheer and utterly scandalous underwear.

He reached for her, his own hands eager, almost clumsy as he lifted that T-shirt up and off, revealing a bra that was every bit as sheer and sexy as her panties. And he felt his heart squeeze, knowing they were both brand-new, and meant only for him.

She gave him a small crooked smile, her bravado slipping as she stepped back, suddenly shy in her scandalous underwear. Michael felt an odd jolt, as though he'd seen that same look before, and felt this same way. He dismissed the thought as quickly as it had come and took hold of her arms, holding them close at her sides.

Her eyes widened with a silent plea but he shook his head. "Just let me look at you," he said and stood back, hearing her whimper as his gaze moved over her with deliberate slowness, lingering on the soft rise and fall of her breasts, the gentle curve of her belly, and the rich, feminine flare of her hips. "You really have no idea how beautiful you are, do you?" he whispered.

She raised her head, met his gaze, her eyes searching his for lies or flattery. And was absurdly pleased when a surprised little smile curved her lips, knowing she'd found only truth.

He drew her closer by degrees, needing her to know exactly how desirable, how lovely she truly was. He slid the thin straps of her bra down while he kissed her lips, her throat, the hollow of her shoulder, feeling her shudder when he brushed his knuckles across one taut and waiting nipple, determined to take this slow if it killed him.

The bra fell away with a flick of the clasp, and he backed her up to the bed, followed her down, his mouth closing on one breast while his hand found the other, delighting in the way she ran her hands over his back, and rose to meet him, no longer shy or hesitant.

Sunny's breasts were warm and heavy, her nipples tingling, straining, hungry for the feel of his tongue on her flesh. That he honestly found her, Sunny Anderson, beautiful still amazed her. That he wanted her—really wanted her—thrilled her, made her bold again, and sure that what she was doing was right and good.

He slid his hand down, across her stomach to the panties that had cost her a fortune. And as he stroked her through the lace, she wondered how he'd like the ones she had planned for tomorrow, and the furry pair she'd kept for a special occasion. But when he slid those panties down, she didn't think of anything at all, simply gave herself over to sensation as she lay naked and spread wide before him, panting and greedy, and loving everything he was doing to her.

Michael trembled inside as he kissed her, loved her, but his hands were steady, taking her up again and again, and holding her there on the edge until she grabbed his hand and made him take her over. And when he stood up, pushing down his jeans and briefs in one quick movement, she was right there, pulling him back into bed and filling her hands with him.

He lay back, sucking in a ragged breath as she took control, her fingers unskilled but earnest and learning fast. He cursed softly, gritted his teeth as she kissed his belly, his chest, his shoulders, and finally his mouth, her hand surrounding him still, driving his body to the brink while she filled his mind with the scent, the sound, the taste of her.

"Enough," he muttered and heard her chuckle as he pushed her down, moved between her thighs. But her laughter caught in her throat when he drove himself into her in one swift move, only to come out as a sigh when he stayed there, locked deep inside, afraid to move for fear that it would all be over too soon.

She ran her fingers down his back, over his buttocks, holding him to her as her hips rose and retreated, rose and retreated in a slow, sensuous rhythm that threatened to undo him.

He rose up over her, upping the ante and the beat, pushing himself into her again and again, taking them both farther, higher. Loving the way she wrapped her arms and legs around him, meeting him thrust for thrust, and holding on tight when release finally came.

His arms gave out and he buried his face in her hair, her neck, breathing her in as he struggled to gain control, to calm. But when she opened her eyes and smiled, Michael knew they hadn't even taken the edge off yet.

He rolled away, propped himself up on an elbow, watching her stretch luxuriously with no sign of regret or shyness anywhere on that angel face—and certainly not in the way she reached for him.

"Again?" she murmured, and he was there, surprising himself more than her it seemed.

She settled back, that smile still on her lips as he moved down the length of her body, trailing kisses across her breasts, her belly, her soft, sweet thighs. She shivered when he opened her legs, gasped at the first touch of his tongue, then gave herself over to him completely, as anxious to learn as he was to teach. But his hands were shaking as he lifted her, his heart pounding too hard, too fast, and he realized then that he was on new ground himself here. Wanting her, needing her in ways he hadn't needed for years.

A dangerous woman, he reminded himself, but his body simply wasn't listening.

Sunny sat up slowly, pushed at her hair, blinked to clear her head. "That was, that was . . ." She sighed and flopped back down. "Absolutely sinful."

Michael ran a fingertip down between her breasts. "Just a little something I thought you'd enjoy."

"You're right." Obviously recovered, she launched herself at him, pushing him down onto the pillows. "Which leaves me no choice but to find something you'll enjoy equally well."

Michael linked his fingers behind his neck, willing to let her imagination take over, but then suddenly she was sitting back on her heels and frowning.

"But right now," she said. "I have got to eat."

Michael rolled over, telling himself anticipation would make it even better as he pulled a menu from the night-stand drawer. "The bar fridge is stocked with beer and soda, and we can order up something to go with it, or we can go out, whichever you want."

"Lunch in bed sounds suitably decadent." She kissed him hard and quick, then swung her feet over the side of the bed. "You take care of the main course, and I'll take care of the beverages." She eyed the overalls and the tangled underwear at her feet, decided she wasn't ready for that yet, and grabbed his shirt instead. "Do you mind?"

He dragged the phone over to the bed. "Not as long as you take it off again once you're back."

She laughed. "Try and stop me," she said, pushing her arms into the sleeves, but purposely leaving the buttons undone so he could see just what he'd be missing while she was gone.

And as she'd hoped, his eyes stayed on her all the way to the door. "But we'll have to be quick, because I have to be home at three. I'm on car-pool duty today."

"Can't you call someone? Hugh, maybe, or Sean. Your mother?"

"My brothers are on a job somewhere, and can you imagine me trying to explain this to Moyra?"

He shrugged. "So we'll pick Jess up together and the three of us will go out."

"Don't you have a presentation to do?"

"I'll do it tomorrow." He flipped open the menu. "What do you want to eat?"

"Anything. But we couldn't go out right away. Jess is at camp. She'll need to change, have a snack—"

"Okay, so we'll go back to your place, let her do all that, and then go out."

"You do know that Moyra will be at the tearoom."

He laughed. "Sunny, don't worry about it. I can handle Moyra. Then later, you and I can come back here—"

"I can't leave Jess alone."

"Or we can stay at your place." He smiled. "I always pack a toothbrush."

She folded her arms. "Have you forgotten the rule about sleeping at my place?"

He glanced up, his gaze raking over her, making goose bumps rise on her skin. "I'm hoping I can change your mind."

"You won't," she said and spun away, feeling sexy, powerful, and every bit as desirable as Sonja had.

And, oh, what a heady feeling it was, one she had never known until today, until Michael. And she refused to read anything into the fact that he wanted to pick up Jess, come back to the tearoom. He was simply having a good time, just as she was.

She unplugged the headphones, and switched on the CD, wailing along with Maria as she did up the buttons on his shirt and making up her mind to savor every moment, every long and hungry look, because who knew when anyone would ever make her feel this way again?

She was on her way to the bar, wondering what he'd surprise her with this time, when she spotted her paintbrush drying on the coffee table. She rescued the poor thing, carried it back to the stepladder, and dropped it in the water. While she was there, she checked the yogurt containers of paint she'd mixed earlier, discovering they had survived the neglect just fine.

She swirled the paintbrush in the water, using her fingers to clean off any stubborn bits while she gazed at the mural. It was coming together faster than she'd predicted, although the couple in the gazebo still needed something.

She was thinking about that when her cell phone started to ring. Her heart jumped, but she told it to settle down. It couldn't be Michael for Sonja because she could hear him on the phone to room service. So she flipped back the lid, checked the display, and was pleased to see that her mother hadn't managed to scare Rona off at all.

"Rona, thanks for calling back," she said, and looked over at the mural, knowing exactly what she needed to add while the real estate agent gave her the details of the latest brownstone: parlor floor, great lighting, and a good price, if you could afford it. She started doing the math: regular chalkboards plus a half bath in the Hamptons—she stopped, narrowed her eyes, seeing the perfect spot for her signature.

"I'll make sure I give the feature sheet to your dad," Rona said. "You can see the apartment anytime."

Sunny thanked her, dropped the phone back into the toolbox, and dipped the tip of the brush into the paint. She turned back to the mural, signed it with a flick of the wrist, and focused on the couple again. All they needed was a touch here, and one over there. A little more white behind them wouldn't hurt either. She rinsed the brush, humming now as Marie told Three Dollar Bill to take a hike, and wondering what the secret would be.

# Fifteen

Michael set the menu down quietly and leaned back against the bar, watching her work. Her hair was a wild red cloud, her face a study in concentration, and his shirt was barely long enough to keep her decent. While he couldn't take his eyes off her, Michael knew she was completely unaware of him. No longer the sweet, sexy lover of only minutes ago, she was the artist now, lost in the music and the mural, humming softly and a little off-key, but her strokes deft and sure, making the people in the gazebo come to life before his eyes.

They stood by the railing, a man and a woman of indeterminate age, their heads turned, looking out at the one looking in. They didn't look startled, merely curious. Watching him as though they knew something was about to happen on his side of the frame.

The effect was unnerving, and Michael looked away—to the gardens, the paths, the intricate dome Sunny had created. But found himself drawn back again and again to the couple in the gazebo, wondering what it was that they saw.

Sunny reached across to the stepladder to rinse her brush and Michael glanced over at his desk, thinking he could make it over there without distracting her. Check his e-mail, go through the prospectus, maybe start his presentation. But when she stood in front of the mural again, Michael stayed where he was, wanting to do nothing more than watch her.

She made a few more adjustments, no longer singing as she focused solely on the painting; then suddenly she drew in a breath and stepped back, obviously finished for the moment. She dropped the brush into the water while she gave the painting a critical going-over—and absently wiped her fingers on his shirt. Michael had to smile as he pushed away from the bar. There were other shirts after all, but only one Sunny.

She glanced at him, her eyes distant, unseeing, then coming sharply into focus. "Hi," she said, her cheeks turning pink and her smile more than a little embarrassed. "I got a little distracted." She winced as she looked down. "And I got paint on your shirt."

"Don't worry about it," he said, and went around the bar. "What do you want to drink?"

"Forgot that too," she murmured, then shook her head and crouched down in front of her paint box. "Just a soda, any kind."

Michael pulled the tabs on two cans and carried them over to where she was rummaging around in the box. "So is the secret there yet, or am I just missing it?"

"It's not there. In fact I have no clue yet what it will even be." She pulled a hair clip from the box, gathered all of that glorious red up on top of her head, and secured it as she got to her feet. "But I'm sure it will come to me."

Michael handed her a can. "Like that couple in the gazebo?"

She nodded, her eyes on the mural as she took a long drink, then gestured to the painting with the can. "They just appeared this morning, but I find I like them."

Michael stood beside her. "To be honest, I don't. It feels like they're watching me."

Sunny laughed. "You're just sensitive." She set the can on the stepladder. "To me they're simply two nice people who . . ."

But Michael didn't hear the rest as he caught sight of a disturbingly familiar book cover inside her toolbox.

He bent to pick it up. "Where did you get this?"

She came toward him. "From Duane. He brought it over for me to have a look. He said it made a big impression on him."

"Only because he's easily impressed."

Michael sat down on the sofa, and when he could, he flipped the book open, going through the pages at random: Bungalow with Veranda—page twenty-one. Cape Cod with Dormers—page fifteen. And without dormers—page sixteen. Two dozen designs in all—and it shocked him to realize that he still remembered exactly where and when each one had been built.

Sunny sank down beside him, curled her feet up under her. "I'm surprised you don't have a copy on your own shelf."

"I don't have one anywhere. There didn't seem any point once I sold the business." He stopped at page five— One and a Half Story with Walk-out Basement. "This one always needed a skylight. The upper hall was too dark without it."

"Do you ever miss the business?"

"I used to."

"Would you ever go back?"

He shook his head. "We cornered the market back then, but it's all different now. Plus, I'd have to gather a team, get the financing, and build a client base all over again. And I'd have to build a house for my brother, and I don't have the energy for that."

Sunny didn't see how that would ever be possible, but kept it to herself as she motioned to the book. "Which one would you choose for him?"

He turned back to page fifteen and leaned closer, holding it so she could see. "With a few modifications, this one would be perfect. Jill loves to entertain but casually, and the layout of the kitchen and family room would work well for her. But they'd need an office for Andy so we'd either have to bump out the back here, or we could lose some space in the living room, probably here." He sat back, a wry smile on his lips. "Of course, knowing Andy, he'd want another floor added. He never did understand the theory behind *Dream Small.*"

"But plenty of others did," she said softly.

He nodded at the page. "It took a while, but eventually they did. Which was a damn good thing because everything we had was on the line when we started out. People thought we were crazy, which we probably were. I gave up a position with a big firm, Kate quit her job as a landscaper, and we turned our apartment into an office. Blueprints in the bedroom, computers in the living room, photocopier in the dining room." He got to his feet and looked around. "The whole place wasn't half as big as this, and we had a staff of four, including the two of us, so we were always tripping over each other trying to get to the phone or the fax or the copier. You should have seen it."

Sunny could see it vividly, just by looking at him.

He was on the move now, talking while he walked with the book in his hand, his face animated, his gestures wide and expansive, painting a picture with words alone and sweeping her up into it.

"A few times, I thought we wouldn't make it, that the experts had been right. But we kept going, working all the house shows, every trade event, writing articles, giving lectures, not ready to give up yet."

"A real dreamer," she murmured, and was pleased when he smiled.

"I guess we were. And then one day, we caught on, we were fashionable. No vaulted ceilings, no wasted space— what a concept. Magazines published the articles, colleges asked me to speak, and it didn't hurt that the newspapers and environmental groups loved us, called us the renegade builders."

"Duane called you a visionary."

He laughed. "And in reality, I was only a pushy bastard who did everything he could to get his name out there."

"I think we refer to that as promotion."

"Or obsession. By the time the book came out, our office was a suite in an executive tower, and my head was so big it barely fit through the front door—something Kate pointed out to me more than a few times." He slowed and looked down at the book. "To be honest, I don't know why she put up with me all that time."

"Because she believed in you," Sunny said softly, not finding it hard at all to understand, because no matter how he tried to hide it, to fight it, Michael was a man of passion and heart. The kind who tilted at windmills and took on giants. She knew exactly why Kate had stayed and why Duane carried that book. And why she would miss him so much when he was gone.

"I guess she did," he said, and sank down beside her on the sofa again, the buoyancy draining away as he turned the book over at last, coming to the picture of himself and Kate, and the house in Maine.

Michael hadn't looked at a picture of Kate in a while, hadn't needed to, because he could see her every time he closed his eyes. That long black hair, those exotic brown eyes. And at night, when he was alone, he was sure he could feel her moving over him in the dark, touching him, loving him, reminding him of everything they'd shared, everything he'd lost. And seeing her on the porch of their house only brought it all into sharper focus, and made it suddenly hard to breathe.

"She was lovely," Sunny said.

"Yes. She was." He dropped the book on the coffee table as he rose and headed for the desk. "I'll check on lunch—"

"Michael," Sunny said, her voice soft enough to make him stop and turn around. She was standing now, the light through the window showing him every curve behind that shirt, and making him wish they could just go back to bed, where everything was simple, straightforward. But then again, that was Sunny over there. And nothing would ever be simple again.

"You told me once," she said, "that if I ever wanted to know anything, all I had to do was ask. Well, I want to know about Kate. And I'm asking you to tell me."

"Why?"

"Because I want to understand you."

"Why?"

That chin rose. "Because I care about you."

"Don't," he said evenly, but she merely shook her head.

"Too late," she said and folded her arms. "So are you a man of your word, or not?"

He hesitated, and she held her breath, not sure what she'd do if he turned away, shut her out again.

Then he was walking toward her, his steps slow and measured.

"You want to know about Kate? Fine. She wasn't just lovely, she was exquisite. But more importantly, she was part of everything I did, everything I was. We were so goddamn happy people used to think we weren't real, but we were, and we knew exactly where we were going, had it all under control. Then one day she went out for groceries, and never came back. A BMW ran a red light and hit her broadside. They said she never felt a thing, and I've always hoped they were right."

He loomed over her, trying to intimidate her again, which was surprising, because it hadn't worked yet, and she'd never figured him for a stupid man. So she met his gaze and held her ground, letting him know nothing had changed, and he wasn't nearly finished. "What did you do then?"

"Do? Well, I moved out of the house because I couldn't stop listening for her car in the driveway. Or reaching for her every time I woke up in our bed. And it took me a long time to forgive her for not watching more closely, not being more careful. For leaving me alone with all our plans, all our dreams. And a business that meant nothing anymore."

"But you loved your work—"

"I loved my wife. And I started to hate the families who came in to see me, resent the fact that they were still together and I was alone. I started making mistakes, really screwing up, but I was lucky. I had a good staff to catch them, to catch me. So I got out before I could do any real damage and promised myself I would never go through that again."

"A business?"

"Love," he said, and was the first to step back, to give way, the fight gone as he walked to the window, stared out at the street. "Do you understand now why I'm not looking for anything permanent? Why we won't ever be a couple?"

"I think so," she said softly.

"Good," he said and turned to her, his eyes moving over her, not with hunger this time but with a soul-deep longing that made her heart ache. "Because the last thing I ever want to do is hurt you."

And it was at that precise moment Sunny realized she was no longer falling in love with him. She couldn't be, because she'd already landed. And there she stood, smack in the middle of a hopeless love with no way to go back, and no desire to try.

But she wouldn't kid herself into believing she could save him, or change his mind or make him take what she wanted to give. He was a hurtin' man, after all, with a sadness that went deep and would take time to heal. And since time was the one thing Sunny didn't have, all she could do was wrap her arms around him and hold on tight. And not give up on him yet.

She walked toward him, knowing he might push her away, call the whole thing off right now, but encouraged by the barest hint of a smile as she drew up in front of him.

"While I appreciate your candor," she said, "I have to say that I think you're an ass." She watched his eyebrows rise. "I understand what it's like to be lonely and betrayed, and scared to death to put your heart on the line again. But the fact is, you can't control your heart any more than I can control mine, and I already know it will hurt like hell when you leave because I love you."

She held up a hand. "Do not interrupt me when I'm on a rant." His smile broadened and there was light in those eyes, she was sure of it. So she edged a little closer, laid a hand on his chest. "I love you," she repeated, at ease with the words because she used them freely with Jess. "And if that makes you uncomfortable, then say so, and I'll leave right now."

"No," he said. "It's fine."

"Then I'll stay, and I won't mention it again. And I won't rant or cry when it's time for you to go. But if you change your mind, and want to say the words to me, then I will be a very good listener." She glanced over her shoulder. "I also think that room service is taking too long. I have to leave soon, and I want to take a shower first, which leaves only one issue to clear up."

He actually gasped when she grabbed hold of his belt. "Are you going to come peacefully, or do I have to use force?"

The tension left his shoulders and that smile turned into a full-out grin. "I think I'd like to see force."

Val leaned back against the fridge with her teacup and the Brownstone feature sheet that Rona had left at the cash desk for Sunny. "So now I've got an appointment for Duane with the tailor in an hour, but he's so set on pin-stripes it's sad." She lowered the page. "This apartment, however, is fabulous."

"No kidding," Sunny said, peering through the order window, checking for signs of Moyra at the front door, and hoping Jess was finished changing soon so she could get Michael out of the tearoom before her mother came back.

She might not know how to explain to her mother what she was doing with Michael, but she didn't have to look at the feature sheet again to know that Val was right about the apartment. It was everything Rona had said, and the rent was . . . possible. Maybe. If more work came in. And it was steady. And Jess didn't kick up a fuss. And . . .

And there was no time to think about it now.

She tucked the feature sheet into her purse. "It's still too early to decide."

Val sipped her tea. "If it's work you're worried about,

you should know that on Saturday every newsstand around the hotel and the one inside will have copies of the *Banner.* Your picture will be everywhere."

"Pictures are one thing, jobs are another." She took a step toward Val. "What I really wanted to ask you about is a little more personal."

Val put down her cup. "I'm all ears."

"I need a . . ." Sunny paused, not sure how to put this. "A really great move. Something that will knock Michael's socks off in . . . you know . . ."

Val grinned. "In bed."

Sunny winced. "Not so loud. Jess will hear you."

"Jess is on the third floor."

"Then Michael will hear you." Sunny looked into the tearoom, making sure Michael was still occupied. "I want something that will . . . surprise him."

"Surprise him, huh?" Val shrugged. "Well, I usually like to start with feathers, or a scarf—"

"No props. I just want something simple but devastating."

Val frowned and picked up her cup. "Let me think a minute."

Sunny sighed. She'd been lucky to have time to change herself, let alone think.

The SORRY WE'RE CLOSED SIGN had been hanging on the front door when she'd arrived at the Isles with Jess and Michael. The Glasgow ladies had been inside, packing tarts in a box, and duly recording their sins on a piece of paper at the cash desk. They'd explained to Sunny that things had been a little slow so Moyra had popped out to the bank and the deli—locking the door behind her because Jack and Hugh were both there and she didn't trust either one to serve her customers. But Jack had let them in, of course. After all, why wouldn't he?

But he'd slipped out himself moments later—the ladies had been sure he had something up his sleeve again—and Hugh was in the back with the gawky fellow and that pretty blonde.

They'd brought Jess up to date on Lilli and André, reporting that they'd last been heard fighting about the wedding date. Seems her mother had discovered the day was bad luck but André didn't believe in such things and now the grandmother wasn't coming.

Then they'd picked up their boxes and headed for the door, telling Michael how nice it was to see him again, and how pleased Moyra would be when she came back.

Sunny knew Moyra wouldn't be pleased at all, and glanced into the tearoom, wondering how much longer Jess was going to be.

"Okay, I've got it," Val said. "Give me a pen and I'll write it down, because you need to do this in exactly the order I tell you, understood?"

Sunny nodded, and handed Val both pen and paper.

Michael sat at the table with Duane and Hugh and a stack of men's fashion magazines, sinking his teeth into a butter tart while around him serious discussion was going on. Double-breasted versus single. Belt or suspenders. But Michael's only contribution to the conversation so far had been "pass the teapot" when his cup ran dry.

Every now and then, however, he'd look over at the kitchen, his smile warm and real, and only for her. Sunny still blushed when she thought about the shower and his idea of good clean fun, but she wasn't embarrassed at all about telling him she loved him. They hadn't talked about it since, which was fine. She'd simply given him something new to think about. The rest was up to him.

Val dropped the pen. "All right, let's go through this. But be warned, it can be addictive."

Sunny smiled as she turned. "Sounds absolutely perfect."

Val held the paper close to her chest, her eyes narrowing. "Before we do this, look me in the eye and tell me you're being careful."

"Of course I'm being—"

"I mean with your heart," Val said softly.

"Don't worry about me. I know the rules." She drew the page from Val's fingers. "Now show me all."

Michael watched the two women huddle over a piece of paper, Sunny's eyes growing wider as Val talked, and he couldn't help wondering what was going on in there. But he stayed where he was, watching Hugh try to talk Nugent out of pinstripes.

"Pinstripes are unpredictable," Hugh said. "One year they're in, the next they're out. . . ." He turned a page in the magazine. "You're better to stick to classics like this."

Duane was still shaking his head when Jack came around the corner with a paper bag. "Hugh, I'm ready to start," he called, then raised a hand and smiled at Michael. "Good to see you again, lad."

Michael smiled back as Hugh got to his feet.

"Gotta go," he said. "The old man is preparing a candlelight dinner for Moyra, and I'm helping him with the main course."

"Sounds romantic," Duane said.

"Actually, it's an act of extreme masochism," Hugh said. "But don't tell Jack. He just bought an expensive bottle of wine. Keep thinking about what I said. Val will be back soon and she'll want an answer."

"I'll be ready," Duane said, and went right back to the pinstripe suit in the magazine.

"So, Nugent," Michael said, to distract him. "How'd it go today?"

"Fine, sir. The mantel will be back next week with the right trim, and I'm halfway through the invoices." He closed the magazine and set it aside. "I know you inspected each job, sir, but I went over what I could as well, to familiarize myself with the way you like things done. I have to say, I was impressed, sir."

"Me too. We really lucked into some fine tradesmen." Michael eyed the tarts on the tea tray. "I think I'm in real danger of addiction."

"I know. I come for my fix once a day now."

Michael grinned and went for seconds. "So, are you all geared up for the meeting?"

"I suppose so, sir. Do you think they'll get the approvals?"

"Why wouldn't they? The hotel is a viable use of land, the Carillon is a mess at the moment, and the prospectus looks good. With a little punching up and some enthusiastic conversation with the one reluctant planner, I don't see how it can miss."

"That's what I thought." Duane sat back. "But I can't help thinking they could have done something else with that ballroom. And the fountains. There's no reason they had to get rid of them completely."

"It's a simple matter of economics, Nugent. Bulldozing the fountains is cheaper than building around them."

"Not so," Duane said, and took a pen and small notebook from his jacket. He turned to a blank page and drew a quick layout of the Carillon and the grounds around it. "If they had simply taken the water slide out here, like this, and swung the parking lot around this way, they could have saved at least one fountain, and not cost themselves anything extra."

"True." Michael took the pen. "But if they had been really smart, they would have switched the water slide to the back, leaving this area as it was, and turned it into a rooftop garden or a restaurant. Then the parking lot could have gone here, saving not only the fountain, but part of the original gardens as well."

Duane grabbed the pen back. "And if they did that, then they could have put the mini-golf there, and made the ballroom into a dining room."

"A fantasy room of gold and mirrors," Michael added.

"Exactly what I was thinking."

Both men grinned at each other, then sat back and sighed.

"You know none of this is going to happen, don't you?"

Duane nodded and clicked his pen shut.

"But who knows?" Michael added. "Maybe we'll have more input on the next project."

"I hope so, sir." Duane slipped his notebook back in his pocket. "I almost forgot to give you this," he added, taking out Michael's cell phone. "It rang eleven times and I took care of each call, as directed. Mrs. Hill was surprised to hear my voice, but pleased with your decision to let me be part of things. She told me to tell you she'll be here on Friday morning at ten."

"I'll be sure to mark that on my calendar," Michael said, and turned when Sunny's laughter drifted out from the kitchen. She was leaning back against the stove, fanning her face with a slip of paper. When she saw him watching her, she gave him a smile so openly sexual he found it hard to breathe. And even harder to keep from going to her.

He still couldn't believe she'd told him she loved him, even though she knew he wasn't going to love her back. Not the way she wanted him to. She winked and tucked a piece of paper into her back pocket as she turned away. The woman had more heart, more courage than most men he knew. Including himself. He was lucky to have her for the time he did.

He slid the cell phone back to Duane. "Why don't you keep it for the rest of the day? Handle any emergencies that might come up."

"Certainly, sir." He smiled as he pocketed the phone again. "I guess there's not much chance of Sonja calling you now anyway."

"Why?" Michael asked. "What have you heard?"

"Nothing, sir," he said quickly. "She's just so far away. And you and Sunny seem to . . ."

He stopped, color rising into his face as Michael raised a brow. "What I mean is, does it really matter anymore if she calls, sir?"

Michael looked over as Jess came down the stairs and Sunny went over to meet her. But Jess wasn't smiling, and for the first time, she was dragging her feet as she walked.

"Is something wrong?" Sunny asked quietly.

Jess looked down at her shoes. "I talked to Natalie. Her mom and her are coming to Arts Night, *and* they're bringing her new boyfriend."

"But that's good news. More people to root for you."

Jess raised her head. "But what if I mess up?"

"How could you mess up?" Michael asked, winning a very surprised hoot of laughter from Jess as he hoisted her up in his arms. "You're too much like your mother. Beautiful and talented, and everyone is going to love you. In fact, I'll bet they throw roses at your feet."

"Now that would be neat," she said, and looked straight at him. "You're coming for sure, aren't you?"

"I wouldn't miss it for the world," he said, taking Sunny's hand as the three of them headed for the door.

"Good luck with the suit," he called back to Duane. "And you're absolutely right, by the way. It doesn't matter at all."

# Sixteen

Michael yawned and looked up from his keyboard. "How does this sound? 'I heartily recommend the addition of a Grant Hall hotel to the city of Sundridge. It will make a fine contribution to the growth and stability of the area.' "

Sunny frowned and closed the front door behind her. "Not exactly punchy, is it?"

She wore jeans and a tank top, and carried her overalls and a change of clothes for herself and Jess in her bag. As Michael watched her cross to her corner of the penthouse, he couldn't help wondering what was under those jeans today.

Black silk, red lace. Nothing at all.

He made himself focus on the screen. "Okay, how about 'I can *really* heartily recommend'?"

She laughed and dropped her purse beside the paint box. "Much better."

"So I'm off to a great start." He put his fingers on the keyboard again, checked his notes, and was about to start the second line of his presentation when the flag went up on his e-mail.

He clicked over, in case it was something he needed for the meeting, but it was only Andy with a message titled *Not Happy with Bill*.

Andy could only mean Bill Johnson, the man Michael

had sold the business to. Curious, Michael opened the message.

> *Met with Bill, not impressed. Do you have any other names? Will pack up van next week if we don't get a date from you before then. Remember, cottage season is upon us. Hugs, Andy.*

Michael smiled and typed.

> *Can't think of a name offhand. Give me some time. Will have better idea of when I can visit after today. Kisses, Mike.*

As he pressed SEND, Michael found he wanted to see the cottage again. Wanted to eat Jill's great cooking, and hug the boys before they were too old for such things. And strangely enough, he wanted to see Andy.

Michael looked up to see Sunny smiling at him. "Whatever is on there must be good."

"Just Andy. Threatening to visit again."

"Family's like that." Sunny flipped on the CD player and pulled a case from her purse.

"How's Jess? Is she still nervous?"

"She has butterflies, but for the most part she's excited. And the cheering section is growing by the day. So are you coming over here, or am I coming there?"

He gestured to the computer. "I've got to finish this."

"Your place then," she said, and pressed PLAY.

Michael raised his head as a flute began. She was playing something new this morning, soft jazz he liked but didn't recognize. As she came toward him, Michael realized how much he liked hearing the music in the morning, because it meant that Sunny was back.

He glanced over at the mural behind her, knowing she would finish all too soon.

He rolled the chair away from the desk and she sat down on his lap. "Jess also told me to make sure you know the time and the place for tonight."

"Seven o'clock, Lloyd Elgin Elementary. I have it written down, and I am always on time."

She cupped his face in her hands, touched her lips to his. "I find punctuality so attractive in a man."

He smiled and wrapped his arms around her, kissing her thoroughly, deeply, enjoying his first taste of her that day.

He still hadn't adjusted to the fact that they would never spend a night together, but he had to admit that the mornings were worth waiting for. With the head office staff gone and Duane cleaning up the last of the paperwork and dealing with the trades, Michael had trained the front desk to hold his calls until nine, and hung a brand-new DO NOT DISTURB sign on the door. Even Duane had learned to knock. And Michael had learned the value of time off.

He ran a hand up under the tank top to her breast, loving the way she moved into his touch, welcoming him, wanting him, as much as he wanted her.

They'd spent every evening with Jess—dinner, a movie, concerts in the park. But the days had been strictly the two of them. In between pizza on her drop cloths and sushi in the tub, they'd worked, sharing an office, conversations, and silences that were never awkward. Without meaning to, Michael had come to know how Sunny took her coffee, what she liked on her burgers, and why she hated hotel tea.

He also knew she had another job lined up in Brooklyn Heights but was still waffling on the brownstone, despite the fact that they'd been over to see it three times. Twice with Jess, who had decided she could live there if she could have a dog. All Sunny had to do was sign the papers, but she wouldn't take that step. And he only hoped the apartment would be available a while longer.

She broke the kiss and sat up straighter, her breathing already ragged, her pulse racing as he stroked a thumb across one taut, waiting nipple. "So how much work do you have left?"

"Not much," he said and reluctantly took his hand away. "Just this speech."

"Want some help?"

"Don't you have to work too?"

She got to her feet and smoothed down her tank top. "I can finish the mural while you're at the meeting."

"You'll finish today?"

She glanced over. "It went faster than I expected."

Michael wasn't surprised. She worked with a level of concentration he hadn't been able to find all week, giving the garden depth with roses and hedges, and small birds that weren't immediately visible. But the focal point was still the couple in the gazebo. Michael had started calling them Fred and Ethel when Sunny wasn't around, and talking to them on more than one occasion, asking if they knew where the secret was or where she'd signed her name, and what the hell they were looking for. And he'd wished that he could be there to see the reactions of guests when they first encountered Sunny's painting.

"So are you going to tell me where the secret is?" he asked.

"Not a chance," she said, and sat down on the corner of the desk. "Now, how can I help?"

Michael handed her the notes Duane had compiled over the week, listing all the reasons why a Grant Hall hotel was perfect for Sundridge. "Just read those out to me, and I'll type."

*"Grant Hall resorts bring in tourists."* She lowered the card. "You can't be serious."

"Try me."

"I intend to." But because he needed to get the speech done, Sunny read out the points and he took them down.

While he typed, Sunny glanced at the papers and drawings on his desk. Most of them were for the new hotel, but there was one photograph of the Carillon as it had been in its heyday—a palace on a hillside, just as Duane had said. When Michael had shown her the picture a few days ago, Sunny understood why he kept putting off writing the presentation.

His fingers stilled and she read again. *"Grant Hall is a*

*good corporate citizen."* Sunny glanced back at him. "So this project still doesn't bother you?"

"Not in the slightest."

"You still don't care about anything."

He kept typing. "I care about you. And Jess."

Sunny held her breath for a heartbeat.

"And if anyone ever tries to bulldoze either one of you, I swear I'll lay myself in its path." He lifted his head. "Next."

Sunny let her breath out and read on, because there was no point in doing anything else. No point in pouting, or stalking off all hurt and angry, because nothing had changed. Whether or not the Carillon project went ahead made little difference—his job at the Brighton was over. The penthouse was needed for guests and Judith had started making noises about site checks in Dallas, Tampa, and Oahu, and how wonderful it was going to be when he went to work at head office full time.

He'd explained to Sunny that the position he'd held with Concord had only worked because the firm was small and the owner eccentric. But Grant Hall was large, and Judith extremely practical. So it was only a matter of days before he would be packing up his office and moving on. Traveling light, as always.

Yet they'd been together every day, apart only for the hours when they slept, and she'd seen the longing in his eyes, felt it in his touch. He was a man capable of real love and commitment, the kind made for home and family. And it made her ache to think of the life he was making for himself.

The gardening book was back on the shelf and if Duane hadn't taken it back he probably would have a copy of *Dream Small* up there too—solid, constant reminders that he'd loved and lost. And would never leave himself open to that kind of pain again.

So all she could do was show him the other side of love. The side that made him smile and laugh, and would fill up every lonely place, if he'd only let it. And wish him well when it was time for him to go.

She slid off the desk as he typed in the last line. "All finished?" He nodded and she smiled. "Since Judith won't be here until ten, we should have just enough time." She rounded the desk. "I'll race you."

Michael was around the desk before she reached the sofa, and gaining on her as she approached the door. They burst through together and leaped on the bed, laughing and rolling across to the other side. Tank top and T-shirt disappeared, jeans were kicked off, and Michael smiled as he ran a hand over her latest pair of panties. "How many more of these things do you have?"

"Only one." She rolled him over and lay on top of him.

His smile broadened to a grin. "When do I get to see it?"

"I'm saving it for a special occasion." She rose up on her knees, pressing kisses to his chest and his belly before wriggling down a little farther to kiss his hips, his thighs.

It wasn't what he'd expected, wasn't what he'd planned, but he wasn't about to fight her either. And he closed his eyes, his heart pounding faster as her hair tickled and her mouth teased. "This seems pretty special."

"This?" Sunny grinned. "This is just something I think you might enjoy."

"Okay, everything looks good," Judith said, taking a quick look around the conference room before turning to Michael. "Our guests should be down any minute now. They're having lunch with the VP of marketing. A most charming man. You'll like him." Her brow creased. "What are you smiling about?"

"Hmmm? Oh." Michael waved a hand. "Just remembering something from earlier today." He gave his Grant Hall jacket a snap and glanced around the room. "Everything looks good."

"I just said that." Judith shook her head and headed for

the door. "Get it together, Michael. This meeting is too important to mess around with."

Michael turned to Duane. "Was I really smiling?"

He handed him a glass of ice water. "Like the Cheshire Cat, sir."

Michael sipped and told himself it was perfectly natural to be a little preoccupied, a little distracted after the morning he'd had. He felt himself smile again and consciously raised the glass to his lips, taking a long cold drink and a real look around.

The company video was cued and ready to roll, bound copies of the prospectus, complete with Michael's personal endorsement, were stacked in the center of the conference table, and a banner reading GRANT HALL CARILLON was strung above the table where the sketches of the proposed hotel were propped. Michael had his presentation in his briefcase and Duane had on his new suit—pinstripes that might be unpredictable, but looked pretty good to Michael. In fact, his whole outfit looked good, from the shiny loafers to the new haircut. If he didn't know better, he'd say he had a whole new Duane standing there in front of him.

"Come on, Nugent," he said. "We might as well sit down."

Duane stayed where he was. "If you don't mind, sir, I'd like to talk to you about something first."

Michael came back a step. "Is something wrong?"

Duane drew in a breath, looked down at his feet, smoothed a hand over his tie, and finally reached inside his jacket. "I'm sorry, sir, but I can't do it anymore." He held out an envelope to Michael. "I'm tendering my resignation effective the end of next week."

Michael stared at the envelope. "What are you talking about?"

"The Carillon, sir. I tried, I really did, but it's breaking my heart to see what they're doing to that place. I understand it's all about economics and target markets, but I honestly believe *that* property should be restored. It's a treasure, sir. A one-of-a-kind building. And the history alone . . ." He broke off and slumped down in a chair. "I can't in good conscience be part of this project. I'll stay for the meeting and I'll back you up as planned, but I will be leaving next week."

Michael held the envelope in front of him, tapped it against his palm, and finally put it into his own pocket. "Then I'll accept your resignation. And believe it or not, I do understand." He glanced over as Judith came into the conference room with their guests. Michael didn't know which ones were bank and which ones were marketing, but he did recognize the mayor of Sundridge and the planners, and certainly George Lutyk—the holdout. A man the others respected, and Michael had liked. George nodded, gave Michael a wave—a move that was not wasted on Judith.

Michael turned and offered a hand to Duane. "It's been a pleasure working with you, Nugent."

Duane nodded. "You too, sir."

"Michael," Judith called. She smiled slowly and confidently. "I'm sure you remember George."


"And, ladies and gentlemen," Judith said with a smile. "A Grant Hall resort is never just another hotel. It's part of the community."

The presentation had gone off without a hitch so far. The video had captivated, the drawings had intrigued, and marketing's profile of the economic benefits of a Grant Hall resort in Sundridge had made everyone sit up and take notice. Judith was glowing, the bankers were smug, and Duane was playing the enthusiastic team member for all he was worth. And through it all, Michael kept wondering if Sunny would come by, and laugh at him again.

"At this point," Judith was saying, "I'd like to turn the meeting over to the newest member of our design team, Michael Wolfe."

All heads turned. It was up to him to wrap everything up on a high note, leaving no doubt in anyone's mind that the Grant Hall proposal for the Carillon was far superior to Concord's original idea. He slid the chair back and reached for the briefcase beside him, figuring he might need those notes after all.

He walked to the front, set his case on the table, and flipped up the locks. "Ladies and gentlemen," he began, "it's an honor for me to be here." He raised the lid, his gaze moving around the table, making all-important eye contact as he reached for the notes he knew were on top. "Grant Hall is a leader in the resort industry, and I—"

He stopped and looked down as his fingers brushed something furry—a pair of marabou feather panties, bright pink, with a note attached. *What are you thinking about right now?*

Special occasions. Fluttering feathers. A redhead who'd dare to wear pink.

Michael closed the lid, looked around the table, and this time, his smile was real. "And I think the possibilities for a very good time are endless."


Judith raised her coffee cup to her lips and leaned closer to Michael. "That was fabulous. Lighthearted, punchy." She toasted him with her cup. "And I believe this deal is in the bag."

"That's the idea," he said, pouring himself a cup of coffee as Judith headed off to do some post-presentation schmoozing.

The moment the meeting ended, a pastry table had been wheeled in to keep up the momentum and the sugar levels. This was a time for informal discussion and questions, and the hum of conversation indicated that the meeting had gone well.

Duane drew up beside him and reached for a cup. "That was a great wrap-up, sir. Very convincing."

Michael looked over. "Did it convince you?"

"No, sir, but then I can be pretty stubborn."

"Nothing wrong with that," Michael said, and turned at a touch on his shoulder.

George Lutyk held out a hand. "Great wrap-up, Michael. Just what I needed after all those pie charts and statistics."

"Glad you enjoyed it."

"It was more than that," George said. "I appreciated hearing your opinion. I've been dead set against this project because I've wanted to see the Carillon protected, rescued and turned back into a castle. But now I'm beginning to wonder if I haven't been narrow in my thinking."

Michael followed his gaze to the sketches on the table.

"It probably *is* time to move on," George said. "Forget what the property was, and think about what it could be. And what they have in mind isn't so bad when I look at it objectively." He sighed, still wavering, still on the fence. "Just tell me honestly, Michael. Do you really think this is a good idea?"

Here it was then. The champion of the Carillon about to be silenced once and for all.

He saw Duane turn away, saw Judith watching him from across the room, and knew what he had to say. Just three words "Yes, I do" and it would all be over. Crack open the champagne and bring on the bulldozers. Michael Wolfe had done his job.

But the longer he looked into George's earnest, trusting face, the harder it was to lie. Because somewhere deep inside, some stubborn part of himself was still holding on to the dream. Just like Duane and George, Michael wanted to see the Carillon survive. And he couldn't kill its last hope.

"You want to know what I really think?" He sighed and put down his cup. "I think you should keep voting against us."

George blinked twice; then smiled and clapped Michael on the arm. "Thanks," he said quietly. "You've made my day."

Michael watched him walk away, his step light and his shoulders square. A man with a mission again. Michael envied him.

"Sir, I am so proud of you. Just so proud." Duane

grabbed Michael and hugged him, right there in the conference room.

Judith's brows rose, George saluted them with a pastry, and Michael hugged the kid back, because there was nothing else for him to do.

Duane stepped back abruptly, put his hands behind his back as his face grew red. "Sir, I'm sorry—"

Michael held up a hand. "Nugent, it's fine. I was touched. Just don't ever do it again."

"I won't, sir, I promise."

Michael drew in a long breath and let it out slowly as George sauntered over to where Judith and the marketing man were talking. "She'll have to fire me for this."

"Sad but true, sir."

"And my name will be mud in the hotel industry."

"For years to come."

"I'll have to do something else."

"If you want to eat, sir."

Michael turned to look at him. "You ever think about building houses, Nugent?"

Duane smiled. "All the time, sir. All the time."

"So you'll be my assistant." Michael grinned and headed out into the hall, stripping off his Grant Hall jacket as he went. "It won't be easy. We'll have to build a team, get the financing, build a client base." He tossed his jacket on a chair as they crossed the lobby. "We'll start with my brother. He's a pain in the ass, but it's work. And I think I can sell him on the Cape Cod."

"Page fifteen, with dormers?"

Michael laughed and pushed the button for the elevator. "We are going to make a great team, you and I. We'll need a name for the company. Something short, easy to remember. And a logo. Maybe Sunny can come up with something."

They stepped onto the elevator and Michael punched the button twice. "You think of a name while I send an e-mail to my brother."

Michael watched the numbers as the elevator rose. "I'll

let them know I'll be up this weekend to do a site check.
Might as well get started right away. And maybe Sunny can
come up with me. Jill and Andy will love her, and I'm sure
Jess and the boys will get along beautifully. . . ."

The elevator stopped and opened in front of the penthouse. Michael could hear the music and Sunny singing
along. He knew she was mixing paint or cleaning brushes,
because she didn't sing when she was painting, she only
hummed. And when he opened the door she would look
over and smile, drop what she was doing to ask how it went.

She'd come to him, kiss his lips, and he'd tell her everything. All about George and the Carillon, and how he'd
blown away his job in a single moment because she'd been
right from the very beginning—he did care. And now he
was going to build houses, with Nugent, of all people.

Then he'd take her in his arms, tell her how he found
those marabou panties, and all he could think of was her.
And she'd give him one of those wonderful grins, and he'd
want her all over again.

"Are you coming, sir?" Duane asked.

"No," he said, and stepped back, his heart pounding,
aware for the first time that he hadn't thought of Kate.
And when he closed his eyes, it wasn't her face he saw
anymore, wasn't her voice he heard in the night. It was
Sunny's, because he loved her.

"Sir?" Duane said. "Is something wrong?"

Michael jabbed the button. "I forgot my briefcase. You
go in. Send the message to my brother, tell him I'll be up
tomorrow."

"But, Michael—"

"Take your goddamn hand off the door, Nugent, and
go and send the e-mail."

Duane's arm dropped and the door closed. And when
Michael reached the lobby, he headed for the front door,
and kept on going.

# Seventeen

Arts Night had always been a proud tradition at Lloyd Elgin Elementary—an evening dedicated to the celebration of art, music and dance for the under-ten set. Student paintings, drawings and clay sculptures were proudly displayed in the foyer. Original poems and stories were being read aloud in the library, and the choir offered a musical welcome as parents and guests came through the main doors. But all of this was merely a warm-up for the main entertainment that would take place in the cafetorium.

In preparation for the event, the cafeteria tables had been folded and stacked against the wall, and rows of hard-backed chairs set up in front of the stage. By 6:15, ticket takers were at the door and by 6:30, a steady stream of adults and children were on their way down the center aisle. Which is why Sunny was standing at the end of row three, aggressively guarding ten seats while she fanned her face with a program and tried not to think about Jess pacing back and forth in the dressing room.

"Those are taken," she called to a woman on the other end of the row, and relaxed a little when she spotted the Glasgow ladies and the rest of the cheering section at the door: Moyra, Sean, Hugh, Jack, Val, and Duane. The only one missing was Michael.

"Taken," she said to a man who had slowed to count the empty seats, then checked the clock on the back wall, hoping Michael was caught in traffic, and not in a confrontation with Judith.

Duane hadn't said a word about the meeting until Judith roared into the penthouse gunning for Michael, leaving him no choice but to give her a brief rundown of what had happened. While he'd been sketchy on the details—and no help at all in determining where Michael had gone after the meeting—he'd given Sunny enough to have her ordering up champagne and waiting for him longer than she'd planned; intending to toast his career change, model the marabou and find out where he was planning to set up his new venture. Because as her heart had been quick to point out, he didn't need to move to California to build houses. He could do it right here in Brooklyn.

She'd stayed until the ice was almost melted and Jess had called twice. But hours later, when she and Jess left their own flat, she still hadn't heard from him.

"This is so exciting," Mrs. Dempster said.

"And the children are so cute," Mrs. Fitzhenry added. "But if you're holding a spot for Lilli and André, you can stop. They're not coming. She gave him back the ring this morning and hasn't been out of the Lucky Koin since."

"Such a shame," Mrs. Dempster said.

"It's for the best," Moyra said as she came down the aisle. "Wouldn't have lasted a week anyway. And Sunny you've saved too many seats. We only need nine." She herded the Glasgow ladies into the row. "Move straight down to the end, and Trudy, take the program off that last chair—"

"Leave it, Mrs. Dempster," Sunny called. "We'll need ten."

"Why on earth—"

"For that nice looking young man she's been seeing, of course." Mrs. Fitzhenry sat down and smiled at Sunny. "When will he be here?"

"Any time now."

Moyra shook her head. "I can't believe you'd bring him

here. Tonight of all nights. But I should have known, what with the way you've been sneaking around all week."

Sunny felt her face warm as the Glasgow ladies leaned closer to hear. "I was not sneaking."

Granted, she and Jess had been using the street entrance rather than going through the tearoom in the mornings. And Sunny had definitely breathed easier every time she came home to find Moyra already barricaded into her room for the night. But that did not qualify as sneaking.

Moyra lowered her voice. "Call it what you like, but I know what I see. And it can't be good for Jess."

"Good for Jess, yes." Hugh grinned as he sauntered up to them. "That's exactly what I said when I saw her name on the program— Good for Jess. And hey, look at the time. The show's about to start any minute. Mom, why don't you slide right in there and take a seat?"

Sunny stepped back, grateful for the reprieve as Hugh took Moyra's arm. Tonight of all nights, she did not want to fight with her mother.

But Moyra shook him off. "I'll sit when I'm ready. And if that Michael gets here late and thinks he can start climbing over me—"

"Why don't we leave him the aisle seat?" Hugh suggested. "Sunny can sit next to him, which would put you right there, and Dad . . ." He signalled to Jack. "Come on down here, Dad."

Sunny turned to greet him, but her smile faltered as he came closer. His face was pale and there was no trace of the usual Jack Anderson charm. "Moyra," he said softly, but she cut him off with a shake of her head.

"I don't want to hear it. Just take yourself down to the end and leave me alone."

Jack moved along the row to the chair next to Mrs. Dempster, who patted his arm as he sat.

"Silly old fool," Moyra muttered, and plunked herself down in the seat Hugh had indicated. "Hugh, for heaven's sake sit down. And where's the rest of them?"

"They're coming," Sunny said and turned to Hugh. "What is going on?"

"They're fighting, what else?" he said, scanning the audience as he spoke, obviously looking for someone. "Where is Michael?"

"On his way." Sunny smiled. "Heavy date again?"

Hugh shrugged. "He said he'd be here. But I think he's getting tired of hiding all the time. A man has only so much patience."

"What is the hold up?" Sean asked as he thumped down the aisle.

"See what I mean." Hugh slid into the row with Sean right behind him. "Don't worry," he whispered, "we'll keep Moyra away from Michael."

"Thanks," Sunny said and scanned the audience herself, hoping Hugh's date was out there.

"You will never guess what I have," Val said, drawing Sunny around as she and Duane edged past a slow moving family.

"Tickets for a new show?"

"Better." Val pulled a newspaper from her purse. "An advance copy of tomorrow's *Banner*, with you front and center."

"It's a great picture," Duane said.

"Fabulous." Val's smiled widened. "And the article? You couldn't have paid for better promotion. Which you have to milk for all it's worth."

"You have a plan, of course."

"Don't I always?"

The *Banner* was a small tabloid with ten pages at most. An ad for Zack's Auto Body sat the top of page one while the police blotter sat on the bottom. And smack in the middle stood Sunny, arms raised, mouth open, and why hadn't she taken off her baseball cap?

"What have you got there?" Moyra asked.

"Sunny on the front page." Val took the paper and flipped it open so Moyra could see. "And she's going to capitalize on every word."

"For all the good it will do her." Moyra waved the paper away but Hugh reached across and took it from Val.

"Very impressive," he said and the Glasgow ladies leaned across Jack for a better look. "Isn't she lovely?"

"Aye, that she is."

Moyra folded her arms and looked at Sunny. "Don't get a swelled head. Tomorrow that paper will be lining bird cages."

"Statistically speaking," Duane said, "small papers such as the *Banner* typically stay in the home longer than dailies. Up to a week or more."

Moyra scowled at him. "Statistics don't pay the bills do they? Now sit down. You too, Val."

"After you," Duane said to Val.

"Thanks," she muttered, and turned to Sunny, whispering, "I hope you called Rona."

"Not yet," Sunny admitted. "But I'm thinking about it."

"Valerie!" Moyra called.

"Think harder," Val mouthed as she moved along the row.

"Have you heard from Michael?" Duane asked softly. "I was hoping you had."

He shook his head. "I'm sure he'll be here."

Sunny laughed. "Of course he will. He would never disappoint Jess."

The lights flashed and Duane hurried along to his spot between Val and Hugh. Sunny checked the door one more time then sat down next to Moyra and plunked her purse on the aisle seat.

The lights dimmed and Moyra leaned closer. "Just so you know, I've left your father."

Sunny swung around. "You what?"

"I left him for good," Moyra said. "I told him in the car coming over."

"But why?"

"Because we have nothing in common anymore. I hardly know the man, and to be blunt I don't want to. So I moved my suitcase up to your flat—"

"But there's no room."

"Don't be silly. We'll be fine there, the three of us, until he moves out. Then we can spread out, do the whole place over the way we like it."

Sunny's heart beat faster. "What we?"

"You, me and Jess." Moyra's smile was warm and loving as the music director climbed the stairs to the stage. "It'll be good, you'll see. And once you're back at the tearoom—"

"Ladies and gentlemen," the music director said. "Welcome to Arts Night."

"We'll talk later," Moyra said and settled back.

Sunny tapped her fingers on her thighs and looked back at the door, wondering if she could make it to the foyer before the music started. Just grab Jess and run. But where would she go? And where the hell was Michael?

The woman behind her pointed to the stage. "The show is up there."

Sunny tried to focus on what the music director was saying, but found herself glancing over at Jack instead. What was he going to do now? Where would he go? Sunny ran a hand over her mouth, wishing she'd told him to take up golf instead of helping out at the tearoom. And wondering how she was going to keep Moyra from moving in the rest of her things.

But there was nothing she could do now, not with Jess fourth on the list, sandwiched between a fifth grade Hamlet and a pair of singing sisters. So she slumped back in the seat and tried to concentrate on the third grade rendition of "The Lollipop Guild."

She did not check the door when a pint-sized fiddler took to the stage and got everyone's toes tapping, including Moyra's. But she couldn't resist when Hamlet started into his soliloquy.

"You might as well face it," Moyra whispered. "He's not coming."

"He won't let Jess down," Sunny repeated, as much to convince herself as Moyra.

"And now," the music director said. "A taste of the High-lands."

Sunny heard the cheer rise up from their row. Sean stomped his feet, Hugh went "Whoop! Whoop! Whoop!" and Jack said over and over, "That's our girl," as Jess walked onto the stage with her swords—her smile wide and embarrassed and proud all at the same time.

Sunny drew in a breath, looked back one more time, and smiled. Michael was there, standing at the door, his eyes on the stage and a program in his hands.

"He's here," she said to Moyra and settled back while Jess went into position—arms raised, toes pointed, fingers just so.

With the first drone of the pipes, Jess seemed to grow taller, the smile disappeared, and she danced—the steps as old as the music itself, but with a passion that was new and hers alone.

Sunny blinked back tears when Jess took her bow, and the applause from row three was suitably thunderous. But no one was ready when a little boy walked up to the stage and threw a rose at her feet.

Jess stared a moment, then bent to pick it up. And Sunny saw her looking out over the audience, trying to pick him out, both of them knowing exactly who the sender had been.

Sunny turned, sure he'd be on his way to the seat now that they were between numbers, but the spot by the door was empty, and no one was on the way down the aisle.

She caught Hugh and Sean watching her, saw Duane shake his head, and felt her face grow hot. Confusion quickly gave way to anger, and humiliation, making it hard to breathe, harder still to think. And underneath it all, her heart was finally quiet, listening at last to the warnings, as it slowly began to break.

"What did you expect?" Moyra asked as Jess left the stage.

"Nothing at all," Sunny said, which was true.

They weren't a couple, never had been. And if this was

the end, then fine, so be it. As much as it hurt, she'd promised them both she wouldn't cling or beg. Promised herself that this time, she would walk away with her head up and her pride intact. And above all, she would not cry.

Of course, if she had ever imagined the ending, it wouldn't have been like this. It would have been civilized, with champagne and moonlight. The two of them clinking glasses, toasting the good times before he kissed her passionately and boarded the train.

All right, so there wouldn't have been a train, but there would definitely have been a kiss. For luck if nothing else. And she deserved that kiss, or at least a hearty handshake. And if she couldn't have those, at least she deserved the courtesy of a good-bye.

The singing sisters made their entrance. Sunny checked the door. It was now or never. She snatched her purse off the chair and got to her feet.

"For God's sake, don't chase him," Moyra said, drawing curious glances from the people around them.

"I'm not chasing him," Sunny said. She was hunting him down, and there was a difference.

The introduction to "Tomorrow" began. Sunny stepped out of the row. Moyra started to rise, but Hugh grabbed the tail of her blouse and held on tight. "Like the lady said earlier, Mom. The show's up there."

Sunny walked up the aisle, head high, nodding to Natalie, her mom and the new boyfriend. And nearly losing her rhythm when a young man in the last row smiled and gave her two thumbs up.

Hugh's date, she realized, and had to swallow hard as she walked past the ticket taker.

The foyer was empty now and she hurried across to the front door. She stepped out into a warm summer night, and spotted him immediately. He was half-way down the parking lot, walking slowly toward his car, with his cell phone in his hand.

Sunny went down the front stairs, moving quickly, wanting to catch him before he pulled away, because she simply didn't want to get involved in a car chase at this point.

She jumped, startled, when the cell phone in her purse chirped. But she didn't hesitate to pull it out and put it to her ear. And when she answered, she made sure she used a lovely Irish lilt.

"Michael, darlin' how are you?" she said.

"How did you know it was me?"

"I recognize your ring." Sunny slowed her pace when he reached his car. "So why are you calling me now?"

She watched him shrug, shove a hand through his hair. "To talk to you, to hear your voice, find out when you'll be in town because I'd really like to see you."

"Would you now?" she said lightly. "And what will you do when you see me?"

"Do?" He dug his car keys from his pocket. "Anything you like."

"Will you take me in your arms and kiss me the way you did that first night?"

"Sure. Of course."

Sunny stopped one car over from his. "Will you make love to me the way you did that night in your penthouse?"

"Sonja—"

She started toward him again, making sure her steps were light. "Answer me, Michael. Do you want to make love to me again?"

"What do you think?"

"I think you're an ass, but then you already know that."

He swung around and froze, the phone still pressed to his ear and his mouth opening, closing, opening, closing.

Sunny strolled toward him. "Why Michael darlin'. You look as if you've seen a ghost."

"What the hell is going on?" he asked, still speaking to her through the phone.

"I'm letting you talk to Sonja. That's what you wanted isn't it?"

"But I don't understand—"

"Oh come on, it's not that difficult. Now I'm Sonja."

She lowered the phone and pressed END. "And now I'm not."

Michael slowly lowered his own phone. "You're telling me you were Sonja?"

"It's amazing what you can do with a mask and a wig, and a wonderful dress. In fact, if you're interested, you can see that dress again in the next production of *Arsenic and Old Lace* by the New Jersey Players."

"What are you talking about?"

"A theatre company. That's where I got the costume. It was a masquerade ball where we met, remember?"

He shook his head. "I don't believe you."

"You need proof? All right." She dropped the phone into her purse. "How about I describe our tumble on your sofa? Or tell you how I felt when Duane interrupted us. Or maybe you'd rather talk about those three people on the elevator, remember them? Barbie and Ken and—"

"Sunny stop it. Why didn't you tell me?"

She hesitated, unsure of herself for the first time since she left the cafetorium. "At first, I was too embarrassed, and I wasn't sure how you'd take it. Then when I got to know you, there didn't seem to be any point. Sonja was gone, and she wasn't coming back."

"And just how many others knew about this?"

"Hugh and Sean," she said. "Val, of course."

"And Duane."

"I'm not sure about Duane."

"I am." Michael walked the length of his car. "So basically you made a fool of me all week, is that it?"

"Don't get self-righteous with me, Michael Wolfe. Not after what you pulled in there."

"Come on, Sunny, you can't compare the two at all."

"You're right. I never set out to hurt or embarrass you. But what you did tonight was intentional, and it will sting for a very long time."

He held out the phone. "Do you honestly believe this won't? You lied to me from the start. Set me up like a chump from the moment we met at the ball. And don't tell me you weren't enjoying yourself just now. Playing me for a fool on the phone, stringing me along so you could hit me with the truth."

"I was angry and hurt—"

"Then you'll understand exactly how I feel right now. I just hope it was everything you hoped for when you came out here."

Sunny took a step toward him. "That's not why I came out. I had no way of knowing you'd call Sonja again. When my phone rang, I didn't think, I just reacted. And you're right, for that moment, I enjoyed seeing you as confused as you'd made me in there. But believe me, I didn't plan any of this. I went to the ball to promote the mural, that's all. I didn't intend to meet you, or go upstairs, or lose the earrings. And I certainly didn't intend to fall in love with you. But I did and I'm sorry. Not for loving you, but for keeping Sonja a secret."

"And that's supposed to make everything all right? I don't think so." He slipped the phone into his pocket. "But I am curious. If you didn't come out to play Sonja, why are you here?"

"To say goodbye, of course."

Michael shook his head. "What are you talking about?"

She gave a short laugh and walked a few steps away. "In my mind it was all going to be very civilized, very mature. It's been fun. Call if you're ever in town, that sort of thing. Then one last kiss and we'd go our separate ways." She leaned against the fender and looked over at the school. "Sounds silly now but it sure made a lot of sense when I was sitting in there with an empty chair beside me."

Michael's shoulders drooped. "Okay, so I owe you an apology for that. But I told you from the start that I don't want anything permanent. I don't want you to save seats for me, or make me part of the family outing, or count on me to be there for anything at all. And when I saw you there—"

"It was easier just to walk away."

He nodded, caught. "I guess it was."

"And I suppose it's easier to keep walking if you're angry with me about Sonja."

He wandered over to the car and leaned against the fender beside her. "I am angry about that." At least he thought he was. Or should be. But it was hard to know what he was feeling when the evening sun was on her hair, and she was looking up at him that way. Harder still to think of her as Sonja, the woman who was supposed to be his escape. He shrugged. "I guess I'm getting over it."

"So now what?" she asked, blunt as always and every bit Sunny again.

"Now I leave."

"Where will you go?"

"Back to Maine. I spent a lot of time thinking about it, and I think it's time I went back."

"Duane will be disappointed. He really likes it here."

"So do I," he said quietly.

"How long before you go?"

"Judith gave me twenty-four hours to get out of the hotel, so I'll be packing tonight."

"Doesn't give you much time."

"I don't have a lot to pack."

Her smile was sad. "The man who travels light."

"It's the only way I know."

"So, this is it then." She pushed away from the car and stood in front of him. "But before you go, I want you to look me in the eye and tell me you don't love me."

"I can't do that. Because I do love you."

"But you don't want to."

"No, I don't. I don't want to start to dream with you, and plan with you. I don't want to picture myself with you and Jess in a Brownstone apartment surrounded by afghans and babies, only to have it all ripped away. I can't go through that again."

"But how do you know that will happen? How do you know we won't grow old together, just like Moyra and Jack. Well, not exactly like Moyra and Jack, but you know what I mean."

Michael had to smile. Everything sounded so simple when she said it. Just jump in, and damn the consequences. But he'd done that once before, and he'd learned the hard way that it was best to be cautious. Best to leave now, before his heart could change his mind.

"I'm sorry Sunny. I'm just not ready to take that kind of chance."

"Then there's only one thing left to do."

"And what's that?"

"A civilized goodbye."

Michael watched her step back, her chin lifted and her shoulders square. No tears, no recriminations, and it humbled him to think that he'd been ready to walk away, to deny her this, in order to save himself the pain.

"You go first," she said.

He couldn't stop himself from reaching out, touching her hair one last time. "Goodbye Sunny. I'll miss you."

"Yes, you will," she said softly. Then she moved in closer, and looped her arms around his neck.

Without thinking, he wrapped his own arms around her, drawing her in and fitting her against him.

"This is the part where you kiss me," she said. "Just once, then you get in your car and drive away. And I won't watch you go, and I won't call you later, because this is what you want." She drew him to her. "Goodbye, Michael."

He didn't realize until that moment how much he wanted this, needed this. He crushed her to him, holding her fast while he kissed her one last time.

She pulled away at last, her eyes wide and dazed as she stepped back. "Now get in your car," she said. "And drive away."

She turned then, and walked toward the school.

Michael sighed and got into his car, the taste of her still in his mind and on his lips. And when he pulled away, she stayed true to her word, and never once looked back.

# Eighteen

Sunny had almost reached the school when Moyra came through the front door and headed down the stairs. When she saw her daughter, she slowed and folded her arms, saying, "He's left you, then."

Sunny's throat ached from holding back tears and her chest was so tight it was an effort to simply breathe. But she forced herself to meet her mother's eyes and keep on walking. "I don't want to do this now, Mom. The show is still on and Jess has a finale to do."

Moyra stepped in front of her, blocking her path to the door. "Surely you're not going back in there? Have some pride, lass. There's not a soul who didn't see what happened."

Sunny drew herself up straighter. "I should stay here, is that it? Hang around the parking lot until the show's over?"

"Of course not. We'll get Jess and go home, just the three of us, and put this whole thing behind us where it belongs. We'll get you working on the pastry again, and talk about what we're going to do with the Isles. Make some real plans for the future."

Moyra smiled for what might have been the first time in weeks, and reached out to brush a strand of hair from Sunny's face. "We'll be fine. And in time, you'll see that this was all for the best."

Sunny pushed her hand away and started for the door. "Best for you obviously, because you get to be right again."

"Sunny, come back here," Moyra said, but it was only the sight of Hugh bursting through the door that brought Sunny to a stop.

He walked to the top of the stairs, looking from one woman to the other before focusing on Sunny. "Are you all right?"

"Of course she is," Moyra answered for her. "Go back inside. We don't need you here."

"Hugh, stay," Sunny said, her voice rising. "I need you here. And no, I'm not all right because Michael is moving back to Maine."

"Jesus Christ," he muttered and glanced out at the parking lot. "Men can be such jerks."

"I told her from the start he wasn't her type."

Sunny rounded on her. "And this just makes your day, doesn't it?"

Moyra drew her head back as though she'd been slapped. "How can you say such a thing? I was only trying to save you from yourself. I only ever wanted you to be happy."

"Is that a fact?" Sunny strolled back to where Moyra stood. "Well, then you'll be pleased to know that I was happier this past week than I've been in six years."

"Don't talk rubbish. Makes you sound pathetic when you're standing out here alone."

Sunny almost laughed. "You want to know what's really pathetic, Mom? Forgetting what it's like to be in love is pathetic. And sitting in a flat for six years, listening to you remind me in a hundred subtle ways about what a fool I'd been, that's pathetic. But if I stayed any longer and let you do it to me again? Now that would be tragic."

Moyra's eyes narrowed. "What is that supposed to mean?"

"It means I'm moving out," Sunny said, surprising herself as much as Moyra.

"You're just upset," Moyra said. "You're not going anywhere. We both know that."

On any other day, her mother would have been right.

Spot-on in her analysis of a hopeless situation. But now that the words had been said, Sunny liked the sound of them too much to take them back.

"Sorry, Mom, but that's where you're wrong." She felt a smile come to her lips and took strength from the sound of her own voice. "Jess and I are definitely moving out."

Moyra shook her head. "You don't have the money—"

"For a brownstone, no. But I can afford something else, and tomorrow, we are going apartment hunting."

"Amen to that," Val whispered.

Sunny and Moyra swung around and saw her and Duane standing beside Hugh and Sean at the top of the stairs, while the Glasgow ladies hovered in the background.

Sunny held up her hands. "What? Is it intermission?"

Val gave her a sheepish smile. "It's baton twirlers. You know how I hate those."

"Me too," Duane said.

Sean shrugged. "I don't mind if they're throwing fire—"

"Stop it, all of you," Moyra yelled, shocking them into silence as she turned back to Sunny.

Her brow was pinched, her mouth tight, and Sunny couldn't remember when she'd last looked so pale. "That's your plan then, is it? Just up and go, taking Jess away, and leaving me to run the tearoom on my own." She turned her head and stared out at the street. "I never dreamed you'd be so heartless."

Sunny took a step toward her, her voice firm but gentle. "It's not heartless, mom, it's realistic. The tearoom was never my dream, it was yours. And you don't have to run the tearoom alone if you don't want to."

"I'll no be bringing in outsiders—"

"I wouldn't expect you to. Not when Hugh can roll pastry so thin and even, it would make you weep. But then, you wouldn't know that because you've been pushing him away for years. And now you're pushing Dad away too."

"Only because he's impossible," she said, and raised her chin in the way of all Anderson women. That stubborn side that made them strong and determined, and sometimes difficult to love.

"Dad's made mistakes, yes, but all he wants is to be part of your life again, to rebuild what you had. But for some reason, you're trying to put me in that spot, trying to build a life with Jess and me, and I can't let you do that. And I'm telling you now, if you keep on the way you're going, you'll end up a bitter old woman with nothing but your recipes and tablecloths, and a good sturdy lock that no one ever challenges."

Moyra's eyes were wide and hurt. "Are you quite finished?"

Sunny raised a hand and let it fall. "Yes."

"Thank God for that," Moyra murmured. She looked across to the silent cheering section on the stairs, then quickly down at her shoes. "Well, then," she said, and put a hand to her throat, her fingers rubbing back and forth while she drew in a few deep breaths, and said, "Well, then," one more time.

Sunny had never seen her mother subdued, had never known her to be lost or confused, uncertain about what to do next. And she knew a moment of guilt, almost wishing she'd waited, held her tongue, at least until they were alone. But then Hugh sent her a single nod, and Sunny knew she'd had no choice.

Moyra raised her head, and Sunny was half-afraid she'd simply walk away and leave them all there, but then Jack stepped forward and called her name, just once, but it was enough to make her turn around.

He motioned to the door. "The tap dancers are up next. We'd better get inside."

Moyra nodded. "Yes, of course." She gave her blouse a sharp tug and headed for the stairs. "Thank you for reminding me, Jack. I'd hate to miss them." She stopped on the bottom step and turned to Sunny. "You'd best get in too. The finale will be soon."

Sunny smiled, her throat tightening all over again. "I'll be along in a minute. You go ahead."

Moyra marched to the top. She stopped briefly beside Hugh. "Are you really that good with the pastry?"

Hugh smiled. "Almost as good as you."

She hesitated a moment, then squared her shoulders. "I find that hard to believe," she said, and turned to Jack. "Let's go before it's over."

"Moyra," Mrs. Dempster said, and hurried after her. "If you need some help in the tea room, we're available most days."

"What do you think, Jack?" Moyra asked.

He offered his arm. "Whatever you like."

Moyra slipped her arm through his, and Sunny's heart squeezed as they went through the door together.

"Well done," Hugh said as he came down the stairs. "Except she's still not budging on you."

"Give it time," a voice said, and Sunny looked over to see a young man with dark hair and gentle eyes standing in the doorway.

She nudged Hugh with an elbow. "Is that your date?"

He nodded, clearly surprised. "That's him. That's Des."

Des sent Hugh a quick but discreet nod, then closed the door and went back to the cafetorium.

"Looks like he's willing to hide a while longer," Sunny said.

"A patient man," Hugh agreed.

It was then that her tears finally came.

"I'm happy for you," she said, dabbing her eyes and sniffing loudly. "I'm jealous of course, but deep down, I really am happy."

Hugh laughed and wrapped an arm around her shoulder. "I can tell."

Sean wandered up beside them. "You want me to beat Michael up for you now?"

"Yes," she said, then held up a hand. "But don't." She frowned. "I mean that, Sean."

Val sauntered over and handed her a tissue. "Michael is an idiot, we all agree. But the great news is that I know where we can find you a fabulous apartment."

"You may have to fight me for it," Duane said and shrugged when Sunny raised a brow. "I'm not going to Maine. If Michael wants to start up there, then I'll wish him luck, because I like it just fine here."

"You guys coming or not?" Sean said on his way to the stairs.

"Yeah," Sunny said, glancing back at the parking lot one last time. "I guess I am."


Michael's hair was still wet from the shower when he poured a second cup of coffee and sat down at the desk with a bottle of aspirin. He snapped off the lid and cursed the pounding in his head.

Popping the cork on Sunny's champagne had seemed like a rational choice when he came home last night—there was so much to celebrate, after all. His new venture, her mural, and their oh-so-civilized parting. That alone had been worth a couple of glasses.

What difference did it make that he'd celebrated alone? Wasn't the first time. Probably wouldn't be the last. He was the man who travelled light. And if you couldn't toast your own success, then who'd do it for you?

The only difference was that this time he hadn't stopped at one glass. Or even two. He'd polished off the whole bottle—drinking to the filing cabinets Judith had sealed, the suitcases he'd packed, and the delivery tag he'd attached to a box so the courier would know where to take it while he was up in Toronto with his brother's family.

"Hailey, Maine," he'd told the couple in the mural. "That's where it's going. Little house on the coast. You'd like it."

They hadn't had a lot to say. Mostly they just watched his every move, waiting to see what was going to happen next. But he would have sworn he heard them laugh when he sank down on Sunny's drop cloths, toasting her success too while he sang "Midnight at the Oasis" with Maria Muldaur and searched for the damn secret in the mural.

Of course, the couple knew where it was, but they hadn't given him the smallest clue. Not even as a reward for finding the tiny *S.A. Anderson* in the petals of a rose. So he'd thumbed his nose at them and toasted her signature, and when he passed out next to her toolbox, the secret had remained exactly that.

"I'll find it without you," Michael muttered, then popped two aspirins into his mouth and washed them down with half the coffee. He turned slowly at the sound of a card in the lock and even managed a smile when Duane stepped into the room. "Just the man I want to see. Did you get my message about the move to Maine?"

"Yes sir, and I wanted to—" Duane closed the door and walked toward the desk. "Are you all right?"

"I'm fine. I was just up all night packing."

Duane glanced over at the bar but wisely said nothing about the empty bottle lying on its side. "About the move, sir—"

"Don't worry, I've arranged everything." Michael rose and walked carefully to the sofa where he'd left his suitcase lying open last night. "Your flight is booked and directions to the house are in the envelope on the desk along with a list of things I'd like you to take care of while I'm in Toronto." He closed his eyes as he bent to do up the zipper. "I'm going to spend a week with my brother's family, take a trip up to the cottage with them, before I head back."

"That's wonderful, sir. Can I carry that for you?"

Michael stifled a groan as he straightened with the case. "I told you, I'm fine. I want you to treat the week like a holiday too. While you're at it, get some prices on signs, stationery, and business cards. I'm leaning toward *Wolfe Design and Construction*, what do you think?"

"I like it, sir, but I really—"

"Judith sent me an e-mail, did I tell you that in the message?" Michael dropped the case by the door. "Turns out they gave her approval in principle on the Carillon project, which means final approval is only a matter of time." He headed back to the desk. "Apparently my speech made such an impact on the other two planners, it didn't matter which way the third one voted. So, there's no happy ending for the Carillon, Nugent."

"No, but at least we tried. And sometimes all you can do is write a happy ending for yourself."

Michael laughed, then thought better of it and headed back to the desk. "That's very profound."

"Just the truth sir, which brings me to why I'm here." Duane drew in a deep breath. "I'm not going with you to Maine. As much as I appreciate your job offer, I have to decline."

Michael sank into the chair and rested his head on his hands. "And why is that?"

"It's been a long time since I've felt at home anywhere, sir. Even longer since I've had real friends, but I think I've finally found both of those things. And while I know you're offering me the kind of opportunity that doesn't come along often, I also know I'd always regret it if I left now, because I may never again find what I have here."

Maybe it was the headache or maybe he was just bone-tired, but for some reason, Michael couldn't help but be touched by the earnest expression on the kid's face. He was so young and optimistic, ready to follow his heart instead of his head, and convinced it was the right thing to do. Michael sighed, remembering what it was to feel that way, and knowing there was nothing to do now but wish him well.

He got to his feet, but slowly, and offered his hand. "Then I'll say good luck, and ask you what your plans are."

Duane beamed. "We're apartment hunting today. Val's got some great places lined up, but Sunny wanted to stop by and pick up her gear first—"

Michael stilled. "Is Sunny here?"

"She's outside. With the van."

"Is she coming up?" Michael asked as he walked to the window. Sure enough, she was there, standing beside the van with Jess and Val—talking, laughing, not looking for him at all.

Duane shuffled his feet. "She wasn't comfortable coming in, sir, under the circumstances. So I told her I'd bring everything down."

Michael lingered a moment, his heart aching as he watched her and Jess start into a tap dance routine, and wished he was close enough to see those matching grins. But what was the point? He'd made his choice, and as hard as it was to turn away, he knew he'd made the right one.

"That's probably the best bet," Michael said, and wandered back to the desk. He glanced over at Duane as he sat down. "I guess you knew she was Sonja, didn't you?"

"Not the whole time. But once I looked a little closer, it was easy to see they were the same person."

"Well, I managed to miss it." Michael dragged what was left of his coffee toward him. "Just say hi to her for me."

"Sir, maybe if you went downstairs—"

That earnest expression was back, but this time Michael was not moved. "Nugent. Just say hi."

"Yes, sir," he said softly, and turned at a knock at the door. "Maybe she's changed her mind . . ."

"She has a key," Michael called after him. But couldn't deny the sting of disappointment when the voice he heard was decidedly male.

"I'm looking for Michael Wolfe."

Duane motioned to Michael and a young man sporting an eyebrow ring and a ponytail came into the room. "I'm from Pro Painters. Got a work order from a Judith Hill to repaint a wall. Do you know which one?"

Michael stared at him. "I hope not. Let me see the order."

The young man pulled a slip of paper from his pocket. "Something about scuff marks . . ."

Michael relaxed. Even Judith wasn't short-sighted enough to ruin another work of art. He pointed to the wall behind the Queen Anne desk. "She must mean over there."

The painter glanced around the room. "I can see why

she's concerned. This is a great suite. And that mural is something else. Can I take a closer look?"

"Be my guest," Michael said, as Duane started rolling the drop cloths.

Michael watched the painter and Duane nodding and smiling while they discussed Sunny's mural. Michael closed his eyes and massaged his temples, pleased that he'd seen the first outside reaction to Sunny's mural, but not surprised that it was positive.

"That's quite a piece," the painter said as he came back to the desk. Michael opened his eyes and the young man held out the work order. "If you sign this, I'll match the color and fix the wall today."

"Great," Michael said and scribbled his name while the painter studied the mural from a distance.

"Sure is a beauty. I really like that nosy couple in the gazebo."

"That's because you haven't spent time with them." Michael handed the work order back and the young man took a business card from his shirt pocket. "I'll give you this, in case you need to call me."

"There's not much point since I'll be leaving shortly."

"You starting another hotel somewhere?"

"They are, but I'm not. I design houses. Small ones."

"No kidding? Well, give me your card instead. My dad is talking about building a smaller house in Connecticut. You go that far?"

"I go where there's work," Michael said as Duane walked out with Sunny's box of paint and a pile of drop cloths. He could barely see around the cloths, and Michael knew that box was heavy. But Duane's step was light and he was whistling softly.

Michael watched until the door clicked shut behind him. That was one happy guy.

He rose and pulled his wallet from his pocket. "I don't have my new cards yet, but I'll write my cell phone number on an old one. Tell your dad to call any time."

He took out a card, and with it came the folded strip of

pictures from mini-golf night. He'd forgotten what he'd done with it until that moment. He smiled, remembering the three of them huddled in that booth—Jess laughing, Sunny snuggled close against him, her hair in his face, her skin like silk—

"Your family?" the painter asked, tilting his head for a better look.

Michael shook his head. "No," he said softly. "I don't have a family."

"But shouldn't I at least go up and say thank you for the rose?" Jess asked.

"No," Sunny said, and crawled into the back of the van with the drop cloths. "It'll be better if you send him a note. Because when a man and a woman stop seeing each other, it's awkward if they do see each other, so they try not to see each other as much as possible." She stuck her head out and looked down at Jess. "Do you know what I'm trying to say?"

"I think so." Jess turned to Val. "But it's so silly. When Natalie and I have a fight, we just yell at each other and get over it. We don't hide on each other."

Sunny rolled her eyes and climbed back out. If she'd thought it was hard explaining dating to Jess, breaking-up, was proving impossible. "I'm not hiding. I'm merely helping the transition to go as smoothly as possible."

"She's hiding," Val said to Jess. "But only because it's part of the whole process. At first you want to spend every waking minute together, then you break up and pretend you never met. It's an art if you do it right."

"Then I guess Michael's not doing it right," Jess said.

Sunny laughed and loaded the box of paint into the van. "Of course he is."

"Then why is he running across the lobby, and leaping over that lady's suitcase?" She winced. "And knocking into that old man?"

"What are you talking about?"

When Jess pointed to the front window of the Brighton, Sunny took a few steps closer. Jess was right, he had knocked into an old man. And now he was on his way to the front door. She turned and walked back to her van. Wherever he was heading, she did not want to be in his way.

She dug her keys out of her jacket. "We should move the van."

"Now she's running away," Jess said.

"I am not—" She stopped and leaned back against the van. "All right, I'm not hiding or running. Now you wait and see, he's not coming for—"

"Sunny," he called from the door. "I have to talk . . ." but the rest was lost behind a group of women going into the hotel.

"Wait there!" he yelled.

Heat rushed into her face as her pulse picked up on the urgency in his tone.

Jess opened her mouth. "Do not jump to conclusions," Sunny said and forced herself to stay where she was, to remain calm and collected. To lean harder against the van so she didn't fall down as Michael squeezed around the group and walked toward her.

"Michael," Jess hollered and launched herself at him.

Michael rewarded her with a hug that made even the most pinch-faced passer-by crack a smile.

"I loved the rose," she said, her arms around his neck as he carried her to the van. "Everyone was green."

"My favorite color," Michael said, looking into Sunny's eyes as they drew up in front of her. "I've been an idiot."

"That's the general opinion," Val muttered. "Jess, come with me."

Michael set Jess down and she took Val's hand. "Can I use your phone?" Jess asked, and cast a quick glance back at Michael as they walked away. "I have got to call Natalie."

Michael turned to Sunny. She raised a brow. "I'm in trouble if I blow this again, aren't I?" he asked.

"I'd say so." She folded her arms to keep from reaching for him. "You look terrible."

He gave a careful nod. "I'm fine."

She shrugged, crossed her ankles so she wouldn't be tempted to take a step toward him, and said, "What brings you out here?"

He glanced around at the crowded street. "It's a long story. Can we go somewhere?"

"I can't leave the van. They'll tow it. Besides, I like it right here," she said, refusing to make it easy for him. This time, he was on his own. "So talk."

Michael drew in a breath and let it out slowly. "Okay. I came out because I was upstairs with this other painter, a guy. And when he asked for my card, I pulled out my wallet and I saw this picture."

He held out the strip of pictures. Sunny saw it was the one they'd taken in the instant photo booth. "And . . ."

"And the guy asked if this was my family. I said no, of course. But the thing is, I wanted to say, 'yes, that's my wife, the one who painted the mural. And this is our daughter, and you should see her dance.' "

He drew the picture back. "But I couldn't say any of that, because it wasn't true. So I told him you were the artist, and the guy got really excited. Started talking about all the wonderful things in the painting. This wasn't news to me until he said it was sad about the two people by the hedges. I didn't know what he meant, so he showed them to me. A woman and a little girl with their backs to me, walking away. The secret was right there in front of me and I couldn't see it. The same way I couldn't see that you were Sonja, when it should have been so clear. And I had this strip of pictures in my hand, and I started to sweat, and I thought it was because I drank too much, but then Duane came back in and he was whistling and whistling, and I wanted to hit him because he was so happy, and I was so goddamn jealous. And it was then that I knew. I want to be part of a couple again. I want to have a family."

He held out his hands. "Am I saying anything right here?"

Sunny smiled and looped her arms around his neck. "You're doing fine so far. But I think I need to hear the rest."

"I love you," he said softly. "I love you so much it scares the hell out of me, but the idea of being without you is so much worse. I want to marry you if you're up for that. Or we can just live together—"

"Marriage is good," she said, drawing him closer and kissing his lips, lightly, tenderly.

"And I want to adopt Jess, and have more kids. We'll buy a brownstone, and set up shop right here. But more than anything, I want the two of you to come and meet my family. I want them to know that I've fallen in love, and I'm happy, truly happy for the first time in years."

Sunny kissed him again. "When do we leave?"

"Today, tomorrow. I don't care."

"Today," she said. "Right after we go to the tearoom and introduce you to Moyra."

Jess raced toward them with Val's phone. "Are you seeing each other again?"

Michael lifted her up. "Oh, yes. And we have some news for you."

Jess waved a hand. "You have news? I just heard that Lilli and André eloped. What can top that?"

Sunny laughed as they walked into the hotel. "Just wait till you hear."